ED AND JO

Love, Art and Gloucester in the Summer of 1923

WAYNE SOINI

—

A HISTORICAL NOVEL

Note about Characters

Readers are warned **not** to take characters and their deeds or words **literally**. Or too seriously.

The degree to which research can cover any of the people described herein varies but the usual rubric very often applies that "any resemblance of the **fictional** characters of this **novel** to real persons is purely coincidental."

The times I worked to represent in this book were veritably Dickensian, i.e., "the best of times, the worst of times, the age of wisdom, the age of foolishness, the epoch of belief, the epoch of incredulity, the season of Life, the season of Darkness, the winter of despair, we had everything before us, we had nothing before us, we were all going to Heaven, we were all going direct the other way—in short, the period was so far like the present period that some of its noisiest authorities insisted on its being received, for good or evil, in the superlative degree of comparison only."

I offer readers a window on the crazy and contradictory era now known as the Roaring Twenties, the Jazz Age, the Age of Wonderful Nonsense, and to 1923 specifically as the Year that Clarence Bird-

seye invented frozen food, and that Summer specifically, forever the Summer that Harding Died, and,
not least, the Summer that Ed painted Gloucester
houses and fell in love with Jo.

Dedicated to Henry Cockeram

———

In England, in 1623, Henry Cockeram published the English Dictionarie, in which "Jubilie" was defined as "a rejoicing yeer, sometime every hundred yeere, sometime every fiftie yeere, sometime every twentie yeere."

Alongside Cockeram's dictionary, Gloucester in 1923 celebrated a rejoicing yeer, its three hundredth jubilie.

Chapter One

Edward Hopper was forty, when many alert men taste life's bitterness and a gifted few of this mass of aging desperadoes reach the moment when they sense that change might be their best friend. Was he destined to be so lucky?

Perhaps. It was a new year. In early January, 1923 in any case Ed broke away from his apartment and walked to the studio he called his "garret" despite its location on the third floor of a seven-story building near which El trains rumbled.

He worked best alone. He shared his studio with no one. Once inside, he put his hand on the light switch.

"Electricity," he said aloud. Like everyone else his age, he had grown up without any light but what the sun and fire provided.

"Let there be light," he said, flicking the switch. Seeing that it was good, he next lowered his collar and slowly undid the four black silver-dollar-sized buttons of his heavy wool Navy surplus peacoat. He wished he had an ulster with a loose, wide belt, but prices mattered to him. Not this year. He did not doff his homburg, nor did he touch the thick

sweater his mother had knitted for her only son but
reached for his neck.

"Jeanne," he said as he began to peel off a pa-
thetic souvenir of his romantic disaster with Jeanne,
a wool scarf which was poignantly soft and warm.
He recalled how she said in her deep and husky
voice when she gave it to him, "*Jeanne est votre bergère,
vous ne voudrez pas.*" Despite that honey-tongued
promise, Jeanne was his shepherd no more, and he
languished, a stray lamb, lost in a cold city with her
mocking token of love around his neck.

His love having abandoned him, life offered Ed
no delight greater than a sunlit white wall. Surfaces
at rest pleased him best. Not often lately did the sea
in storm or imitations of movement occupy his
mind, set his hands to work or comprise his paintings. Gadabouts Ed observed with a silent and in-
ternal horror. To his complete disgust, the earth
and its people continued in 1923 to chase wind and
one another. Walk, walk, walk. The mere sight of
shoes made him sick, even shoes at rest.

At his apartment window in Greenwich Village,
stunned each morning as Washington Square
wearily emerged from darkness to shadows to light,
Ed stood and stared. Below him blur-faced bodies
moved, riding, walking, striding, lurching, even
skipping and dancing. When snow fell his high
hope of an unblemished, motionless cover proved
false when the white carpet, no matter how thick,
soon pocked and erupted into slush or blistered as
ice in spots while the pus of mud exuded and either
glopped or froze, too. "New York Nightmare," a
masterpiece depicting the horror of this chaos
formed in his mind, but its execution eluded him.

In France before the War, he had studied to see
how some knew the secret of still life. It was *stillness.*
For example, Cezanne said, "With an apple I will

astonish Paris," and was true to his word. He anatomized. But Van Gogh, ho, set *fixed stars* spinning out into a rippling night sky. He was incapable of being still or of painting a still life. Ed had stood transfixed in horror before one of Van Gogh's paintings of old shoes. A museum guard approached him, first to ask if he was all right, and then to please move on. Ed had moved but those mute brown shoes, still warm, shaking, tossed to the floor seconds before, shoes that danced haunted him.

Artists like Van Gogh lived to capture the hint of movement or motion's residue. Not Ed. No artist understood Monet's haystacks on airless days and his ceaseless worship of the impassive *façade* of the cathedral at Rouen better than Ed. Ed sought to sabotage the Creator God Aquinas had posited, the First Mover. Ed lived to defy Whoever or Whatever pulled invisible strings to make the universe and its puppets *move*.

Ironically, Ed liked *movies*. Perhaps because they did not really move but were frozen frames that gave the illusion of motion, he was drawn to the flickers, the fledglings that thrummed and shook stubby wings but never really flew. In the theater, though, any movement, buttocks shifting in seats—how conscious he was of this—and whispering, yakking bothered him. As he watched a film, his eyes would drift from the shimmering screen to the theater's still wallpaper or to its frozen, bored usher. Walking home from the Palace or the Strand, he could sketch the foyer from memory, or the pattern of the carpet but he could not always have named the movie. His dates found him absent, monosyllabic and except for Jeanne nobody went with him to a movie more than once.

Since Jeanne's absence, numbed, shattered Ed

merely *was*. Strong human bonds had fallen like so
many leaves in autumn. Then the cold crept into
everything, and he needed more coal for his stove
than he could afford, and sometimes he shivered
for hours under both of his blankets, where he once
had Jeanne. Why must everything change? Why
must *he* change? Could nothing and no one stand
still?

Once, in his callow youth, he had dreamed of
becoming a naval architect. Ed was not drawn to
draw fleets of frigates, their sails billowing, and
flags flying; no, he wished to flatten boats into two
dimensions like so many pinned butterflies. He
never launched his boat business. In vain, he sought
sameness in the sea itself. The roiling sea was the
red flag to this bull, but he flailed and failed. The
sea would not yield to his incessant charges. Like
Canute, Ed could not command the waves to stop.
God knew he tried, leaving behind canvas waters
littered with lifeless cardboard waves and seas of
frozen, blue sacks of flour, the most immobile salt
water that anybody ever painted.

In time, gasping, drowning on land, Ed found
that it was not company that misery loved: it was
art. Marooned ashore, a bit above the ashcans and
gritty streets, up at a distance that always magically
stilled city noises, diverting himself away from
Jeanne and the sea he could usually sketch his way
to near contentment or at least less pain with
bunches of grapes or the distant cityscape visible
from his garret. *Usually*.

"Too cold," Ed said, touching with his forefinger windows that were frosted over. Nothing here
savored of balm here.

"Not today," Ed said, speaking to a letter that
he absolutely refused to open, Jeanne's last letter,
postmarked New Orleans. It lay dead on a side

table because Ed, taking it from the postman, saw his name and address in her thin and spidery handwriting and immediately resolved to bring it to his studio. Because she had left off any return address, why read it?

"No hope," Ed said, thinking that if he forced himself to take a seat on the high stool in front of his drawing board, he would breathe and stare with eyes fixed on nothing. In lucid moments, he would study blemishes in the drawing board, then, overwhelmed, forget them as he drifted, only to come to and renew the same study endlessly. His fingers already felt weighted.

Deciding not to stay, he slowly buttoned up his coat again. Putting one foot in front of the other, shutting out the lights and locking the studio behind him, Ed turned himself into a salesman. In his extra-long peacoat, in the semi-dark of early January, once outside feeling slush under thin soles, his light brown pinewood portmanteau dangling, Ed whistled "I Ain't Got Nobody" to lighten his spirits.

He was in no mood to sell but then he never was. He needed two-thousand dollars a year and he had no savings left. It was tap city, drum up some business or starve. He would have to endure cold but that was hardly the worst of it. Worse was a shy and quiet man's exquisite torture by way of forced smiles, false cheer and hearty handshakes, surfaces that only formed like waves and soon broke. If he had his way, he would live alone in a cave, carefully studying its creviced, eternal walls.

The Biblical verse ran through his mind, "Vanity, vanity, all is vanity and a chase after wind." He was cold. He was old. In the City, he survived but he did not live.

Chapter Two

The cold was getting through his shoes and his
thick coat, and it was time to duck into some building. Having passed enough blocks to gather mo-
mentum, he realized that he was near the Haskell
Building, a warren of manic theatrical agents, ver-
bose one-man mail order houses, morose coin
dealers and other potential advertisers, He had not
tried his luck in months in this building, where
change ruled like a god. They came and went here,
departing without notice or forwarding addresses,
evicted for nonpayment of rent. Ed felt eerie
knocking on doors of empty offices, offices un-
staffed by secretaries, phones inside ringing,
unanswered.

He always started at the top and worked his
way down. Going six nos for six hellos on the sev-
enth floor, he mentally designated his next prospec-
tive customer on the sixth floor to serve as an
omen. If he made a sale, he would ride that mo-
mentum forward; if not, he was done selling for the
day. The ominous customer turned out to be billed
on its frosted glass door the ATOMIC NOVEL-
TIES mail order company, whose stated owner and
operator, Henry Marx, a man new to him, turned

out to be a smiling gentleman who wore a handlebar moustache, decked out in a gray sweater over a yellow-and-black striped vest, whose white shirt billowed in puffy upper sleeves.

Their meeting began auspiciously.

"Happy New Year, sir," Marx said.

"Happy 1923 to you, sir," Ed said, then in a crisp, business-like, and almost confident tone explaining that he was a commercial artist who made illustrations for catalogs. Marx, eyeing him with pleasing excitement, quickly asked Ed to look at his latest novelty catalogue, which was at least two years old. Upon review, Ed pointed out how flat its line drawings were and said that he could improve, greatly improve the paper display of the goods that Marx was selling.

"If I draw with shadows, they become three dimensional and at the same time they stand out," Ed said, after which he opened his portmanteau and showed Marx some of his drawings of small objects.

"How long did it take you to draw these?" Marx asked, his unblinking eyes on Ed's.

Ed decided to use an old joke, grinning broadly, and saying that it took him an hour "plus twenty years of training and practice."

Marx did not smile. He asked, "How much do you charge for an hour?"

Feeling a gutful of failure forming in his belly, Ed spoke in haste. He thought that he might make Mr. Marx a great four-page catalogue for twenty-five dollars. Marx handed the pictures back, saying nothing more.

"All right," Ed said. "I will not bother you further."

"Wait. You like boats? You got a son?"

Before Ed could answer, Marx had rooted

around a pile of toys to find a powerboat five or six inches long, its deck blue, its hull white.

"Fill it here with carbonate of soda, put it in the bathtub and it'll run for five minutes. Kids love 'em."

Ed put the boat in his jacket pocket and took it as a bad omen. He thought on the elevator, alone, as he descended of naval architecture, the road not taken. He hated illustrating and he hated selling. Why not take up a spot behind a drawing board and, with all of the instruments of measurement, draw a dream of a yacht for someone? Or a canoe for mass manufacture? Or a schooner? Was it too late? Could he thrive at a new game?

An atom again in the crowd milling around Times Square, Ed thought about his joke. So he was not much of a comedian, but it was more than true. His sketches really were the tips of icebergs of years of training and experience, of time spent in Paris, in the country, in the city, sketching from his boyhood up to today. And had he not studied here in New York at the famed Chase School for years under Robert Henri? At forty, he had spent more than half of his life studying and practicing art. Mostly, that meant staring, a lot of staring. If Ed were of a morbid turn of mind, he might propose as his fantasy epitaph, "HERE LIES EDWARD HOPPER: HE STARED."

But truly, it was a professional skill. "Many have eyes, but few see," the great Henri had told crowded classes of glittery eyed admirers, all of whom at first tried hard to see as Henri saw, which was precisely what Henri did not want. In Henri's classes "You are painting like me," was not a compliment; it was the professor's strongest criticism. Who was better than Henri? None of them, but Henri insisted that they were to see with their own eyes and paint with their own hands, not using his eyes or his hands.

"If you want to make your mark in art, you must do it in your own way," Henri said every class, in different words. Then, if their strokes of pencil, ink or paint seemed to Henri to copy his work or that of anyone else, he came as close as he ever did to barking. Henri would clear his throat in a growl, the more extended and louder, the worse the displeasure he intended to express.

"See what is to be seen." That was another Henri saying. Ed strove to see things as they were, and himself as he was, realistically. No, today, he was not about to start a new career. He was never going to design boats. Since the War, times had been improving. Why should he chuck away so much of his investment in time and energy when he could stage his own recovery from failure? Sherman & Bryan would welcome him back at a high salary, but he was not going back to work for an agency, even the largest, even the best.

As he walked feeling slush through thin soles, increasingly wet, increasingly cold, Ed was grateful that Henri was not here to see him. Or to know that Ed was no longer snagging orders for four-color lobby posters from movie theaters, for which he charged a princely hundred apiece. Only last year he swam in dollar bills. Now the studios made their own, sending the lobby cards out along with copies of their films. Ed did not require Henri to know what his old teacher would have said, as he did in his classes—that Art was feast or famine.

"You are all riding a roller-coaster," Henri told them, gesturing with his thick arms up and down. "You are all in competition in a city of ever-changing tastes. But" he would conclude, raising his hands up over his head in classic jubilation, "you are also living in the art capital of the world."

New York, New York. Yes. The roller coaster moved up as well as down, today's streak of bad luck would end, and he would get some orders. He made money as an illustrator, he paid the rent, and kept food on the table more often than most of the fine artists with whom he chummed. They asked *him* for loans. Ed prized his record as an illustrator as much as he despised its inherent incidents of humiliation. He knew how to make a living with ink and paint in New York. What he had done, he could do again. With optimism that he could wrest a surplus out of this cold city, he pondered what to do with the chickens that would hatch.

If he was not to turn anarchist and bomb Wall Street, he must flee New York for some summer sanctuary. He was not staying in New York, that was definite. He never did. New York was too hot, too crowded, and now, too full of memories of Jeanne. Jeanne. With her he had spoken French. Although her birthday gift to him in July had been a volume of Verlaine's erotic poetry, she had promptly thereafter vanished like smoke for no reason Ed would ever understand. He kept the book. No matter his feelings about Jeanne, he still liked Verlaine.

But *sa maudite letter,* given that the envelope containing it had no return address, was certainly no suggestion that they be friends. He would be traveling alone. If being alone was painful, at least it was an old and familiar pain; indeed, his oldest and most familiar. It was his happiness with Jeanne that had been unfamiliar, unbelievable, and finally nonexistent. A bell ought to have gone off in his head. He knew better. Stupid, stupid, stupid. How could he have chased a flapper, let alone a French one who wore silk scarves and gave him a wool one, ludicrously tying it around his head when she did. "My bald pirate," she had said, *"mon pirate chauve."* although he had not lost all of his hair.

He could forgive his sins but not his stupidity. He had burned his many sketches of Jeanne. They were not that good anyway. Portraits came out poorly, as did his nudes. Again, his ambition had been to design boats. If it had been up to Ed in Eden, women would have had flatter backs, broader, longer hips, pointed heads and they would have floated with a stable, easy equilibrium. He found that women, as designed by God, had all of the balance and reliability of tumbling puppies.

They spoke French together but when she wanted him to listen closely, she spoke a sort of English. Perhaps in her letter she had urged him, as she often did, to become "the architect of the ships," which she pronounced like "sheeps." She asked him far too often why, if he was unhappy, he did not change jobs. He recalled how she would say, gesturing with dismissive waves of her hands, "I shall not maintain in anything what made me unhappy to be."

To flee New York to a cave overlooking the Hudson might be ideal but it was impractical. He would sell and sell until, with enough money in the bank, he could break off producing headache tablet brochures, shirt advertisements, and catalogs, and for a time leave every building, every newsstand, every grocery in this city that mocked him and his dead-end career.

To clinch it, Ed could easily sublet his Washington Square apartment, and even his studio to some unlucky artist or draftsman required to stay in the city. He also awaited a hundred dollars overdue from slow payers for two magazine covers and he was a finalist for the design of a new breakfast cereal box. If he won, he would have a thousand dollars from a Battle Creek baron and could swing this summer in Paris.

But then, was he really up for Paris? To hear nasal chatter in a vowel-rich tongue spoken over bread, cheese, and wine? The possibility existed that he might even meet Jeanne. She would not stay long in New Orleans and, if she did, in Paris Ed would certainly see many twins of that slim, short-haired girl in a cloche hat swathed in a long silk scarf.

Memories excluded Provincetown, where Jeanne and he had planned to summer. She had seriously wished to visit the place, saying in English, "At Cape Cod we could devour scallops fried." Ogunquit he quickly disposed of because they had gone there together last summer. The artists there knew all about her and him. If he went to Ogunquit, he would be constantly running into them and they would ask him where Jeanne was, where was that French girl, you know, the *joie de vivre* girl, Ed, who sang the sad songs. None would mention her absence of underwear, although all would have this in mind. No, no, *non*.

By the time Ed got back to his office, he had decided upon Gloucester, a fishing town he had visited one summer before the War, a place he had hardly begun to explore. He recalled many surfaces at rest in Gloucester. As he set his electric heater on high and pointed it at his stool, he thought summer thoughts after a while, smelling leather as his shoes warmed to swampy temperatures. Bent over his drawing board, teasing a line into a curve, easing a bunch of grapes into existence, coaxing a wine ad into existence, he varied thick and thin pencil strokes into a rhythmic composition. Too bad, with

Prohibition, his bacchanalian scene was unsalable. Speakeasies did not need illustrations to move their product and the country's liquor stores were boarded up. Change, change, change. Was nothing sacred?

Setting his ornate grapes aside, and his pencil, he began pen-and-ink sketches, daring ads for hosiery intended to lure the glances of passengers on the El. They made him think of Miss Silk Stockings, Jeanne. He would visit Gloucester without Jeanne. The stockings done and drying, he moved on to dip into his India inkwell and draw out of it celluloid collars and jut-jawed men with gelled hair.

Time passed. For hours, skipping supper and well after dark, Ed drew ads aimed at smokers in the upscale market. The casual readers of newspapers and magazines must be baited as one baits mice or hooks fish. He felt like a mechanic or a technician operating a great baiting machine. He seethed within a perfect loathing for the art capital of the world in which he labored before he paused, his head throbbing, closing his aching eyes, putting his pen down, bringing his fists up to his forehead, his elbows on the easel. What was it all for? He was forty years old and still asking.

A late train rumbled by and passengers on the El looking at his building saw the light in one of its third-floor offices on a man hunched over, his head down, possibly thinking intently, possibly napping. Nobody thought that they were witnessing an artist at work or a man facing a crisis.

Chapter Three

Ed subleased his flat, a small apartment at 3 Washington Square North, in Greenwich Village, cheaply to another artist, Robert Mandel, on condition that he not bring in anyone who smoked. Mandel was fine with that as long as he could drink. Ed countered that Mandel could drink but not spill, and to keep the place clean and to open the windows in good weather. Exit Ed from New York, pursued by his demons.

As dawn broke on his first day in Gloucester in over ten years, after the fitful sleep of a tall man in a short bed, Ed woke in dim light and cursed under his breath. Night was ending, day was beginning, and he had overslept. In the shared bathroom of the full house, blessedly uninterrupted, he hurriedly but quietly lathered up his soap mug, gently stropped his razor and shaved. He was forty but his hands remained supple and steady.

He had three full months prepaid, June through August, in a "single room with shared bath" at Mrs. Post's small boarding house on Middle Street. He intended to sketch today, and he was running late. Down in the kitchen, Mrs. Post was already serving two other New Yorkers on holiday, one of whom wore thick glasses and was fat enough to be a butcher, the other a small-built man, perhaps a tailor. From her Ed sought only a half mug of coffee with sugar while smelling what the others wanted to devour before making their way to a charter boat for a day of fishing. Each one might do better at sea on an empty stomach, but Ed spoke no warning as their fried eggs and bacon steamed and popped. Ed usually said nothing. Ed was no good at small talk. In truth, he was no good at any talk. He quaffed his hot coffee, silently nodding as they made utterances in his direction until one remark seemed to require an answer.

"What is so rare as a day in June?" one of them asked Ed. He was too loud, and Mrs. Post said, quietly, "Shhh. Please, others are sleeping."

Ed was full of poems, in English and French, and could have completely recited this one. But he was not going to.

"Nothing," Ed said quietly, as if answering the riddle definitively.

"No," the bespectacled one said, grinning, quietly as if sharing a secret, "a fishing boat with fish instead of liquor."

Prohibition, a law more honored in the breach than in the observance by 1923, had tempted some of Gloucester's fleet to haul liquid cargo.

"I suppose that you are an artist," the small one said to Ed, his voice properly muted.

"I suppose myself to be an artist," Ed said, in a serious remark, looking at both with a glare that communicated, as he intended, that their conversation was over upon a sore point. Had he sold a painting since the Armory Show in 1913, Ed might have simply said yes. He did not count—he resented—so many years bent over drawing boards as a commercial artist, in the medium of pen and ink.

Ed said no more while the men debated—quietly—their chances of catching anything worthwhile. His ears perked up a bit when they talked about the rum runners and the local Coast Guard base, though.

One said, "We'll want to see if their plane comes out of the hangar on Ten Pound Island."

"What sort of plane is it?" his friend asked.

"A sea plane," the other said. "It must be something to see one land in the water."

Ed chose not to regale the fishermen planewatchers with tales of how he supported himself; hence, no tales shared of the horrors of forced smiles as he went door to door seeking customers among Manhattan businesses, nor legitimate boasts about magazines that ran covers signed by E. Hopper, or his prize as a semi-finalist for the design of the box of America's newest breakfast cereal, a year's supply of Butteroats. He likewise left unsaid that shirt companies sold their wares with his bold profiles of jut-jawed men of probity wearing their shirts and their detachable celluloid collars. He was mum about American Express, for whom he had so many times drawn their branch office in Paris that he could do it in his sleep. And so long after the Armistice Ed declined to mention his first prize for "SMASH THE HUN!" in the national contest for war posters.

The two men were talking about the mystery reported in the *Times* of the day before. The body of a young man, Wendell "Bag o' rocks" Birkelder, had been found floating off Marblehead. The police chief had the local physician, Dr. Adam Blythe, perform an autopsy, after which the doctor concluded that the cause of death was "accidental drowning."

"But how would he know the drowning was accidental?" one asked, to which the other said, "I don't know."

Ed had other things to think about. Once done with coffee, outside at last, carefully closing the front door, Ed disembarked, stepping off the granite front step onto Middle Street. He took a right and found himself on the wrong street, on Whale Avenue headed to the City Hall. Reversing course, he moved apace along the narrow sidewalk until his way was blocked. A young man and a young woman, she with bobbed hair, wearing a flapper skirt that hung just above her knees, he nicely dressed, a white shirt with frills, possibly a member of a band, gazed into one another's eyes. Disregarding dawn, this couple's night obviously had yet to end. The two of them hugged and kissed, too involved with one another to realize Ed's presence. It happens.

Ed marched invisibly past them in the middle of Middle Street to Cod Street and quickly came upon the new bronze statue of Joan of Arc. Her sword was raised up to salute the flag flying over the white pillared American Legion Hall, once the town hall of Gloucester. Joan reminded him of Jeanne, of course, and that he ought to have been in France this summer. Traveling light, his sketch pad under his arm, charcoal, pencils, and erasers in his pockets, whistling "I'm Nobody's Baby," intent upon capturing a Gloucester house in the morning sun, Ed trudged on past Joan, down Washington Street until, in another fifteen minutes, crossed over to Centennial Avenue to take on "Portagee Hill."

See what is to be seen. The sky's texture and hue, the quality of light and shade, the thready strands that filled the unseeing eyes of the people in Gloucester's streets around him he was to translate into lines on paper. These poor passersby cheated themselves of a heady experience. The sun had risen over Gloucester but they all may as well have been blind. The sunlight on surfaces here—how it could not be seen, not be stared at, even though— especially because—no artist could really capture light on paper by any means in any media.

Where else would he have found light like this but in Gloucester, where the sparkling salt waters around the island reflected back up into the sky their amplifying and intensifying brightness.

Ed took great strides at top speed toward an ironically unknown destination. He was guessing that there, atop the hill, he would find a scene to preserve, a passing moment fast falling like water through his fingers, no matter how closely cupped, no matter if he made fists. It was scandalous that he had not risen earlier, that he had paused for coffee and a chat with the amateur fishermen who asked if he was an artist. If he did not see now, Gloucester now would not be seen. If he did not sketch, this morning in Gloucester would not last long. Was this or was this not a morning to last?

Ed, who would never give birth, nonetheless knew the pain of labor, his sketchpad in his lap, in the throes of sketching, something that mothers need not do. Sitting on a stone wall, Ed, his sketchpad open, always liked the feeling, the tingle of touching open pages, blank and subject to his will to fill. What he could control, he did control. He wasn't in New York anymore.

He took out up out of his pocket vine charcoal. Curious, he thought to evoke the effects of sun over Gloucester, light and shadow, with the faint grays and firmer black streaks of a soft black charcoal stick. A phrase by Rudyard Kipling, "sludgy, squdgy," came to Ed's mind. He never pressed soft charcoal to paper without thinking those words. He was a river on legs at such times, flowing upon the surface of a sheet of paper, the source of marks with that fluid-seeming, greasy black medium. It was like uncorking a champagne to feel the flow of art through the fingers of his hand this sunny morning on the blank white that waited, passive, for his animating touch.

Or it would have been so—had he not kept *breaking* his charcoal. Having dried over the winter, it crumbled and fragmented now. He switched to pencil, which was too hard, then all of the series of pencils he had with him failed. The ends of burnt sticks were what he needed. His cheeks reddened, not from sun but from rage. He was failing at what he had risen to do, what he was born for, what he had trained with Henri to accomplish.

He had to act quickly. That morning in Gloucester, Ed glanced up at frequent intervals, checking how high above the horizon the great lamp of the universe hung. It seemed to keep far ahead of him. In Gloucester, sunlight was a dramatic unfolding, each different shade illuminating the city only once per day and not before or after that point.

See what is to be seen. The house attracted him, but he was fumbling. He felt a perfect fool, inept as a child. For a time, he sat on a wall, his hopes fading. Gradually he felt overwhelmed. Inertia hit his leaden hands. He stared down his resistant opponents, the house across the street and a ridiculously flat and fragile piece of paper. The saying about someone who could not fight their way out of a paper bag fit him for the moment. He could arrest nothing, no matter how immobile. The morning chill was long gone. If he cared to, he knew that he could close his eyes and sense the warmth. His nose, his ears might buoy him up with a lively sense of today in Gloucester. But if he opened his eyes, he would study the open sketchpad, measuring the evenness of its margins, then forget that he had done that, and repeat. If he did not rise, for an hour he sit more zombie than human.

He rose and decisively closed his sketchpad, then with a dancer's grace folded up his easel and seat, preparing to leave. As he did, he wondered about the people who lived here in this house before him, perhaps in its rooms just now, bustling in the kitchen, dealing with laundry in the cellar, a baby sleeping, a mother watching, a grandmother knitting the winter's mittens in June, a gray-haired and bewhiskered retired sea captain turning through the pages of a book of saints, the gift of a granddaughter. Nothing important or interesting any more than everything was important and interesting and made up the world of this day here in Gloucester, a day that had never come before and would never come again—unless he were to realize a capacity to draw, and now he could no more draw than a fish could fly.

He truly, secretly hoped, though, that the house was empty and unoccupied. Empty houses interested him most. The vacuity, the gap, the space was the miracle to make vivid in a drawing or a painting. The viewer must sense not the robe or fabric but the curving edge of the twisted robe where it ends. Henri had them draw and redraw to the end of their patience to get onto a two-dimensional sheet of paper some living vestige of *nothing*. He thought he did achieve nothing sometimes, but only rarely. The curve of the cloth was rightly and loosely drawn, projecting outward, with an edge that was sharply realized, and from an angle embodied—what? —the snap of a sail over the sailboat, the breeze one feels but does not see, the

nothing that you know exists and that will yet over-
come you, as you die, disintegrate, dematerialize
and are less than dust and ashes, resolved to
nothing.

But it was not that, really. Actually, he was
simply shy and did not want to face anybody. That
was why he wanted the house empty, so that nobody would pop open the door and step out and
see him, and engage in talk. The natives said the
name of their city as if it were "Gloss-tah" and had
other quaint words and accents somewhat toward a
Down East or Cape Cod dialect but actually neither of those, its own. To Ed's ears, they spoke as if
a troupe of dialect comedians for his amusement,
but he lacked all patience with that idea this
morning.

Did no one see but him? Ed could have
screamed if he were certain to be unheard. Here, it
had been just him versus the house in a duel, and
the house had won. Although the day was lost, he
could return. He claimed the house as his own,
lastly marking its location in his mind, noting the
mailbox on which "ADAM" appeared with other
letters rubbed off. He wondered whether an S had
once ended the name, worn by winds and snows, a
mystery. No doubt, winters could be hard on this
spit of land on the edge of the roiling seas.

Nothing to be done but go. The spirit, his muse,
had withdrawn. He felt the fatigue of failure. His
bleak mood had followed him from New York. He
was no more content this morning in Gloucester
than he had been in the Haskell Building in January. He walked down Centennial Avenue—a
twisting roller coaster of a street finally paved in
1876 and then named after the one-hundredth anniversary of American independence—another ten
minutes down Washington Street, the greatest,

longest street in Gloucester, named for General and later President George Washington, to return from his historical progress to Mrs. Post's for lunch and then to read, nap or simply to sit and stare out the window practicing fully and consciously the art of self-loathing.

Chapter Four

As the luggage for her summer in Gloucester moved out of sight within the Boston & Maine system, Josephine Nivison stood before a one-armed young vendor at Penn Station. She thought that he got back but lost an arm Over There.

"Have you the current *Harper's Bazaar*?" she asked.

"Had it, but have it no more, lady. Another Anita Loos story, it went real fast, zoom," the vendor said.

"Darn, that's why I wanted it. Have you any novels?"

"You don't want a novel, ma'am. Novels are wastes of time. Go for something factual, something solid. Here's a new one, *Liberty*, general interest, current events, only a nickel."

"No, thanks."

"Well, you need something to read—let's see now—we got *Photoplay*, Valentino's life story written by himself, with pictures, ma'am, what do you think?"

"I think he didn't really write it."

"You a fan of *Literary Digest*?"

"No political chewing gum for me, thanks."

"Well, okay, baby, perfect for you, the *Saturday Evening Post* has an article on how to make money in stocks."

"So you do carry fiction. Still, no sale, my friend."

"My last guess, my friend, *Vanity Fair*, nice cover by John Held," he said, holding it out for her to take.

"No, thanks, I really only wanted *Harper's Bazaar* and I have a train to catch."

"Where ya going, may I ask."

"To Gloucester."

"Ah, if I could, I would, too. Never been but my hero, Roger Babson, lives there, the Wall Street Wizard. Say hello to him for me."

"I will."

"You want a tip on stocks? On the square, seriously."

"No, thanks."

Jo then walked away, but he shouted to her retreating figure, "RCA, radio is the future. You'll never regret it, lady. Quadruple your money. See you when you get back from Gloucester."

What a salesman. Jo wondered how Lorelei would have handled him. Anita Loos's heroine, Lorelei Lee, between the lines of her diary gave women volumes of advice on how men behaved and how to deal with them. Jo liked to keep up. She started to keep a diary like Lorelei, recording her daily life and any wisdom she observed, heard, or thought of herself. Straddling the fence, should she be an intelligent, disciplined, prim woman or a crafty, jaded, modern flapper? The frau in the kitchen and kids idea was definitely out for Lorelei and for her, though she did take in a cat.

Falling in line for a ticket, Jo exulted in seeing and being seen—as Arthur's owner. Loud meows started to come clamoring from the box she was holding, which was a wooden cat carrier with a shoulder strap, its sides factory-punctured all over for ventilation. Jo had covered the bottom of the carrier with newspaper and an old towel. Behind Jo in the line a girl, six or eight, kept asking, "Where is the cat? And why is he meowing, mommy?"

Her mother kept telling her to shush, that it was not her business, but the little girl's questions continued. Jo turned to the person behind her in line, a man with an extraordinarily long neck and a large Adam's apple, whose receding chin and sad beagle eyes suggested a portrait, if she ever did portraits, but Jo considered portraits beyond reach. She asked if he would save her place in line. He nodded and Jo dashed to the little girl.

"Would you like to meet Arthur?" Jo asked.

When the girl turned shy and looked away, grasping her mother's hand, Jo addressed the mother.

"Would she like to see my cat, do you think?"

The woman smiled, "I think it would answer her questions, yes."

Jo told the girl to join her on the end of a bench nearby. Once seated, she unlocked the brass snaps that held the lid down and reached in to pick up and hold Arthur, who actually stopped meowing.

"See how he looks around. All cats are curious but Arthur especially. And he likes to be petted. Would you like to pet him?" Jo asked.

Before lifting a hand, the little girl asked, "Is his name really Arthur?"

"After King Arthur because he is the ruler. What's your name?"

"Susan. What's yours?"

"Jo."

"Joe's not a girl's name."

"Short for Josephine. Pleased to meet you, Susan, and so is Arthur pleased to meet you. He
doesn't like just anybody. But, you see, he stopped
crying. He must like you."

The girl reached to touch Arthur's head and he
bent his head to enable her to reach a spot behind
his ears.

"Arthur likes to be scratched behind his ears,
Susan, dear," Jo, who had several years' experience teaching art to children this age, said. After
a bit—Jo had never left off from monitoring the
progress of the line—Jo said, "I am afraid I must
put Arthur back into his carrier and get into
line."

"Does Arthur need a ticket, too?"

"Yes, dear, because I am going to place him in a
seat beside me. I will not let them take him into the
baggage car."

"Can I ask you another question?" Susan
asked.

"Of course. Go ahead."

"Why are you so short?"

Jo, at five feet, was like a pixie. The little girl
hardly had to look up at her.

"Because my heart is so big," Jo said, laughing
and running toward the beagle man, whose arms
were waving as he was next. After the encounter
with her young interrogator, Jo's trip itself from
New York to Boston was uneventful for both her
and Arthur. He only awoke in Boston, where they
had to cross town to take a train at North Station
for the North Shore. She found a seat in an
arrangement of paired seats facing one another.
Opposite Jo and Arthur was a man in his thirties
with a neatly trimmed bearded who looked to Jo
like a professor, a married professor wearing a gold
wedding band. He greeted her, "Hello, ma'am,"

and asked if she minded conversation. She said, "Please."

"I'm Leo Sands. Where are you headed?"

"To Gloucester. I'm Josephine Nivison and my cat is Arthur."

"Hello, Arthur. Ah, Gloucester. Almost the end of the line, just before Rockport."

"Yes, I had a tough time deciding between them."

"This is Gloucester's 300th, you know, Josephine."

"Really, Leo?"

"Have you visited Gloucester before?"

"Only once, ten years ago."

"Well, it's changed, spruced up, made up like a, um, alluring damsel. For the celebrations, 300 years of Gloucester."

"Will there be crowds?"

"I very much hope so. Sometimes I play in Gloucester, used to be their piano, but now they have a Hammond organ at the North Shore theater. Are you a tourist?"

"I draw and paint, Leo."

"An artist? I guessed right. You look like an artist. All redheads are artistic, sparks flying from their heads, you know. Plenty going in in Gloucester, not just art this year."

Once the locomotive started up, they had to choose between suffocating in heat by closing the window or enduring frequent blasts of smoke and even sparks through an open window. They left the window open at her choice, and sat in occasional smoke without speaking more because after Jo told Leo about Arthur, perhaps too much, the man occupied himself by reading the *Gloucester Daily Times* until his stop, which was Beverly, birthplace of the American Navy.

"I hope that you and your cat have a wonderful time in Gloucester, miss."

Miss. So he had noticed the absence of a ring upon her hand. As he put on a straw boater with a red ribbon, she thought about his profession. An entertainer, almost a vaudevillian as an off-stage musician, one of the organists who accompanied the movies and live acts. Apparently, he liked people.

"I play in Gloucester," he said, repeating himself. "Perhaps we'll meet again, Josephine. Goodbye for now."

"Thank you, Leo. A good summer to you," Jo said.

"Most pleased," he said, rushing to get out before the locomotive restarted.

Their short exchange had drawn some of the life out of Jo. The doctors she consulted in New York said that her heart was good, and her frequent fatigue was an aftereffect of her illness during the War. She had volunteered to be a Red Cross nurse and almost immediately been set back for months, in need of being nursed herself. Since then, she intermittently fell into a sluggish and sad state. A couple of years malnourished as a "starving artist" had not helped and, as she reached forty, her summer trips were like roller coasters. Today, as late afternoon preceded, she felt a weariness that was normal to her on any journey, but which usually held off flooding her until she lay down or sat in a chair at her destination. This time, as she gazed out the train windows at the passing landscape of trees and houses in a blur, she felt tired and a bit doleful even before she arrived. Notwithstanding Arthur, she felt alone.

From her earlier visit to Gloucester she recalled the beaches, the harbor, the boats, the sea, the children playing. She only sketched with pencil and charcoal in 1912. This time, she brought watercolors. This time she would introduce herself as an "artist" rather than as an "art student." She was actually making her name and a living, although a spare one, as an artist in New York.

It was not that she emanated confidence. She still felt a degree of intimidation when facing blank paper. Lines did not come easily. Her drawings often seemed to her to be stiff and unhappy. A line she intended to flow like Isadora Duncan instead wilted and wobbled. It was not perfectionism that inhibited her: Jo was no perfectionist. She simply found herself admiring details in the world of still lifes and flowers that she could see but not quite pluck. She hoped for change, that this time beautiful sites, happy groups, and lively people might enter her work as she summered in Gloucester, nearly the end of the line. She smiled at her pun. Arthur began to meow. She must do better this summer.

"It's all right, Arthurkitty, all right, moofykins."

He meowed louder, his complaining, outraged meow.

"I know you're hungry. We'll be there soon. Mrs. Murphy will give you some fresh fish, won't that be nice?"

Arthur meowed more mutely, half soothed.

She told Leo that she was an artist but, if she chose to introduce herself as such, she was also a teacher on vacation. In the city, she taught art part-time to public elementary school students. The youths after the War were either too timid to move into art or too bold for her to discipline. She had difficulty connecting with any of them, but it was a job. She had been jobless and homeless and knew how that was. She had saved a tidy sum for a rainy day and also had a coin or two for her summer expenses.

Oddly, Ed Hopper came to mind as she looked out at the boats of Manchester harbor. She recalled the fact that he had wanted to be a boat architect, but he never said more on that topic, which she found sad. He seemed to be brooding over disappointments when they had both been in Gloucester in 1912, and before and after that in classes with Professor Henri. People who saw Ed in Ogunquit last summer said that he looked older, being almost bald now, as he was being hauled around ridiculously by a short-cropped French woman with a Gallic nose who favored what looked like a gauzy yellow cheesecloth cape or shoulder wrap. Her friend had said, "She was too young and too lively for him, Jo, but there is no arguing anybody into a taste for beer or a love of cats, as they say." She wondered if the French girl had moved on after a summer romance. Jo herself knew about summer romances. They often ended when she drew lines of permissible touching. Was she getting too old herself? In Provincetown the previous summer, she had only had Arthur for real company.

Arthur meowed. He sounded sad. Could he read her thoughts?

She did not require a dream man. He need not be handsome, certainly not, she felt herself to be no classic beauty herself. He could be bald and wear glasses, but he should be smart, literate, able to hold up his end of a conversation, dance. As Lorelei might add, it did not matter if he smoked or drank, or spilled soup on his shirt and did not know how to cook—he could not expect much from her in terms of domesticity or housekeeping. She was looking for compatible company as she reached forty. An artist, a musician, a poet—just not one of those biographers or historical novelists. A girl has to draw the line somewhere, and as is well known, biographers and historical novelists live in the past and are jingle-brained.

Arthur meowed.

"Almost there, moofykins, we've just left Manchester," Jo said.

But he must be modern and think of a woman as an equal partner in life's adventure, with no desire or hope of any children. She possessed talents. Her red hair was gorgeous. She was good with people, not in a pushy way either, but with an ability to intuit another person's feelings and to match those feeling appropriately. She could keep books, balance accounts and handle business matters. If she had not taught, she would have become a private secretary, and a good one, too. last, although it seemed unnatural in 1923, she had remained a mademoiselle intact and not a madam.

Arthur meowed as the conductor at the end of the car shouted, "Next stop, Gloucester. Now arriving, Gloucester. This way out, please."

Chapter Five

Donald Nash, Jr., who won his mother a five-dollar
bank account as the first baby born in the mater-
nity wing of the Addison Gilbert Hospital in 1900,
had been straddling the nineteenth and twentieth
centuries awkwardly ever since.

A fifth generation Gloucesterite, Don was the
latest of a long line that ran from his great-great-
grandfather, the lawyer and state senator, Lonson
Nash, who spotted a sea serpent in Gloucester
Harbor in 1817, and wrote about it. It did not
matter that two-hundred other people saw the
same thing, that ten or twelve signed sworn affi-
davits, and a committee of scientists under a Federal judge's supervision in Boston affirmed that the
marine creature actually did visit Gloucester
Harbor for three weeks, Lonson Nash was never
elected to any public office again. Lonson's son
dove deeply into marine insurance, though he fa-
mously declined to cover perils at sea for the
Gloucester's owners of slave ships. His son was a
ship's chandler and Gloucester's best and fastest
marine chronometer repairman, followed by Don's
father, another marine insurance agent who got
lucky and came to be named the first director of

the great consolidated fleet of five hundred vessels for Gorton-Pew, the company that dominated the Gloucester waterfront from its launch in 1906. Don, who bore the Nash family's Roman nose and its traditional flair for observation and writing, did not enjoy his visits to his father's office, with its large windows that overlooked Five Pound Island and the Inner Harbor.

"Look," his father would command him. "Take those binoculars and look at all of the schooners out there. I'm the captain of the captains, Donny—and, someday, you'll sit in my chair and your signature will launch a thousand ships."

Don would look but he could not see a marine career. It gave him a stomachache to imagine directing these ships. What he really enjoyed was the local Carnegie library, the Sawyer Free Library and Lyceum. Its stacks were open to him, beginning with the top left front, books on the occult. He read first all about ghosts and spiritualism. His father would insist that he bring back home volumes of Frederick Marryat's rousing sea tales, and so he did. But it was other stuff that interested him.

"Did you know that Henry David Thoreau spoke in Gloucester, Father?" he asked the old man, who gave him a baleful look in exchange.

Despite his father's silence, twelve-year-old Don rattled on that Thoreau gave his Gloucester audience a preview of his upcoming book about Walden Pond, with a humorous twist.

"The paper said that he brought down the house. He must have been very funny to hear in person," Don said.

His father finally spoke, "That nonsense is never going to get you anywhere in life. Study the fluctuations of the prices of cod, my boy. Look at the landings, judge whether this season is as good, worse, or better than last season in volume. Make it a point to know the state of the tides. I ask you, is it low tide or high tide?"

Don shrugged and said he did not know.

"A Gloucester boy who does not know the tides," his father said, shaking his head. Rising from his chair to his full height, his father told Don, "You have as good a brain as mine. It was my legacy to you, my gift. I am only asking that you put your brain to use in the fields in which I can be of greatest help in your education and in which, in time, you can thrive more quickly and rise higher than in any other field. Do you understand?"

"I do, Father," Don said.

"Do you believe that you can just as easily study what I said as you can study any other subject?"

"I do, Father," Don said.

His father took their conversation to have amounted to a negotiation in which his son yielded to superior reason and logic. Both father and son knew what was best from that moment. When Don went off to college, to his father's college, to Harvard in Cambridge, he took the courses his father suggested but found himself losing interest. One day in 1918, he had had enough. He found his way to the Army recruiter and joined up to go Over There. As he trained in Plattsburg, he got a letter from his mother about quitting Harvard, a letter which made no reference to his enlistment and the War. His mother wrote:

"Your father loves you very much and, as you know, from your birth his heart was set on your working together. He feels (to use his word, not one I agree with) 'betrayed.' I hope that you can understand and act accordingly. I am unsure that his anger will pass soon, as he has consulted with our attorney to disown you."

Don's unit shipped out and they landed in France in the summer of 1918, where the Influenza floored him and lots of others in huge tents of suffering victims, many of whom died. He was still recovering, without having fired a shot during the Great War, when word came that the guns were silenced: the war ended in an Armistice on the eleventh hour of the eleventh day of the eleventh month.

When Don returned to Gloucester, it was not to the homestead but to a summer rental on Long Beach, a house on a lot leased from the Town of Rockport. When he moved to take a room at the YMCA, he still took long walks to various beaches in early morning even during the winter. One foggy morning, just as the mist cleared off Good Harbor beach, Don saw an amazing sight: a battleship. No mirage, it turned out to be the *George Washington*, carrying President Wilson back from the Versailles peace conference. Rumors flew around Gloucester that the Presidential ship had gone off course, although the captain realized as much shortly before plowing ashore. Don found himself itching to write up such events, to turn each day into reading matter.

He thereafter fully disgraced the family name by becoming a reporter for the local newspaper, the *Times*. His son a newshawk? The old man in the Nash homestead on Rocky Neck—from the second floor of which the maid had seen a sea serpent one morning in 1817, which set Lonson in motion toward political doom—immediately canceled his subscription. He never wished to see the Nash name in a byline.

No matter, it was by writing that the now-disowned family disgracer Don Nash made a living. In time, by skipping meals and saving seriously, Don scraped together enough to buy his own automobile, a nearly new and still shiny scarlet red-and-sparkling-chrome Stutz Bearcat, in which he tooled about town and took breezy rides by Bass Rocks on hot summer days as he made rounds. He collected autopsy reports from Dr. Egan, got a glimpse at local crime through the desk sergeant and his log at the station off Main Street, jabbered with the Mayor or councilors during their interminable feuds, covered ship launches, Catholic events like the Blessing of the Fleet, worked up details of storms, fires, wrecks and fatalities on the rail track, and, lately, stories of rum running and Prohibition agents.

"What year is it, Don?" his editor, Garret Bean, also known as "Chief," asked.

"Is this a test?"

"Need I repeat?"

"It is 1923, sir."

"What does that mean, Don?"

"I am due for a raise, Garret?"

"Try again."

"I have no idea what you are fishing for."

"Here's a hint: 1623, 1923."

"Why didn't you just tell me that you want a story about the Tricentennial?"

"Because I did tell you and I have been waiting. Two weeks now. Well?"

"I am still working on it."

"We do not have three hundred years, son. When might I expect a story?"

"I did one yesterday on Mike O'Brien, the singing postman."

"Yes, I know, Obee, who sings on his route and weekends, the Irish tenor. His favorite song is 'Tessie,' which he learned from his father before he could walk. He named his dog, a rat terrier,

Caruso. Nothing worth printing," the Chief said, displaying his recollection of the article and his judgment of its value. He never passed it on to run as a story.

"What do you want?"

"My story on the Tricentennial, Donny."

"Tomorrow."

"Really?" Garret said, unable to squelch a grin. So Don had something up his sleeve. Good.

"Really. My military band scoop," Don said. "Half written."

"What military band?"

"See? You don't even know about it. The greatest group since John Philip Sousa, the Marine Corps band."

"The Marine Corps band is coming here?"

"Tuba, drums, flutes, the works. All because of James Centennial Nutt."

"Who's he?"

"Got you again, Chief. Captain Nutt of G Company, the War of 1898, all volunteers. Born on the Fourth of July, 1876. On his 47th birthday, he will be the honored guest, along with survivors of Company G, at a concert in Stage Fort Park. The Secretary of War was impressed by that history and, out of all requests for the band on the Fourth, he decided to honor Gloucester's request."

"Nice story, human interest, local color."

"Beats the band."

"Comedian. Everybody's in vaudeville now."

"By the way, Garret, there are people here from New York, artists, musicians, bohemians."

"No kidding."

"I could interview them."

"No."

"One of them is 'Sabrina, the Mystic Artistic

Dance Interpreter.' She studied under Isadora Duncan."

"Absolutely not."

"The great choreographer."

"I heard that she is a Red. Besides, we are not a tabloid, and the *Times* does not practice yellow journalism."

"You need something better for the front page than the Birkelder case."

"That case was solved. Accidental drowning."

"So said Dr. Blythe. Well, anyhow, I was scouting for a piece, and I told the dancer that we could probably at least run her photo along with a caption of where she is going to perform."

"A piece, indeed. Donny, I would not run a photo of Sabrina naked in a nest on top of the City Hall clock tower. Clear?"

"Very clear. Very disappointing, but very clear as well. You know, Chief, I've always heard that journalism is—"

"Stifle yourself, lad. Journalism is most emphatically *not* literature on a deadline. The Tricentennial will unfold in our pages like clockwork."

"But not Sabrina."

"The Tricentennial is going to uplift our spirits by calling to mind the one-hundred-thousand days and nights since the earliest settlers, think of the compassion of the immortal Isabelle Babson as a midwife, think of the bravery of those soldiers who will proudly parade by us, think of the hopes and dreams of anybody else we ought to honor, not forgetting men in peril even now on the indifferent sea."

"You could write the Mayor's speech."

"I already did. I'll give you a copy of His Honor's address soon. But get moving now."

"You are not cynical, are you?"

"Of the glorious celebration of our city's glorious past? Donny, Donny, Donny."

Don shook his head, smiling. The editor was mocking him, but he only left the *Times* office when the Chief pointed at the door and said, "Go get today's news before it goes bad."

Chapter Six

Jo was organized but only after the fact. Predictions were not her strength, and she could not plan for beans, but like Lorelei Lee she could order and make careful notes of whatever actually happened. She moved fastest in reverse. It was both a skill and her joy to document her life, every day refreshing her huge archival inventory with a few more notes, sketch book entries, updates in journals, or at least one good letter.

Anticipating joy, she wrote a cousin before she left New York, "Besides giving Arthur a bit of salt air and fresh fish, which he loves, my mission is to draw and to paint flowers before they fade, and the sun sets on my side of the world. Do you know that in Gloucester the light is so much better? Every artist says so. Gloucester roses are dazzling in June, incandescent with a glow that appears nowhere else, nowhere. In Gloucester in 1912, when I was but a student, I learned that. Then I had an eye but not much of a hand, but now I am proudly up on the first rung climbed by all professional artists.

"Everything's jake. My artwork sells, my name is becoming known, and, best of all, through me roses live in galleries in December. Everyone has a journey to make and mine is through roses. Can't you hear the Lorelei Lee in that motto? I shall see to it that Gloucester flowers of 1923 do not live in vain. Dear cousin, keep this to yourself but I am to present my artwork this winter by invitation as part of the annual show at the Brooklyn Museum. By ensuring that these natural Gloucester beauties are never forgotten, I do no harm with my brush and daubs of paint and, I hope, I may do some good. Even for my own career. Meanwhile, as they say, I follow my nose."

Thus, as June began, Jo's nose—and her cat's—arrived in front of Mrs. Murphy's rooming house on Washington Street in Gloucester. As they got out of the cab, they took from the railroad station (the distance was short, but she had the cat and her luggage), Arthur smelled fish before Jo did, and commenced a ruckus and loud crying meows as if from two cats from inside his carrier, a din that only increased as soon as Mrs. Murphy opened the door.

"You made it," Mrs. Murphy said. She was a voluble woman who favored declaring the obvious with a degree of surprised pleasure and touch of dismay. "And you have cats."

"We did, Mrs. Murphy, and I have one cat," Jo said, adding by way of breathless introduction, "Josephine Nivison and Arthur."

Arthur meowed a long, mournful meow. The cab driver, one of Gloucester's fisherman too old to fish but too poor to retire, held Jo's luggage until Mrs. Murphy gestured for him to bring it on into the parlor, where Jo set Arthur in his carrier down on the sofa and dealt with her large pocketbook and small wallet to offer more than twice his due, a whole dollar—"Keep the change"—and a bright smile.

"Have a good time in town, ma'am," the driver said, pocketing the bill and wishing, despite the safety of an occupation on shore, and despite the income that was nearly the same as at sea, that he was out on George's Banks in the fresh and bracing air, where he and other men and everything around him had seemed somehow both bigger and more than on land.

"First things first," Mrs. Murphy said, escorting Jo to the kitchen. The driver was left dropping off the baggage and leaving without a tip as the ladies tended to the needs of Arthur the cat. Immediately when freed, Arthur padded about between hiding under chairs and acting frightened, eating nothing although a plate of flaky pieces of boiled flounder placed on the floor just then was plainly within his smell zone and sight.

"Shall we eat? I have fish chowder hot on the stove and fresh bread, still warm," Mrs. Murphy said. But Jo suggested that her new landlady show her to her room, where she could unpack while Arthur ate.

"He likes to eat alone," Jo said. "He doesn't like to be watched."

"Fish is all right, then, Miss Nivison?"

"Oh, please call me Jo. It's not the fish, he's hungry, but he's shy, my dear Moofy."

"Of course. But isn't that strange, dear, a shy New Yorker?"

Jo agreed that it was strange. Jo noticed Mrs. Murphy had magazines out on her parlor table. Happily spotting *Harper's Bazaar*, Jo asked if she might take it up to her room to read. Mrs, Murphy said, "Of course. I think it has a new Lorelei story."

"Isn't she wonderful?" Jo said.

"And full of surprises. I read it to know how the world is changing for you girls."

"I'm hardly a girl, Mrs. Murphy."

"To me, you are. Woman are set but girls continue to change, that's how I see things."

Jo smiled (Lorelei's ironic and goofy motto was, "Smile, smile, smile") as they climbed the stairs, each toting a piece of luggage, Jo carrying her scriptures, *Harper's Bazaar*. Jo was flooded with thoughts she had held off while on the train. Flowers were wonderful, and children at the beach buoyed up her spirits, Gloucester breezes refreshed her, but would she meet someone? Of course, she would meet a hundred people and renew many old acquaintances, but—a special someone? She had last visited Gloucester before the war, a girl still in her twenties. That summer, she and other artists had shared the same boarding house in Rocky Neck. She would meet some of them again. But so what? She was ten years older and so were they.

It struck her with certainty that Ed Hopper had been in Gloucester way back. She remembered how Ed sketched a lot but never showed anybody anything, and she never saw him paint at all, not once. Stiff and wooden, he walked like the Nutcracker soldier in the ballet. Too tall for her, really. In Gloucester that summer, she dressed as the blossom she was, in glad rags, light and creamy colors, brilliant scarves, and floppy hats running amok with red and purple swathes. Too gaudy to please his eyes though she pleased others. In the end, who cared? *Sic transit Ed Hopper.*

Now, in the late spring of 1923, Jo's kitten was a full-grown tomcat ensconced in Mrs. Murphy's house that she advertised as being "on a quiet street, pets permitted, references required." A quiet street—somewhat exaggerated, as Washington

Street, though quiet enough by night, the city's busiest street by day, rumbled with a degree to traffic—*was* quieter than Brooklyn. Once Jo arrived, Mrs. Murphy praised her guest house as being "only steps away, my dear, from the trolley that runs all along Washington Street and 'round the Cape.'" Jo shared how she could not bear to leave Arthur in sweltering New York City for the summer.

"I don't blame you at all at all," Mrs. Murphy said in reply, adding that there would always be scraps of fresh fish for "the little darlin'."

"Have you other guests?"

"It's early in the season, for tonight just yourself, but others are coming next week and through the Fiesta week at the end of the month. July will be busy except for two weeks when a man comes from Vermont. He books two rooms, one for himself and one for his trunks. He's a writer, but very shy."

Jo asked questions about the Fiesta, which led Mrs. Murphy to tell her about a concert coming up "just down the street, at Stage Fort Park" on the Fourth and about the Tricentennial and activities in August, "a parade, a pageant, fireworks and everything." To Jo, it seemed like too much, too distracting. She wanted to see, hear, smell, touch, taste the city of Gloucester as immersed in it as any local resident, rather than gawk and stand in a crowd of other tourists from out of town.

Meanwhile, none of this bothered her cat. Downstairs, Arthur ate every scrap before him in great, hasty gulps and then, showing just how well fish agreed with him, before he curled up contentedly on the puffy blue and white checked Chambray sofa in the parlor.

"Oh, the darlin'," Mrs. Murphy said of him as

Jo picked him up and held him close to bring him to her room upstairs.

"I've left a box in your room for his use, with torn newspaper," Mrs. Murphy said.

"I saw, Mrs. Murphy. Thank you," Jo said, hoping that Arthur would orient himself quickly. Nocturnal evacuation was his habit.

Chapter Seven

Ed took a brisk walk down the Boulevard, straying at the new green railing up over a long beachfront of granite blocks that were not here in 1912. He recalled instead a row of snug seaside homes that had dotted this stretch, the ruins of an old rope factory, and what someone pointed out had been the site of a windmill that ground salt. Today about halfway down the Boulevard Ed passed the pedestal, under wraps of a dark tarp, which awaited the installation of a much-publicized Fishermen's Memorial. With nothing but tarp to see yet, Ed stood at the railing and looked the other way, at the waves coming in, with glances at activity on Ten Pound Island, where crews to man a fast motorboat and a seaplane prepared to undertake surveillance for rum runners. He had dreamed of a quiet, even motionless sanctuary from the hectic City but Gloucester in 1923 was turning out to be no still life.

Ed returned to Middle Street and, as soon as he came in the door, Mrs. Post said, "You had a visitor. He left a message."

Thus, Ed found out that Guy Pène Du Bois had

been by and hoped to see him. His old friend's boarding house was not far, up on Main Street. Ed, carrying a sketch pad and some pencils, found Guy in his room, the door open, as he lay back on his bed, propped up by pillows, reading some French publication, which made Ed think instantly of Jeanne. Guy looked up and told Ed, as if they were in mid-conversation, "The French art critics are so much more advanced than ours."

"You would know," Ed said. Guy himself straddled two worlds as an artist whose art criticism appeared in several publications, including a newspaper for which he also drew cartoons.

Guy said, "I'm here for three weeks, more or less. I came to see Craske and his statue. And anyone else I know who comes here, including recluses like Ed Hopper."

Ed said, "I'd like an early view of that statue myself."

"Are you doing anything tonight, Father Time?"

"Nothing."

"Cat's meow. We can knock on Craske's door and see how close we can get to the greatest secret in Gloucester."

Leonard Craske's statue in honor of Gloucester's fishermen was to be unveiled the next month, but the *Times* was utterly silent about its current location. Rumors had it under wraps in the backyard of Craske's studio, in the lighthouse at Eastern Point, up in the solarium of the Addison Gilbert Hospital, and a half dozen other unlikely places. Craske, born in England but now settled in Gloucester, had most appropriately won the commission for a memorial to the city's fishermen, the first of whom had been English-born transatlantic adventurers who, in 1623, dried cod at what was now Tablet Rock in Stage Fort Park.

"By the way, Ed, did you know that Jo Nivison is in Gloucester, too?"

"Really?" Ed said. Jo, once his fellow art student, always fussing with flowers and bright colors, had been making a name for herself in New York while he struggled to sell shirts. Life was unfair.

"With her cat."

"Really?" Ed said, unable not to smile now.

"The old maid with her cat was walking around the Boulevard this morning holding it. No kidding, if I had my brownie Kodak with me, I'd have snapped a picture."

"How did I miss her, and you?"

"You slept late, of course. We were up with the birds. You don't know what a bird sounds like, do you?"

"I like Jo," Ed said, in a vague monotone. He got up earlier than either of them, but he was not about to get into how little he slept, how early he awoke, or what he did. Guy understood only that Ed did not dislike Jo. In a *non sequitur* response, now closing his magazine and putting it down on a nearby table, piled high with books, magazines, and newspapers, Guy said, "You have to consider your audience in writing."

"Not so in painting?"

Guy painted, favoring richly attired couples. His group figures exuded wealth, attended theater, ate well at restaurants, but were otherwise poignantly outside communication, unable to speak, clearly separated. Were they happy? Their expressions were blank or foggy, blurred by intentionally clumsy strokes, or, when (rarely) Guy brought their expressions out clearly, distant and passive. However, this aspect Ed thought reflected

the best of Guy's genius, and at a show the previous year he had told Guy so. Guy, unimpressed
with himself, told Ed that he was making a study of
couples and painted only what he saw, "audience
be damned." He quoted their teacher, Robert
Henri, "See what is to be seen."

Ed steered clear of abstract discussion—Guy
was notorious for hours of talk over a flyspeck of a
dot on a single painting, exploring its many possible
meanings, pondering the artist's original options—
and said that he was about to leave to sketch.

"May I join you?" Guy asked.

"If you want to go to Rockport on the trolley,
'round the Cape," Ed said.

At the Main Street terminus, the jovial conduc-
tor-driver, like Gloucester's old town crier but
without the bell, announced to passengers who
boarded, "Trolley to Taraville and points north,
through Pigeonhole Cove to Rockport, Rockport
being our last and final destination. From Rockport, change trolleys for your return trip to civilization."

Thus it was that the two men rode a packed
trolley past the Addison Gilbert Hospital, around
the Mills, which featured no tidal mills now but
only a couple of small stores, up Meeting House
Hill, he Methodist church with its Paul Revere bell,
down through the shade of the Riverdale Willows,
planted on each side of the road to hold it from
melting away each spring, past the old Hodgkins
grist mill and the long stone bridge to Annisquam,
up and around twists and past coves, roaring faster
than seemed safe over the tracks up on a trestle
next to Plum Cove, through the village, around the
bend at the Lanesville post office, soon beside Folly
Cove, sparkling and broad, and its granite wharf
where hundreds of Finnish quarrymen had

marched on strike and had won higher wages about twenty years earlier, on up the hilly stretch to Rockport, then past several hotels and the booming, banging Cape Ann Tool Company, Savinen's bakery—the scent of cardamom forever in the yeasty air just here—Antti Niemi's cobbler shop, past the red granite bank-like solid Rockport Granite Company's offices, next rushing over the Keystone Bridge, and then, just as Pigeon Cove ended, at the stop in front of Rockport's volunteer fire station, they alighted. They got off the trolley on Granite Street because Guy said that he wanted to walk, to which Ed nodded. Guy had been babbling for the entire trip, as Ed had been nodding. As they walked down the slope and not only Back Beach came into view but also a veritable bevy of bathing beauties, Ed realized Guy's motive.

"You've been here before," Ed said, creeping up on articulating his realization.

"Nothing like this on the East Coast until you hit Coney Island," Guy said, throwing his arms out as if to embrace all of the girls at the beach.

"Big waves," Ed said, being risqué without risk. In fact, the beach was so enclosed that its waves were ostentatiously minimal, although "big" was a dimension not without presence on Back Beach and the next strand of sand, Front Beach, as well.

"Shall we stop and draw?" Guy said.

"And draw flies? Guy, you do not even have a sketchpad."

"I'm gathering ideas."

"You said walk, and walk we shall."

"We're here to see the sights," Guy grumbled.

"You ain't seen nuthin' yet," Ed said, imitating Al Jolson. Passing Front Beach, rather than skip by "Oker the Haberdasher, Tailoring done on premises," Guy insisted that they stop. He had spied a straw hat among goods in the front window. Once properly attired in a new straw boater with a blue ribbon, Guy was beaming. For himself, Ed perked up at the turn of Main Street upon reaching a shoe store. Van Gogh's shoes did not come into his mind, nor the bile he tasted on contemplating all of the unnecessary walking that ground soles down to nothing. Rather, the display in the window of "John Tarr, Dry Goods, Wearing Apparel and Footwear" caught Ed's eye because of his father. It was an odd link, but real to Ed. He told Guy, "Imagine this store around dawn, in the early light of long shadows. What could outdo a closed store shortly after dawn?"

In an instant, Ed was far from Gloucester, far from 1923. Ed saw his father's store as it was before 1900. In life, his father had tread water, holding his place in society only on his father-in-law's money and as a storekeeper, a sweeper with an apron who maintained a modest dry goods store. Despising such an occupation, Ed maintained distance. He looked at stores from outside, he sketched store-fronts. In his paintings, nobody was entering, purchasing, or coming out of a store, let alone smiling. Not for Ed was the busy emporium, or men on cracker boxes gathered around a pot-belly stove. He never once depicted a customer anywhere. When Ed at seventeen had signed up for a correspondence course, he knew exactly what he was doing: he was drawing a line that he would not cross: business was not for him.

His father shut down the store shortly after Ed began receiving and sending back his assignments, it turned out that his father retired, although in good health, because he had never liked his work either. Ed asked him why he had persisted in the trade for so long. "I thought you might want to keep a store," he said. His father's words hurt. How little he had known his son, who had on several occasions distinctly stated his ambition to become a naval architect or, at least, a designer of yachts, certainly a draftsman. When he reminded his father years later, the old man had shrugged and told him in a glum tone, "After I saw you drawing those boats, then I knew. Best laid plans, you know." Ed asked, "You had to see me draw?" His father's reply redeemed him. The old man, although quite ill by then, looked him hard in the eyes—they had staring in common—and said, "I did. You learn a lot from watching customers, Eddie. Use your eyes." He had to mean nothing less than that he saw his son as an artist in his very first crude drawings. Ed's childhood admiration of his father flooded back into him from that point and never left. He buried a father he loved more than ever, and missed him now in Rockport.

Ed had needed this paternal encouragement, but not the old man's specific instruction. Ed did use his eyes. The Hoppers' family legacy was staring. No day dawned in which he did not use his eyes. He also used his legs. When the family store had been closed for over a year, its goods gathering dust, to that vacant ruin Ed was drawn as if to ancient Rome. He did not walk, he bicycled alone up to HOPPER'S DRY GOODS. So said the sign still, but it was truly neither Hopper's then nor a dry goods.

He never told his father about his visit (which became a series of visits) and his reveries before the crude but colorfully painted wooden Indian. Holding a handful of cigars, it had once stood proudly by the door, a sign that tobacco could be had within. Now the fallen chief shrank in the shadows behind the display window, as if guarding an inventory, but an inventory that never moved and instead lingered on, unsold, headed toward an indefinite but surely a humbling, if not an utterly catastrophic fate. The contrasting dimness of the unlit building with its dusty—was that a spider dangling from a cobweb? —outsized windows was haunting. His father never told him later when the store was sold and its inventory was taken out, dumped unceremoniously to make space for a women's tailor. One day, Ed rode his bike up to find that the store had blossomed into many shades of pink and purple dresses—the colors of the season —under a great green awning. He did not venture inside.

His father and the old wooden Indian came to mind now as he and Guy walked along Main Street in Rockport. For Ed, the wooden figure's motionlessness, and silence embodied stuckness. The Indian suggested something too awful to articulate in any but a metaphorical way. Garishly displayed, humankind's limits, his species' frozen, bound, trapped state challenged Ed to drop any comforting illusion of free will. Ed walked in conscious pain on Main Street, among fellow pitiable creatures, barely living; if breathing, nothing more than surviving. The time to view a shoe store was when it was closed, in the early morning, empty, before anybody walked by or looked in its windows, inert shoes, motionless shoes.

Guy would never know, because Ed would never utter, how he felt staring into the window of Tarr's store. Did Guy think that he was considering buying a new pair of shoes? He was, rather, thinking of death, of being among the walking, shod dead. Money was dead. Goods were dead. Had Ed in his young manhood confided in his father (he never had) he would have shared thoughts that the exchange of money for goods constituted a particularly lifeless livelihood. He sympathized with his now-dead father as he stared in Rockport.

But then the two men moved on, Guy walking smartly, his straw hat having gone to his head, while Ed trudged, his glumpy old shoes dragging. To Ed's fallen spirits Rockport offered a respite, if not a living rebuttal. It moved. Grains of sand at the beach shifted, waves surged and fell back, winds raised sails. Life beckoned here along the shore in a gap between the bank and L.E. Smith's three-story whitewashed building with a broad striped awning. He took in a broad view of rushing, incoming waves. The sparkling, foaming blue waters reminded him of his ambition to be a naval architect. His high hopes had come to nothing, but he never forgot his effervescent spirits. He suddenly felt a surge of good cheer. In that moment, Cape Ann was his crossroads. What lay ahead of him but an open horizon?

Not hearing Guy discourse on the weather and seagulls (he hoped none would "spot" his straw hat), Ed stared at this slice of sea for a moment while his mind wandered all about his past, his present and his future. As a facilitator of commerce, as a cog in the great American illustrations marketing machine, he might have pleased his old man. But his father knew better before he died. He saw a future in his son's sketches. Ed's ambition to draw his way up and into vessels had itself sailed away before he went to Paris. Now, in 1923 Ed wanted, no, he *craved* to be an artist. He would be the king of vacant houses, mastering them, evoking their stillness, seeing, and painting raw and bleak exteriors as the insoluble mysteries they were. He wanted to nail stuckness so perfectly that his father's wooden Indian would be but his father's wooden Indian. Ed, in short, wanted to show others the corner into which life painted them all. When Ed's seething brain ceased to pump out this series of bleak reveries, he realized that he was walking, and that Guy was talking.

"But what of living, I say? Don't we all really look for paintings that display life? I mean paintings that make us think and respond, ah, yes, life is like that, people engaged with people. Right, Ed?"

Talkativeness seemed suddenly contagious under the Rockport skies. Ed said, "I like light and shadows, Guy. Did you grasp the poignance of the window display of Tarr's store yourself? Weren't you moved?"

"Not so much. I saw that winter boots were on sale."

Ed went on undeterred, "Imagine the owner of that store, his hope to sell those shoes, coveting customers as he placed that line of drab children's shoes out on the step-like levels of black-carpeted shelves. Did you notice those shoes' colors, in this light?"

"Various browns and tans, Ed," Guy said, but Ed was barely listening.

"There is so much pathos in a painting of this empty shoe store and its empty shoes. To use one of your terms—pointillistic—a pointillistic spectrum of brown shades, a prism of broken dreams."

"Prisms have more colors."

"How much more moving and realistic is Tarr's store that than a painting of two tiny figures of boys flying a kite under a darkening sky."

"Ed, you're dead wrong and you know better. What about Norman Rockwell? Canvases with two boys and a kite sell very well."

"Winslow Homer, too, I suppose. Bring him up

if you want, Guy, but I hear that he never painted
except for money."

"You heard that from me. Commissions drove
his brush, but he was a great artist. We're both
artists enough to know the difference between art
and illustration. We have been illustrators."

Guy unintentionally stung Ed, hitting a sore
spot: Guy had moved on. Guy had *been* an illustrator while, unless Ed changed his life at age forty,
Ed was *still* an illustrator. Commercial art that
saved him from starving to death, which enabled
him to summer in Gloucester, did not feed his soul
—but illustrating was nonetheless what he continued to *do*. He went silent, as did Guy, thank God.

They walked on, passing art galleries, niches of
culture in a street that otherwise offered the public
shoes, hats, Tuck's taffy and no fewer than three
breakfast establishments. The ham and eggs place
—over which was a bowling alley that opened at
noon—"10 a.m. on rainy days"—was cheek by
jowl next to doughnuts, nisu and pastries served
with coffee or tea, and a few doors down from the
fanciest red-checked tablecloth option of fresh local
blueberries, strawberries and cream, cinnamon-
sprinkled oatmeal, or pancakes with maple syrup.

However, neither Ed nor Guy suggested breakfast and they only stopped finally at the end of
Main Street, approaching the start of Bearskin
Neck, where a colonial had slain the last bear in
these parts and hung its hide up to dry. Declining to
explore the Neck, they then traipsed on past shops
of silversmiths and pewter artisans, locally made
quilts, penny candies, artist's supplies and souvenirs
up toward T Wharf. There, at the granitic edge of
the continent, next stop England, they took seats
atop granite blocks, on which thrones they were
monarchs of all that they surveyed. They looked

across Rockport's inner harbor over to a barn-red shack loaded with lobster buoys.

"Would you paint it?" Ed asked Guy.

Guy paused, squinted, then frowned and shook his head, "This would never be anybody's first choice of a motif. What do you say?"

"I say you know your onions."

Wordless, Guy watched as Ed sketched the lobster boats and dories moored or moving into or out of Rockport harbor this fine summer day. It was a good hour before either said anything more, then it was, surprisingly, Ed.

"This is too jolly for me," Ed said, sighing. He had dutifully transcribed morning in Rockport in rhythmic lines upon his sketchpad, but no sketch possessed the power to move that was inherent in the window of John Tarr's store. Nuanced and squiggly lines of reflections on nearly calm water might please him some other time but Ed lacked patience for another hour of it, despite the weather, the clear light and the artist-beckoning seascape.

"Don't worry, I can see that I wouldn't do much with this either," Guy said as they both rose up from their respective granite blocks. "A flapper checking out a con man is worth an acre of boats in Rockport. What do you say to that, Ed?"

"I say that artists say the silliest things and that you should write a book."

As they walked back to catch the trolley back to civilization, it came to Ed that he ought to be on the lookout for Jo, but he asked Guy about Craske and the Man at the Wheel.

"Are we still going to seek out the statue?"

"Don't say it so loudly," Guy said, "but yes. Tonight, come over to my place at seven and we'll take a cab to East Gloucester. I don't think Craske will let that statue out of his sight. And I bet he will be unable to resist showing it to two artists from New York."

However, when they knocked on his door, nobody answered. Craske was not at home and, if his famous statue was, they never learned it.

Chapter Eight

Ed awoke from a dream. In it, he floated outside, above and around a house with impossibly many eaves and cornices, terrifying light and shadows, walls radiant wherever the sun touched, even incandescent, reflecting, glowing, shimmering infinitely subtle reds, blues and yellows, all the while he was searching in all of his pockets, finding no pockets, finding no pencil, no charcoal, no means to draw—and then the house suddenly groaned in seeming pain and began to melt, more swiftly than an ice cream in the sun, colors fading fast, everything merging into liquid, shades of Payne's gray engulfing and overwhelming, no corners defined and longer, all murk, not a line surviving. He awoke with a start.

Skipping any coffee after he shaved in haste, after verifying that he had pencils *and* a pencil sharpener, leaving the boarding house to lumber along with a wooden box of brushes and paints, an easel hanging from a strap over his shoulder, traversing the roads beside the houses of Gloucester— and also the Marchant Box Factory, which had four electric generators, more than any other box factory in the world, and more famous than Ed—Ed, as determined to sketch and to paint as the sun was determined to shine that day, all unwittingly and circuitously wended his way toward Jo, Jo of New York, whom he had not even guessed to be in Gloucester.

At the stop for the trolley, Ed, ever staring, unable to turn off his eyes, scanned and spotted an artistic pen and ink notice, with sketch, of LOST CAT. From its neat and careful lettering, he discerned the name of this lost cat's owner, Josephine Nivison. She listed her local address, a boarding house a few blocks away run by one Mrs. Murphy. Then, in the bushes near the telephone pole and sign, Ed spotted a cat like the one in the poster, meowing.

Ed said, "Oh, shit."

He alone seemed to be standing here, elected by fate of all men and women on earth to rescue said cat, whose name was indicated on the sign to be "Arthur."

Ed found himself squatting and holding out a hand, although he had no food to offer, feeling foolish, saying "Arthur" repeatedly. The cat did the cat thing of looking suspiciously, but looking nonetheless, waving its tail about in its turmoil, then slowly and warily approaching the proffered hand.

"Do not bite me, Arthur. I am a friend of your mother's."

His voice had startled the feline, who turned and dashed back under the bushes, where it crouched, as if hidden but actually perfectly visible.

"Damn," Ed said, as he saw the trolley coming along and clanging its bell.

With an agility he retained from his youth, Ed bent low and scooped the cat up into both hands, holding it, especially its paws, soothing it by saying, "Arthurkitty, Arthurkitty."

The trolley operator opened the door to the orange painted vehicle from which two poles stood up like antennae, sparking occasionally from the overhanging lines. Ed loped up the three steps.

"Oh, no animals allowed aboard, sir," the driver said.

"It's no animal, it's a lost cat," Ed said. "I'm taking it back to its owner. If you will get out and look at the poster there on the telephone pole, you'll see. I am on a mission of mercy."

"Where is the owner?"

After Ed said the address, the driver closed the door and set the controls and the trolley lurched forward. He told Ed, "Well, that is not very far. Three stops. Five cents each."

"He won't need a seat," Ed said, holding the cat in one hand and fishing in his pocket for a nickel in change.

"Ten cents," the driver said.

Ed put the nickel into the collection machine. As it clinked, Ed said, "Children are free."

The driver said, "He is no kitten."

"Neither am I," Ed said. "I am a Good Samaritan. Good Samaritans ride free."

"You want to pay or get off at the next stop?" the driver asked.

Ed stood, found another nickel, pushed it in the slot, and after the clink said, "There is your ten cents, and I am taking up two seats."

"Two seats are fine, sir. Just hold onto the cat," the driver said. "Some people are allergic."

"Yes, and I am allergic to people," Ed said.

"You like cats?" a woman passenger asked from across the aisle.

"Less by the minute," Ed asked. The trolley was arriving at the first of the three stops before he would get off with the cat.

"What is his name?" the woman asked.

"Balls," Ed said. "His name is 'Balls,' and do not ask why or I will tell you."

The trolley went the next two stops in silence all around until the driver announced, "Third stop, men with cats may leave us now. Thank you for taking the trolley today."

He struggled now to hold the cat, along with everything else. Perhaps the cat understood how near it was to being reunited with Jo. In any case, Ed swore freely while trying, with difficulty, to maintain control of the cat, which scratched him vigorously on both forearms, drawing blood.

A white sign with black printed letters "ROOMS *for Tourists*" stood hanging from a post in the small front yard behind sunlit hedges of many shades of green. The many windows of the two-story house were secured from intrusive eyes by dark green awnings and, on each side, by green shutters to batten down at season's end. He walked four steps up the stoop, standing then under a jutting overhead to prevent rain and snow from covering the steps. After he knocked, Mrs. Murphy promptly let him in, and he asked for Jo Nivison.

"Who shall I tell her is calling?" Mrs. Murphy asked.

"Her cat," Ed said. He then endured fully five minutes of soprano singing, welcoming greetings by Mrs. Murphy to Arthur in a baby voice that "Arthur kitty, Arthur kitty. Arthur came back, Arthur darlin is home now," and such expressions of delight.

"Please stop," Ed said. "Can you get Jo now, please?"

"And how. She will be so happy."

"No less happy than I, madam."

In a few minutes, Jo came downstairs in nightdress and bathrobe, her red hair all askew. She was as Ed last saw her, though less clothed and more breathless.

"Oh, Arthur," she wailed, her hands out to take the cat from him, as she bellowed, "look at you, my darling."

Standing aside, ignored, Ed finally cleared his throat and said, "You're welcome very much. Do you have a Band-Aid or two handy?"

"Oh, thank you, darling Eddie. May I kiss you?"

"You may hug your cat," Ed said. "Mercurochrome and band-aids would be appropriate for me."

"Oh, yes, yes, I will, hug my cat. Oh, yes. How are you doing, Ed? It's been a while."

"It has been a while. I'm bleeding. Have you anything for scratches?"

"Oh, my," she said, calling Mrs. Murphy to root about for medical supplies. She then hugged her cat as Ed stared at her.

He finally said, "And, as for how I am doing, I was delayed this morning by an errand, to return a lost cat to its owner."

"Oh, I am sorry. On such a nice day."

"He couldn't be lost on a rainy day. He picked a day without clouds, with such sunlight that it lights walls into incandescence and sharpens shadows to black. But Ed Hopper, of course, instead of painting rides a trolley with a cat and pays ten cents for the privilege."

"He didn't need his own seat."

"That's what I said."

"I'll repay you."

"Don't bother. And they let children ride free."

Jo kissed her cat and then, as Ed moved to

leave, she raised her hand to his neck and offered to
kiss him.

"Um, not after the cat," Ed said.

Jo let him go, saying, "Oh."

"Do you often kiss the cat?"

"We haven't seen each other in three days. I
was worried he was D-E-A-D."

"I thought about making him D-E-A-D myself.
But then they have seven lives, don't they?" Ed
asked.

"And we but one. Pity," Jo said.

"My, you're poetic this morning," Ed said. After
Mrs. Murphy appeared with rubbing alcohol "for
the infection," which stung and burned when applied, and bandaged his forearms by winding gauze
around each, finally making it look like he had
slashed his wrists. Ed was then discharged and free
to go.

His hand on the brass doorknob and turning it,
carrying his wooden box and the easel dangling
from the strap around one shoulder, he said, addressing Jo and ignoring Arthur, "Well, Jo, see you
around, kid."

"Yes, see you, Ed. Wave bye-bye, Arthurkins,"
Jo said, raising the cat's paw up and down as if in a
bye-bye. The cat's expression, like Ed's, was sour as
they stared each other down. Then the door closed,
she heard his feet trot down the steps, he was gone,
and she was holding the cat.

Chapter Nine

In another part of the city, East Gloucester, a place of shipyards, restaurants, residences, and rumor had it (rightly), speakeasies, the itinerant *Times* reporter was parking his red roadster on East Main Street and getting out to approach the door of a ramshackle two-story shingled house. Here lived a sculptor.

As the door opened, Don faced a tall man dressed much like a fisherman between trips in a dark blue, worn jersey crisscrossed by white streaks and corduroy pants of the color known among the locals as "shit brown." His shoes were as formidable as boots. Don introduced himself and said, "Thank you for meeting with me, Mr. Craske."

When Craske answered, he exposed his British origins with a London accent that remained strong some fifteen years after his immigration.

"I am flattered, Nash," he said, sounding much like an actor in an Oscar Wilde play. "You call me Craske or Leonard, or Lenny or Len, as you choose, righto?"

Don opted for a simple "yes." They sat in the sculptor's living room on cushioned chairs, with permission to make notes, ("Sketch me if you want"), in a few comfortable minutes, Don nailed down that Craske was 47 years old, had been born in Kensington, "not within the shadow of Trafalgar Square but not far either from the center of the City" of London. He first undertook medical studies in his early twenties but found that he was not cut out to be a doctor.

"It offended my sensibilities to cut or to saw away at the human body, although anatomy itself I found absolutely fascinating. I went from two years immersed in the study of bodies, living and dead, to a study of sculpting human beings. I remain forever grateful for my medical studies. My anatomy work helps me any time I sculpt."

Don wrote down that Craske had studied under Paul Raphael Montford and "the Dicksee family," whoever they were. Mention of the Dicksee family reminded him involuntarily of his own, a family that he now never saw. If he ever saw the Nash family again, it would be by accident. His mother and brother and sister were too much under the thumb of the tyrant at the head of the household to buck the prohibition against communicating with Don.

"I also acted," Craske said, with a swirling gesture of his right hand, "primarily in farces or Shakespeare. A bit of music hall stuff, too, as I could sing in those days. Not so much lately, you know, with Prohibition. It dries your throat or something, you never sound better than when you are drunk."

He decided against asking Craske how he got along with his family. Instead, he asked questions about the statue, which paid off handsomely. He was sure to use every crumb of detail that Craske offered him. For starters, the statue had been assembled in parts, he said.

"It has the legs of one man, the back and neck of another, the head of a fishing captain you would know but I don't want to give names. That would take the story away from the representational aspect of what I did. It would also reduce the excitement of mystery and guessing, you understand. Mystery is the ticket. Like Shakespeare's 'dark lady.' The very point of assemblage, which is what I call my technique, is that the result is anonymous, bearing the impression of the type rather than any part-i-cu-lar re-cog-niz-able rump."

Don was writing notes, which made Craske wary.

"I think 'rump' was incautious. Let's say 'face,' shall we?"

"My editor would never let me go with 'rump,'" Don said.

"Have you tried? I'd like to know that I was interviewed by a young man who tried to break into print in the *Gloucester Daily Times* with 'rump,'" Craske said.

Don said that he was sorry, he had not actually tried, unfortunately.

"I'm sorry, too," Craske said, his blue eyes twinkling, "On the supposition that your editor will resist the temptation to print, I grant you my permission to try with my quotation. I am already the winner of the competition, and the state is going to pay me ten thousand dollars for the work. I do not face much risk with 'rump.' Go ahead and give it a go."

They talked further and he found that the American Legion had allowed him space in which to sketch fishermen who posed in boots and wearing a variety of gear, open shirts, slickers, sou'westers, and tousled hair blowing in the sea breeze. Don heard about the evolution of the statue from a feisty young man out to challenge the sea with a degree of boldness to a more crouched, wary, stern-faced older fisherman with a sou'wester.

"Let's go and visit," Craske said. "The original is under wraps at the Legion Hall. You can see the father of the monument, much younger and braver on his face than the older, wiser man. You know the saying, don't you?"

Don asked Craske to tell him.

"There are bold sailors, and there are old sailors, but there are no old, bold sailors."

"Some truth in that."

"Much truth," Craske said. "A truth I've tried to show in the older, wiser mien of the man I depicted, not a bold sailor but a wise one."

With that much for his article, Don drove them both in his red Stutz Bearcat over to the Legion Hall. The Joan of Arc statue being prominent and nearby, Don asked Craske what he thought of it. Craske leaned back and looked up, his admiration obvious.

"The sculptor did a wonderful job but it's not a Medieval French lass from the country fitted into armor, it's a London tailor-made suit of armor for which a Victorian lady was fitted," Craske said. "Please do not quote me but as a former citizen of the United Kingdom, I would say that here you have someone who could ride out of *Country Life*, that periodical's frontispiece of Lady Fermor-Hesketh mounted."

The two men then entered the Hall and went upstairs, where Craske casually unveiled the plaster original and pointed out various features, including describing those that he changed in the monument to be unveiled the following week.

Craske told Don, "The man at the wheel you

will see unveiled at the Boulevard is older than this one, deeper lines in his face. And I have changed the weather to rough seas. You will see that my man at the wheel is steering through a storm, high waves and heavy rain coming down, him hardly able to see, or to judge where he is. It's a true story that has had different endings. On some ships, the man went down. On others, 'given sea room enough,' you know, the helmsman weathered the gale, the ship reached home. Don, those men were equally brave, whatever fate they met."

"Will you be speaking at the unveiling?" Don asked.

"I have no great desire to address the crowd other than visually," Craske said, replacing the tarp over the statue. "I greatly enjoy the tete-a-tete and meetings with a few friends, confidentially, off the record, over drinks. Conversation, you know, rather than public addresses. Public addresses got us all into no end of trouble, the War, you know."

The sculptor had lived in Gloucester long enough to ask a question of Don, "The French officers who came here for the dedication of Joan, they did not make an address, did they?"

Don, home from Harvard for the purpose, had stood alongside his family at the dedication, one of their last times all together. He said that they had only said a few respectful words to convey the "eternal gratitude" of the French people for the American fighting forces that helped the country to stay free.

Craske said, "That is all that we can say, we who survived the war. My statue represents the fishermen who, although wary, although cautious, although wise, nonetheless went down to the sea in ships. You know, I never stopped thinking about the loss of men, so many men to bring fish to market, so many. That was in my mind each moment I worked on the body that would represent them all, the living and the dead."

"You thought about your time in medical school, then?"

"Impossible not to, working with the human body. Sick or well, our bodies are so many transient vessels in which we sail about in life. Medical studies, anatomy, dissections, but don't let's get into all that. You have enough of a job already to run the gauntlet with my 'rump.' To that end, I wish you well."

Don thought that Craske had to be the most amusing man he had ever interviewed. In imagination and articulation, Craske was great, but born or gifted with a great modesty and humility also and an openness to what Gloucester was about, and the greater world—clearly, he was not finished.

"The War changed the outer world more than it changed Gloucester," Craske told Don as they descended the stairs and got into his car. "Here, the tides go in, the tides go out, storms and fair weather come and go, back-breaking hauls and empty nets, good trips, bad trips, all the rhythm of Gloucester. The man at the wheel is not old fashioned or ever going to be dated. My man at the wheel stands the same now as men at sea a hundred years ago, nay, three hundred years ago, and I dare predict, will stand as men—and, by then, women, too—go down to the sea in ships a hundred years from now, when Gloucester is four hundred years old."

"You foresee changes."

"More on land than at sea. No, except women at work, and better and bigger ships, out there the struggle will always be against the sea and the risk of storms and the unlucky trips. The changes will come on land, Don, in sprawling cities, Prohibition

will come and go, Rockport will vote wet, young
people will let their hair grow and rebel, jazz will
be universal until other music comes after jazz and
other music after that, and, may I say, what is going
on in the back seat when Junior takes Millie out will
acc-el-e-rate."

"Off the record?" Don said.

"Ab-so-lute-ly not. Print every word if your editor will let you," Craske said as they reached his
home.

"I do not foresee that long an article."

"Neither do I, Nash. You asked me about
change. What did you expect? I don't see human
beings standing still. You'll live longer and see
more. Planes will be flying to the moon in your
lifetime."

"I don't think so."

"I'd bet on it, Don. Cameras will develop pictures themselves. Movies will come with sound and
radios will come with movie attachments. On tele-
phones, you will see who you are talking to."

"You should tell Roger Babson, the investor."

"I already did. He's running with one of my
ideas, an anti-gravity device to prevent plane
crashes."

"That would be great."

"I wish I had an idea like that to prevent ships
from sinking, but I can't figure one out, even in
theory."

Having theoretically solved the problem of
falling planes and placed sinking ships into the list
of projects ahead, Craske was at an end and
home. While Craske urged him to come back
again soon, for which Don was grateful, Don
doubted that a second interview could be even
half as interesting as this one. Don started up his
red roadster and wished for a moment that he

were headed home to see his family. What a story he had to share.

But it was not to be. Checking the rearview mirror as he pulled out, Don saw no vehicle coming. Despite the increasingly high numbers of automobile sales in the country, it was not often that one really needed to look before pulling out into the road. Whenever Don drove from the Boulevard down Western Avenue up and into Essex, as a virtual hobby he monitored incoming traffic. Most times, he did not encounter a single incoming car. He hoped that they would not build a bridge over the Annisquam besides the one already in place at the Blynman Canal. Another bridge, a highway to Boston, would end the island isolation that had insulated Gloucester from changing too much for three hundred years and counting. But not to worry. Don estimated the chances of building a high bridge to span the Annisquam about even with the chance that human beings would walk on the moon in his lifetime or that the Boston Braves would move to Atlanta.

Chapter Ten

Ed was taking the trolley alone this day. Guy had plans to meet someone and, although he asked Ed to join them, it was not in Ed to lose any more sunlight and sketching. He wanted to inspect a building he had noticed when with Guy on their earlier expedition. Drawn to drug stores, Ed got off the streetcar in the center of Lanesville, near the corner to Lane's Cove, at the Foster Brothers' drug store.

A bell jingled over the screen door as he entered. Too clean, this immaculate store had to be owned by an obsessive. The smell of an astringent was in the air, witch hazel. The proprietor of Foster Brothers was reading a book. Ed wondered if he was looking at himself, had he followed his father into keeping a store, a lonely bachelor reading between customers.

"Fred Foster, sir," the old man said, looking up from an open book and marking his place with a receipt. He wore a white coat without a collar of the type favored years ago by surgeons and druggists. Hair remained atop his head, but of a whitish gray that Ed thought he could whip up with titanium white and just a bit of Payne's gray. White

eyebrows and a neatly trimmed white moustache
completed his early snow visage. He wore bifocal
gold-framed spectacles on a neck loop in case they
fell.

"Edward Hopper," Ed said, not to be discourte-
ous. Neither of them made a move to shake hands.

"I like your accent, sir. We get a lot of New
Yorkers here each summer. Are you an artist?"

Ed had replied, "I pass for one in New York,"
and Foster laughed.

After asking if he needed linseed oil, which Ed
declined, Foster asked Ed about the new stadium
that the Yankees were building. Although Foster's
habit was to offer more conversationally than he
asked, this suited Ed just fine.

"I've seen it," Ed said, thinking that the tan-to-
ward-sepia walls of Indiana limestone that impressed him for a painting someday. Had Ed not
feared to trigger a flood of talk he would have told
Foster that, although new, Yankee Stadium was already like an old photograph fading to brown, a
collegiate sort of edifice without the usual insipid
green ivy cover. More surface than shadow, its face
expressing a dare, Yankee Stadium was a bold fist
of a structure. The hindrance was that Ed could
hardly paint it empty; no viewer would ever see it
as anything but filled with fans, the source of a roar
when Babe Ruth hit a home run.

Foster, busy using a wet rag lightly to dust im-
peccably clean glass counters and wipe the glass
doors of cabinets holding medications and patent
remedies, said, "I am hoping maybe the Braves can
get the Babe back. You know that he was sold to
raise funds for a darn Broadway musical? What a
shame. Why, if it was up to me whether we'd have
'Tea for Two' or the Babe in Boston, I'd go for the
Babe in Boston every time. Darn Yankees. My late

brother said that that trade would curse Boston, that we'd never win another pennant, and he was sure as heck right. Ain't it something? We haven't yet. And looks like it might be quite a while, too."

"So far," Ed said, nodding, but Foster was only getting into gear.

"You aren't looking for whiskey, are you?"

"No," Ed said, shaking his head as well.

"Lots of tourists think that the drug stores stock whiskey, but it is by prescription only," Foster said, emphasizing the last three words in a bit louder voice and with slight pauses between each word. Then, he leaned over and asked in a whisper, "You a veteran?"

"No," Ed said.

After looking right and left although Ed was the only other person in the store, Foster said, "Veterans I, uh, don't care if they have the prescription on them. Could be they left it home, right? I figure, anyway, what they saw Over There, they need their medication."

Next looking Ed in the eye, the old man asked simply, "What do you want?"

The question was existential, the one Ed came to Gloucester to answer, and now it was eerie to have it put to him here in the Foster Brothers drug store.

"You have soda pop?" Ed asked, sounding lame even to his own ears.

"Not here, sorry. If anybody told you to come to Foster Brothers' for a soda pop, they were just pulling your leg. No, sir, never. You know that soda pop used to come with corked bottles and how they'd explode?"

Ed recalled those days when soda pop actually popped its corks, but he chose not to speak, only to nod.

"My brother Howard, God rest him, he never wanted soda exploding in our store and we never did stock it, even after those metal caps came in. I suppose I could put some in, but I haven't. Sort of an offense to his memory, you know? Good man, he died of the Spanish flu. This here counter was the front line, with sick folks coming in for medicines. Howie always rooted for the Red Sox. Funny but the Red Sox haven't won a Series since he passed. Did I tell you his prediction?"

"Yes," Ed said.

"I root for the Braves. Say, have you ever been to Braves Field? It is gi-gantic, I'm telling you. Gigantic. It's hard to hit them out of Braves Field. I don't know as any player will ever do it, even Ty Cobb. Of course, anything could happen. You hear about the guy just came up from Rhode Island to play on the team, his first game, Ernie Padgett? He went out to play shortstop, and bang, right into the record books. Un-assisted tri-ple play. His first game, sir. That's baseball, ain't it? Planning ahead is just the same in life, just as presumptuous. You can't plan the fifth inning, can you? That's what I always say. No. And Fenway Park, what a field. You've seen it, haven't you?"

"No," Ed said.

"You got to before you go back to Gotham. Braves Field and Fenway Park both. Fenway's like, you know, one of those Easter eggs you peep into and see all green, sharp, and clean inside, a regular bandbox. If I was ever a writer, a classy author, I'd be a sportswriter, and my summers would be all baseball. Oh, mister, the things I would write about Fenway, like how it is a compromise between Euclid and Nature."

"I like that," Ed said, and he truly did. He was a fanatic for buildings that hit the trademark be-

tween Nature's beguiling irregularities and man's
Euclidean determinations, but just now he was
heading for the door without another word, not
even a good-bye, just nodding, lest he trigger Foster
to go into a litany of the best players of the game
or its New York origins, debating whether it was
delivered by Doubleday in Cooperstown or born in
the Elysian Fields across the river in New Jersey.

As Ed left, Foster said, "You get back, you see
what you can do to pass the word in New York
among your contacts to send the Babe back to Boston. The Braves need him, you know?"

Credited with influence he did not possess Ed
nodded and closed the jingling screen door behind
him. As he made his exit, he did not hear Foster's
last remarks, something about Fenway, perhaps
seeing Fenway, or agreeing about Fenway. Foster
Brothers' store had not passed Ed's inspection. Too
clean, too boxy, and painted gray, not whitewashed,
more like an Odd Fellows Hall in upstate New York
than a local pharmacy, exuding an omnipresent
camaraderie. Not for Ed to paint.

Smiling over Foster's remark that "you can't
plan the fifth inning," in his own unplanned mid-
life Ed passed the small firehouse next door, its
barn door open to show off a gleaming brass engine, motorized now, horse-drawn no more. He
came to the Knights of Pythias hall, a boarded-up
former liquor store—in front of which he stopped,
gazing at it as at a Roman ruin, noting the varying
textures of the boards, the spectrum of browns,
some warm, some cool and dark, inviting him to
linger—almost tempting him to sketch, but then he
could smell cardamon emanating from a Finn
bakery that must have been braiding loops of
dough into *nisu*, sugar-sprinkled sweet bread best
eaten with fresh, strong coffee, which drew him on.

However, although he inhaled, he did not stop, and
he also crossed the street rather than take the road
that turned down to Lane's Cove, certainly a place
to stake out for later that summer,—he must return
for a full day at Lane's Cove among its shacks and
dories, the breakwater, and its old, beached coal
barge—because he wanted to see what was to be
seen elsewhere this morning.

Ed thus walked briskly past the Lanesville station of the United States Post Office, oddly set on
the right side of a duplex apartment-house.
Through a picture window, as if framed, a bald
man with thickish eyeglasses looked out, sunlit
against the dark interior, like a bored animal in a
cage. A painting, but not for him, not today. Ed
spared barely a glance at a barn, a cornfield, and a
huge house, definitely designed as a boarding
house, three sprawling stories, flowers, an apple tree
and a pear tree in its front yard as if to say, "An
Italian family lives here." Too much activity to
please him, with its emanations of people inside,
women cooking, cleaning, tending babies.

He walked by other non-starters, homes that
did not lure him to look, let alone to paint until, at
the top of the hill, a yellow clapboard, two stories,
with two queer-looking old-fashioned arched windows on the front of its third floor or attic, two ce-
ment lions standing on the sides of its four-step
stoop which led to a door of frosted glass on which
a flowery design was traced. It was nonetheless another treasure that he quickly decided that he had
to leave behind. He could never articulate the Victorian voluptuousness of this comfortable residence. He looked until he was satisfyingly filled by
the long, narrow porch roof and pillars, open over
a long row of posts topped by a banister. On the
porch was a rocking chair and a straight chair that

was relocated to the porch for the summer season. Whoever lived here, Ed imagined, had an icebox, took coal deliveries, stored canned goods in a pantry with a floor-length curtain and cooled their pies on the windowsills. Sadly, he envisioned, they had already sacrificed serenity for a squawky telephone with a multi-ring party line, and maybe even a crystal radio set, an old ship refitted for its twentieth century voyage.

Next door, he spotted a backyard sauna—no smoke, not today—and a house that was upright, indeed, as if a dog that wanted to stand on its hind legs, an off-yellow with brown-painted trim, which were magnificent choices. In its front yard, a spectacle by itself, was the sort of curving, curling apple tree that mimicked a serpent's grace in branches, winding about as if intent upon avoiding proximity to Heaven, more horizontal than vertical. He would have liked to draw it but the house, except for its colors, juicy, shiny brown as a chestnut freshly freed of its outer covering, did not move him. It was too simple. And it was not unoccupied, it felt to him that a Finnish woman would be busy inside, pulling sheets through a wringer in its cool cellar, or gathering rugs to hang them on the backyard line and beat them until the dust was gone from each one.

Further on, a tiny sign planted in the center of a small scrubby front yard said, in simple, neat block letters, "LOBSTERS," inviting awareness that here a man lived in part from off the fruit of the sea. The name on the doorplate was Morey. Morey the lobsterman's house was New England neat and trim like a lobster boat in good working condition, no more, no less than needed, Shaker-like as could be, square and featuring a front door in its dead center, fronted by a granite block a foot

above the sidewalk. Ed would have liked to have
seen the man's lobster boat and the man. Both were
at Lane's Cove even now.

Onward, Ed walked past newer houses, then by
Wainola Hall, in front of which stood a tall flagpole
with its American flag flapping and snapping in the
breeze that morning. But for that breeze, Ed would
have been sweating. As it was, he welcomed the
sight ahead of a store, where he might purchase
something to quench his thirst. Between two shady
elm trees, he walked to enter Ranta's Market.

Dry goods stores, groceries and drug stores fascinated Ed, whose father had been a storekeeper,
who had hoped that he might grow up to take over
the store.

"I'll be right with you," a man said from the
backroom, where Ed could see a pot-belly stove,
and a lead-lined sink at which the store's proprietor,
swathed in a white apron, washed his hands. A
meat cleaver gleamed on the butcher block, where
the man had been carving roasts from a side of
beef. Ed noticed strands of black thread tied just
above his elbows to prevent his white shirt sleeves
from slipping and getting into anything. The man,
whose face was round and definitely Finnish,
nodded and smiled.

"How can I help you?" he asked in the husky,
careful accent of Finns.

In the store, the smell of coffee dominated,
from fresh ground. Undertones of vinegar from
what Ed guessed was a pickle barrel, and molasses
—the barrel next to it, there for people to ladle as
much as they wished into containers they brought
from home for the purpose. Another sign indicated
kerosene for sale, and Ed imagined the hand-
cranked pump in the backroom for that purpose.
Ed was happy in this ambience, reminded of his

father's general store. A small rack of a couple of Wonder breads, a Sunbeam bread and a handful of fresh-baked turnovers and chocolate Bismarks suggested that more households baked their own than relied on the store for their daily bread or sweets. Lanesville was the hardest part of the Cape in which to make a living, all ledge and rocks and far from downtown.

Ed said, "I'd like a cold drink."

"Coca Cola?"

"Fine."

The man left the counter to serve up a bottle of coke, from the icy tub on the right of the door. Ed could not help but admire the gaudy cash register, its sides like a carnival organ, except that the keys of this organ went "ka-ching" and each note represented one more turn of the cogs of American commerce. Ed spotted a paper posted on the wall beside the register, a list of names with various figures beside them. The store obviously granted credit, tabs to be paid later in the week or month.

How the ornate brass register held his attention. If Ed were ever able—the cash register was so many lights and shadows and gorgeous shapes and colors here—it would be part of the imagined ideal painting of a store like his father's, closed, at night, or never to reopen. But he soon sensed the kicker, that in his imagined painting of a store closed, unlit, in twilight or in the shadowy dimness the prevailed not long after dawn, this miraculous register's best elements would vanish. Only in bright sunshine, especially the clean and clear light of a cloudless Gloucester sky, here before a large eight-by-eight front window, was the Ranta's Market cash register a thrilling object that repaid every second taken to view it.

Upon receiving his drink, Ed paid his nickel

and was on his way, imbibing sweet, tickling swigs of carbonated, caffeinated caramel from the green glass bottle until it was gone. He was then beside a cemetery that he decided to investigate. Graves never interested him, but the landscaping and trees of a cemetery often did, exemplifying a peaceful place. Here, he found an oddly disquieting, dark pond, around which weeping willows fell like green waterfalls to the sides of its black surface, as disturbing to his psyche as anything he had seen that day. He filled his Coca Cola bottle with dark water and let it go, to sink where it could not be seen. He then walked out to wait for the streetcar.

He returned the Gloucester the long way, via Rockport. Just before the keystone bridge, he saw workmen lined up for their weekly pay envelopes in front of the bank-like granite building of the ROCKPORT GRANITE CO., that company's name carved in bold stone letters above its door. As Ed rode, he mulled over what he had seen. That house he had walked past, the tall one next to the arthritic apple tree, the house with arched windows, he rewarmed for extended admiration. He again and regretfully concluded that it could not be painted, no more than the brass register at Ranta's Market. He retained in memory an ever-enlarging collection of Unpaintables, rich visual attractions resistant to pen or brush, forever dreams, uncatchable will o' wisps. He hoped not to encounter too many more objects so attractive and so far beyond his skills this summer. Even when he painted a perfectly paintable subject, Ed often thought, and occasionally said to himself aloud, "I am never able to paint what I set out to paint."

By the time he shook off such thoughts, he found himself already on Thatcher Road, past Good Harbor Beach, where the season's first harbor seals had begun to cavort, before reaching the district redolent with the smell of fish and diesel, downtown Gloucester, where he made his exit, at that point facing but a short walk to Mrs. Post's.

Ed was downtown, off the streetcar and walking up Main Street. Past the Hotel Gloucester, a narrow, ugly building from which he actually averted his eyes, Ed looked instead at the butcher's shops across the street, with their red and black oil pencil handwritten signs. In Italian and English, he noted that linguica could be had here much more reasonably than in New York; however, here he had no stove. Such was his life, he always seemed to hunger, to lack skills to capture themes on paper or on canvas, feast his eyes only; that hunger persisted her on Main Street before the butcher's, insatiable. Appetite he never lacked, a shark-like hunger that kept him moving and made his days meaningful. They say that sharks never sleep.

At his guest house, after a filling supper of cod-fish cakes and homemade beans, which he enjoyed with several helpings of hot, fresh buttered corn-bread, Ed asked to use Mrs. Post's telephone. Despite feeling squeamish about talking, about using a phone, about asking a woman out, Ed called Jo.

"Hello, Mrs. Murphy," he said, asking for Jo, who came to the phone quickly.

"Hello?" Jo asked.

"Hello, it's Ed," he said.

"Oh, I could not imagine who knew that I was here. Arthur's fine, if you wanted to know."

"I want to know if you want to go to the movies."

"Tonight?"

"Yes. Arthur should be all right alone, don't you think?"

"Do you know what is playing?"

"I saw in the paper, it's the latest Bessie Love movie."

"Not that it matters, it will be so good to see you. We go back a long way, don't we, Eddie?"

"You say yes?"

"I say yes, when will you be by?"

"In about a half hour," he said. "See you then."

"See you then," she said, in a trill that he did not like but with which women seemed always to end their phone calls with him.

Chapter Eleven

Ed knocked at the front door, his Muse alert and mulling idly over the artistic possibilities of Jo's rooming house with its green shutters and green awnings. After six but still light, Gloucester's brilliant sunshine flattened these fabric and wood surfaces. His Muse would not let him be. Paint this, paint this, but darker, just after twilight, take the place on when brightness emanated from Mrs. Murphy's lighted sign, "ROOMS *For Tourists.*" That hazy, dreamlike image, like a candle in a cave, could be phenomenal. He filed it away for later use as the door opened, ludicrously presenting Mrs. Murphy.

"Are you here for Jo?" Mrs. Murphy asked, raising, and holding her hand over her eyes. She thus amused him at a moment that he had been stimulated but not amused. Although Ed hated to be interrogated and most especially hated leading questions that implied that his questioner knew the answer, Mrs. Murphy's gesture distracted him from irritation, transforming her into either The Old Scout out of a Frederick Remington or a rookie in ranks executing a clumsy version of a military salute with curled fingers, whereupon Ed nodded and offered a smile he strove to suppress as he spoke.

"Yes, Mrs. Murphy," he said.

Whereupon Jo's landlady dropped her hand, turned, and rushed away, bustling, and talking without turning her head, "I'll go get her and you just make yourself to home on any seat you choose."

The world in motion having rushed off, Ed took long, slow steps into the parlor, looking all around, studying each piece of furniture, a jumble of periods, nothing thrown away if it had more wear, until he chose the edge of an armchair chair upon which to perch, waiting. He pondered the ignominy to which he had recently fallen, seated, waiting an interminable time for a woman to dress. He could have gone to the movies alone. He could have reclined on his bed and read. Ought he walk out?

He was tempted but something like lassitude kept him from moving. He conserved energy, as he had inside a warm church listening to a boring sermon by a pompous minister. That winter day the bitter cold—it was snowing and blowing outside—led him to stay as long as he could, even attending the post-service reception in the church basement. Such is the power of inertia, when the pull of the chair exceeds anything drawing us into motion. He would see this date through, but make no more. His Gloucester time was too precious. If he was not sketching, he should be painting or looking for houses, reading, or talking about art with Guy. What else was he in Gloucester for?

Two girls of about ten or eleven, dressed alike, seeming to be twins, their brunette hair long, came into the living room and sat staring and silent.

"Waiting for your parents?" Ed asked, smiling politely.

Neither showed having heard him. If they were not deaf and they were not foreign and they were not intentionally rude, then they were being very obedient to their parents' edict not to speak to strangers. Then Jo appeared, her face rosy-hued and grand as never previously. She was the illustration of a girl in love. Her eyes seemed to twinkle, had he seen them before at Good Harbor? No. Anywhere else? No. It was unsettling to Ed, who rose and stepped forward as she stepped forward to hug and kiss him on the cheek. He puckered in air.

Nearby, he heard the girls snickering and one saying, "Tsk-tsk."

Jo said, without turning, "You must have met Rose and Sara."

"Not to speak with," Ed said.

The girls' mother next arrived, saying that they must move fast in order to meet their father's ship. Ed judged that either daddy was due on the boat from Boston, or he was done with a trip out fishing or cruising the waters off Cape Ann. Either way, the trio disappeared out the front door before Ed and Jo ceased to embrace.

"How are you, Eddie?" she asked.

"Well, and you, Jo?" he asked. He chose to echo her words but not her robust good cheer.

"I am very happy in present company," Jo said, turning and flashing teeth before arranging her right arm within his left arm to form the sort of attachment of appendages by which a gentleman escorts a lady. Her teeth were larger than he recalled, not bucktoothed but not tucked behind her lips demurely either. But—were they not beautiful teeth? And she was wearing a fashionably cut red dress that ended short of her knees, a real flapper in a bright yellow cloche hat. It was as if she had walked out of one of her own gaily painted still lifes.

He had no lines prepared and off they went wordlessly, as Mrs. Murphy brought up the rear to the front door saying, "I'll get it, you two go."

"Shall we walk?" Ed asked, with no trolley in sight.

"By all means," Jo said.

"It's not too far," Ed said. It was a fifteen-minute walk and the day, which had been humid and airless, was still hot although a breeze was just starting to come in from the harbor and was about to cool the city.

"Bessie Love. I think she's great. I can't wait, how about you?" Jo asked, eyebrows up and her right arm pressing against his left.

Ed nodded. They then walked, not too quickly but still without stopping, the fifteen minutes to the North Shore Theater. His estimate was right. As Ed purchased two tickets, they could hear an organist inside entertaining people as they gathered. A strip of paper across the movie poster read, "Music by Leo Sands." Deciding afterwards not to share that Leo and she had once shared seats on the train and conversed, Jo kept a secret from Ed while telling him, "Leo Sands. I read about him in the newspaper. People follow him wherever he plays, he's that good."

Ed nodded, already miserable as they walked through the lobby, and he felt obliged to offer. He was not going to praise the organist. It would be as irritating to praise him as it would be not to praise him and, either way being irritating, he chose silence. He always did.

"Coke or popcorn?" he asked, expecting her to choose, hoping against the odds that she would say, "I've just eaten."

She said, "Oh, that sounds wonderful. Coke and popcorn, please."

After Ed shelled out for both refreshments, she asked if he would hold the popcorn while she started the coke. Some women were easier to get than to get rid of. He said, "Fine," but renewed his resolution: this would be their last date. How had he ever encumbered himself with this veritable pixie with bangs? To see "St. Elmo," no less. For God's sakes, his mother had once wept over the dreadful old sin-and-redemption novel by Augusta Evans, three times a failure on the silver screen, now in its fourth attempt, starring John Gilbert and Bessie Love. But he need not watch the screen, he could stare at the curtain, the ceiling, the theater. He did not lack for thrills.

They found seats, Ed adopting a rigid posture, his back straight. A couple behind immediately rose and moved, murmuring and snuffling, once Ed did so, as Ed's head would block their view of "St. Elmo." Jo managed to make her narrow seat seem wide as she sat almost side-saddle, sipping her coke with ice. She shifted and moved about, trying out one position and then another. Ed wondered: would this go on for the entire movie?

As they listened to the organ, and Ed realized how young Leo Sands looked, obviously bearded to look older, Jo asked for him to pass the popcorn, insisting that he take a handful—it was, she said, "dee-liciously salty and buttery"—and, after they were done munching a box that Ed judged was too small for what he had paid, listening to the interminable organ, which she almost alone in the audience applauded, too loudly, the show began.

It turned out that the movie actually held their attention, not only hers but his. Surrounded by the contagious enthusiasm of a full house of Glouces-

terites, it was a magic night like no other. Ed and Jo
followed the unfolding story of an insufferably
stuffy rich man, St. Elmo Thornton, from the moment that he proposed to his fiancé, Agnes Hunt.
He was soon betrayed by Agnes and his best friend,
Murray Hammond, on the surface a young divinity
student destined for the church but in fact a two-
timing utter hypocrite. After St. Elmo caught them
smooching on the divan and overheard them planning to reap a harvest from St. Elmo as part of a
short marriage and a quick divorce, he saw red.
Though the plot was hackneyed and had been
written before any of them had been born, the audience dared to cheer and applaud when St. Elmo
picked a fight with this bad boy and killed him.
Someone in the balcony actually yelled, "Good for
you," as St. Elmo galloped out of town on his
horse.

With cheating Agnes left behind in the dust,
enter the blacksmith's daughter—played with great
verve by the beloved Bessie Love—who had seen
St. Elmo kill his friend. The audience was instantly
as one, asking the same question: Would she tell the
authorities?

Just at this point the film broke and everyone
could hear the slap-slap-slap of a film off-track as
the projector kept turning its reels.

"Moment, folks," the projectionist said, turning
on the house lights and turning off the projector
with a practiced hand. No fool, he kept repeating
the word, "Sorry," as he went about his business
before a hundred eyes, quickly splicing the broken
ends of the film together, using scissors and glue
with astonishing alacrity. Even so, one minute became two and two slid into three as the restive
crowd's members murmured and strangers spoke
to one another, some about "money back," some

about popcorn, and some about whether the girl would tell or ought to tell what she had witnessed. After the word "Okay," the lights went out and the projector began to whir again, and the film resumed on Bessie Love's agonized face of indecision.

She ran after the disappearing man on horseback and in the road found a book he had dropped while riding off, a closed book she picked up and clasped dramatically to her bosom as she looked longingly down the road, where the dust raised by the speeding horse was clearing. No, the audience knew from the closed book, her gesture, and her expressive face, she would never tell. The organist played a several bars, just enough, of his variation of the opening chords of Schumann's "Nachtlied." Indeed, throughout, Leo Sands maintained perfect synchrony with each scene on the screen, from a handcrafted score that included classical music, more recent and melodic scores and, it seemed in a much softer key, romantic riffs. By clothing sunlit and smooth traveling aurally, and imitating the tumultuous crash of thunderclaps and noise of torrential rain, he made the show.

"He plays well," Jo whispered, her hand reaching toward his although she was unconscious of moving a finger.

"Oh, yes," Ed, his fingers gripping hers, his feelings atypically aboil, whispered now himself, "he plays well."

Meanwhile, in the muddled middle of the movie now, St. Elmo, ludicrously costumed in riding attire, in evening clothes, in other formal wear at a casino, at a hotel getting his boots shined, on a riverboat and a train, spent his time on screen demonstrably angry, waving his arms violently and in subtitles expressing his hatred of all women as an indiscriminate brood of vipers. This went longer

than Ed would have liked. Some of the lines hit
close to home, so soon after his affair with Jeanne.

He spoke. Astonishing himself in the course of
a movie, he whispered to Jo, "I'd like to hear him
say any of this stuff out loud."

Misunderstanding perfectly, Jo whispered back,
"Yes, he must have a wonderful voice."

The audience around them formed a rising
tide, more than ready for St. Elmo's return home,
where Bessie Love was serving as his mother's com-
panion. Neither the audience nor St. Elmo needed
more than to look into this girl's shining eyes to understand that all women were not evil and viperous.
But, of course, he set up a test that Bessie must
pass: during the next year he would be away, and
she was not to use the key that he gave her to open
a model of the Taj Mahal, in which he had hidden
his "last letter from Agnes." Seconds later, but
"One year later" according to the magical rules of
Hollywood time and subtitles, St. Elmo returned, at
which moment he found the Taj Mahal intact, the
letter unread, and the girl provably honest and true.
Succumbing to love at last, St. Elmo fell to his
knees to ask her to marry him, at which the audience clapped vigorously and stamped its feet in approval, including Ed and Jo, the latter sobbing with
happiness.

But Ed was unavoidably thinking of *sa maudite
lettre* postmarked from New Orleans. Even as he
joined the exuberant crowd stamping its feet and
cheering, Ed pictured a title card "One year later"
of the couple solemnly before a divorce court
judge. But that was Ed. The rest of the audience
reacted to "St. Elmo" as one of the year's best feel-
good films. After "THE END" came up, the crowd
began to melt away but everyone who had witnessed the movie—almost all of them, excepting

Ed—remained outside for a time part of an exhilarated group glad to be alive and believers in the
power of love.

As they left the theater, Jo said, "Comedy is
other people, you get to laugh by joining in."

"How so?"

"We are most able to laugh when we are with
others."

Ed countered, "But then being alone eliminates
comedy, doesn't it?"

"I suppose, unless a couple of the comedians
get together."

It made Ed laugh, and then Jo laughed, too.

Ed asked Jo, "Do you know Dogtown?"

"Did you say 'Dogtown'?" Jo asked, laughing
again.

"I did."

"What's Dogtown?"

"The original settlers' open lands. They were
abandoned and left untouched and now they form
a great forest in the center of Gloucester, rocks and
trees we might explore someday," he blurted out
before he realized. He could not recall his words.
He had invited her out on another date. Together
under a shady canopy of trees in full leaf. No good
could come of this, what was he thinking.

"Oh, we must, Eddie," Jo said. She was so
happy, and surprised that he was talking, he was
inviting her to explore. And in the woods. The ice-
berg was melting. She who had had increasingly no
hope in the world of romance this summer in
Gloucester, let alone with Ed Hopper, felt like
climbing a tree.

"You know, Jo," Ed said, temporizing, explaining unnecessarily, "I've been thinking that we
should spend more time together since we're both
here, old friends."

If he intended this line as a reasoned buffer between them, it was a poor choice of words to maintain distance.

"Well, I'd like that very much," Jo said simply. Perhaps they would paint the same Dogtown tree. Now she started to remember things she had heard or read. Wasn't there a "Whale's Jaw"? He didn't know. Somebody said that Dogtown was Druidic, Gloucester's Stonehenge. Well, there are rocks. Were blueberries in season? Ed had no idea. Before Jo could ask if there was not at least one secluded grove—a shady grove that was not Ed's aim—Ed cleared his throat and said, "That organist was especially fine."

"Leo Sands? Oh, my, yes, Ed," Jo said, then crossed into sharing. "I met him on the train coming to Gloucester."

"You—met him? Leo Sands?"

"Yes, he was on the same train. We talked, or I talked. Mostly, he just read his newspaper."

Ed paused, reflecting before he said more, but he was itching to ask, "Why didn't you tell me?"

"There was nothing to tell, really," she said.

In the silence of the next several minutes, they walked together, up Whale Avenue, across Prospect then up along the long railroad depot, still open for people headed to Boston, to Washington Street and Mrs. Murphy's.

"You don't have to go, Ed," Jo said.

"Go?" he asked.

"To Dogtown."

"We can go. Why wouldn't I take you?"

"You seemed angry with me."

"About what?"

"Leo Sands."

"Don't know the man. Do you?"

Jo managed to say, "No," before she laughed out loud.

Women are mysteries, Ed thought. He shook his head. He ought to have designed ships. Sheeps. His father's plan was best for him. As an illustrator selling his own goods, he was a merchant without a store, wasn't he?

Jo was aboil with confusion. Instead of being on a sedate visit to Gloucester with Arthur, she was a single lady was caught in the near-universal uncertainty of principles presented to the women of the Nineteen-Twenties except that for Jo the backseat was going to be Dogtown Common. What was a girl to do? Was she a flapper? She had once lived in a church, for God's sakes. St Elmo, help me.

When they neared Mrs. Murphy's, Ed drew her aside, away from the sidewalk, into a shady drive that led to the Oak Grove Cemetery, where trees seethed with breeze, articulating the frustration of the dead buried with unfulfilled longings. Gloucester blew in his ears, and in Jo's. They spent some time getting to know one another much better by touch and lip. Jo and he were as if walking on clouds by the time they actually reached Mrs. Murphy's. The door was only locked if one of the guests particularly requested it; the door tonight was unlocked.

"Thank you for a truly lovely evening, Ed," Jo said.

"Likewise, Jo," Ed said.

"Likewise," Jo said, smiling but not showing her teeth. Did she think them unlovely? Her teeth were beautiful. To Ed tonight she was altogether beautiful.

"Likewise," Ed said, feeling giddy.

"Likewise," Jo said, giggling, not feeling her age at all.

They embraced on the front step and a car passing by on Washington Street tooted its horn as if in celebration. People were noticing them. Ed spoke first.

"Have you anything set yet for Saturday afternoon and evening?" Ed found himself asking her ponderously, like the Secretary of State addressing the President.

"No, I'm a bohemian. I sleep late and I don't plan."

Ignoring her wit, Ed said, "I will see what there is to do."

She wondered if Ed regretted having suggested Dogtown now and was looking for something else.

"Then, thank you for the possible invitation, sir," Jo said.

Then they did part, their hands lingering before breaking off and as Ed turned, his stodgy big shoes shuffling upon the sidewalk, though he felt to be a degree walking on air on his way back slowly to Mrs. Post's on Middle Street. At least they were safely past Leo Sands.

Chapter Twelve

The day after his movie date with Jo and Leo
Sands, Ed staked out a small table in back of a
speakeasy called "The Canary" off Rogers Street, a
bar which may have been a warehouse before a bit
of cleaning, paint and some assorted sticks of furniture turned it into a saloon. Guy had not been interested in joining him at a "dive," as he called The
Canary without seeing.

"Rogers Street?"

"Off Rogers, Duncan, I think."

"No, thank you."

Of course, Guy's term fit this place snugly, as a
dive it was. Ed, however, had a fondness for places
in some way underwater, beyond the respectable, in
a degree of shadow. The Canary fit him. Nobody
bothered him, not even the waiter, a short and stout
kid who seemed to be no more than fifteen. It was a
slow night; nobody needed the table for two and Ed
sipped his way slowly through three beers in almost
two hours. Finally, the time being about ten, Ed
rose to leave, thinking that Guy had missed nothing
when a young lady appeared, unbidden and unexpected, and sat across from him.

"I'm Carol."

"Do I know you?"

"We do now. I just told you."

Ed nodded and resumed his seat. Maybe he had taken on too much of the local strong beer. Maybe he aimed to stick it to Guy for deserting him. Maybe it was Jo, the question mark. Maybe he was simply attracted to this odd duck. The waiter came over with two foaming beers in glass steins, arranged for by Carol. They toasted because Carol raised her stein.

"To Gloucester," Ed said.

"To us," Carol said.

Ed wiped his face and was going to ask if she was a local, but she asked Ed first, "You enjoying Gloucester so far?"

The way she dropped her r's, it was Glostah, and fah, he knew he was sitting beside a local girl, a forward girl whose blond hair might not be genuine, and whose teeth and lips presented interesting challenges to anyone who painted portraits.

"You must meet Leon, he paints models," Ed said, ignoring her question.

"Kroll? He's done me," Carol said, breaking into a giggle, adding, "I don't mean that the way it sounds. Leon's a perfect gentleman."

Tipping her glass up, she drank in long, smooth swallows.

"I don't paint people," Ed said, sounding inane to his own ears. Why was it always so difficult to talk? He ought to ask Carol, who seemed to have figured out ways to evade any difficulty.

"You like boats? The harbor?" Carol asked. With one more tip-up, her beer was empty, but Ed was not about to signal for another round.

"Houses."

"Really. You paint houses?" she said, then she

shrieked with a hyena outburst of laughter. She added, "I didn't mean that the way it sounds."

Ed shook his head and took another sip. He wondered if it would be rude to leave now.

"So, how are the houses of Gloucester?" she asked, each hand holding up a side of her own painted face.

"You're not interested."

"No, I'm not. But you are, and I'm interested in you, handsome."

Oddly appealing in the dim light of this dive, she was not Jeanne, she was not any woman he had ever met, even at parties. She was Pierrot, bold and brassy. Unhindered by a brassiere or, likely, any other underwear, Carol's decolletage was generous, her dress was silk and lace. Her cheeks were slightly though not ruinously rouged by blush from a brush, her heart-shaped pout was generously daubed by lipstick to achieve a startling glare of perfect scarlet. If he painted her, he would have to factor in Max Factor. How could he not allow her to continue to entertain him? But it was only fair to warn her.

"I'm not interesting," Ed said.

"You're from out of town, New York, Manhattan, maybe?"

"I am," Ed said. His glass was half-full.

"Are you here to fish?" she asked, making "fish" sound dirty.

He smiled, "I am an artist."

"An artist, no wonder you know Leon. Mister, you're interesting. You've probably been to Paris."

"Can I ask you a personal question, Carol?"

"Sure, sugar."

"I'm in my forties. Are you even half my age?"

"No fair, but I'm 23. And a hundred-and-ten pounds stripped. I give honesty and I expect honesty from my men. I like wine but I'll settle for beer.

I believe in good times, and my idea of a good time is for both parties, not just one. Capish?"

Ed reiterated mentally that he had never met such a bold and brassy woman.

"You're a fast one," Ed said. It did not faze the painted lady.

"Honest, I am fast. Can you keep up with me, buddy?"

"What does that mean?"

"Take a powder, kiddo, and go somewhere else, just the twosie of usuns."

"I was thinking of leaving."

"Pay the tab?" she asked.

"Of course," Ed said, reaching for his wallet. He showed its few bills and said, "Don't get any big ideas. It's pretty thin."

"No worry, sweetface, here we go, upsiedoodle. I'll leave the tip."

"I have no car."

"That's all right, I do."

Carol walked around the bar to their boy waiter and embraced him with a fervor that he was either hoping for or used to and liked, as he and she kissed away with vigor. Ed figured out that this was his tip. He also thought that they'd wear out their lips, and the waiter would next need a couple of napkins to wipe away the lipstick without looking like a vampire after a good meal.

Tipped off by the tip, feeling tipsy himself, Ed led the way to Paradise as he rarely did that night under the stars in Stage Fort Park. On a blanket Carol spread out in the new mown grassy hill beside the sloping "Tablet Rock" that proclaimed itself to be the site of the first white settlement in Gloucester, he and she brought moaning and gasping fireworks. Nothing that a man and a woman had not done before, it felt fresh and new this night and, especially for Ed, reflected relief after a long time out of the game. He found that Carol had such beautifully shaped long legs, pale and white in the moonlight. He realized belatedly that they had obliviously rolled off the blanket and onto the grass, which felt lush and cool. No pile rug would have been more comfortable. They both smoked her cigarettes as they dressed, thinking their own thoughts until Carol spoke.

"Nice?" Carol asked.

"Nice," Ed said.

After about another half-minute, tossing her cigarette and crushing it underfoot, she said, "You didn't talk."

"Didn't think we were here to converse," he said, arching his eyebrows and pursing his lips as if to shrug with his face. He looked at her, eye to eye in the moonlight, now drained of color, everything about her a shade of gray, many shades of gray now.

"You don't even talk afterward."

"I'm sorry to disappoint you," he said, thinking Payne's gray and white titanium mixed about half and half, which was the basis for her face, with shades darker, of course, running into shadows. He had loved the cool of Payne's gray in his early years as an artist, whenever he did not paint with a spectrum of warm browns. In time, he found that beauty required light to bring it out; reduce light, reduce beauty. Ed drifted, teetering on the brink of clarifying art theory rather than paying close attention to Carol.

"You like me? I have to ask because, you know, you don't T-A-L-K."

"I like you. I just don't like to talk."

Although he had not executed a portrait since the one of Jeanne, the facial expression of this one

was perfect—a smile nearing a laugh, her eyes as
wide as they ought to be, and not a whit wider—
the main danger in his sketches of women's eyes—
but, he had decided, studying it at length after she
disappeared, that her portrait was too colorful,
much too colorful. He may as well have been Egon
Schiele, given those rouged cheeks and the flesh,
too pink. If he were to do anyone's portrait again,
it would be Carol in the moonlight, a series of
varying limited light until only her forehead, in
part, an oval, and cheekbones, nose, tips of lips and
chin, the most prominent features of her face sur-
faced out of a dark Payne's gray background. In
other words, a series at the end of which her
beauty disappeared, having faded away like God in
the Old Testament. A sad series but realistic, and
how Ed strove for realism.

"Tired?" Carol asked, perhaps for the second
time, yawning. He may have been too deep in
thought, she sounded snappish.

"Exhausted."

"I'll take you home now, sugar. Where are you
staying?"

He stated the address and Carol said, "Mrs.
Post's," as if she had been at that address before,
although not necessarily inside it. In Ed's head, any
idea of a series of portraits vanished like the shimmering pieces drizzling after a fireworks explosion
overhead. There was only the night sky. A dark
cloud curtained the moon before he noticed. If Ed
had not been in low spirits earlier, he was certainly
depressed in Carol's car on the way to Mrs. Post's.

"Good night," he said, interpreting her fixed,
straight-backed position at the steering wheel to signal: *Noli me tangere.*

"Mmf," Carol said, exaggerating the minimalist
conversing minimally. No tip for Ed. No embrace,

no penetrating exploration of his oral cavity. They would, Ed was sure, never see one another again. Even if they met, each would look through the other and avert their eyes.

Hell, but relationships were torments. At that moment, invited to pick between revisiting the ATOMIC NOVELTIES office or going to a party, he would have chosen the office. It would be painful, he supposed, but the office he could leave quickly without seeming rude.

He entered the house thinking that, except for Mrs. Post, he had no ongoing relationship with any human being in over a hundred miles. He found himself in his room, undressed and about to go to bed without knowing how he got there or remembering stepping out of Carol's car, closing the door, using his key, coming up the stairs, all a blank. Ought he to see a doctor?

He lay down and closed his eyes and, to his surprise, awoke the next morning rested, smelling bacon and coffee, and feeling hungry.

Chapter Thirteen

In thinking that he had no ongoing relationship with any human being in over a hundred miles, he had blocked out forgotten Jo. As he shook off a hangover (or, more accurately, took care not to shake his head) he came to life again over coffee, eggs, bacon, and toast.

"Mrs. Post, the bacon is crisp," Ed said.

His comments so rarely broke the silence as he ate that Mrs. Post wondered if Ed was all right or, at the least, disappointed by the bacon.

"Too crisp?" she asked, turning as more bacon spattered in her black large frying pan.

"Just right."

"The eggs okay?" she asked, confident about her coffee without asking.

"Great eggs," Ed said. He loved eggs well scrambled, soft and fluffy, over which he put more pepper than salt and a taste of ketchup. What could be better?

"Do you permit guests for breakfast?" he asked, thinking of Jo.

"I have a fee for that, but you have to schedule in advance, no more than one at a sitting," Mrs. Post said, thinking that her guest was all right, just

in love. It happened. Over the years, Mrs. Post was
witness to so many summer romances that she had
a theory about Gloucester being extra magnetic,
where people were more attracted to one another
than a lot of places.

"Care for seconds?" Mrs. Post asked.

"Thanks, no. I'm full and happy."

As for Ed, full and in a good mood, he could
see Jo sitting at this table and gabbling away with
Mrs. Post. She never lacked for things to say. He
had to admit that Jo was something more in his life
than she had been. She was no satellite in a distant
orbit who had been his fellow student at the Chase
School, hardly more than a nodding acquaintance.
He had found her cat, for God's sakes, and they
had attended a movie. They had touched and
kissed, and their eyes had locked more than briefly.
Weren't they going out this weekend? And hadn't
she hoped for him to take her to Dogtown? A
fleeting recollection of Carol's bare legs in the
moonlight from the night before emerged and embarrassed him. He put the napkin down on the
table and fled.

"I'll let you know," Ed told Mrs. Post.

The phone rang. Saved by the bell, it was for
Ed. Leon Kroll apologized for his late invitation,
but he hadn't known that Ed was in town. He was
inviting as many artists as he could find for a party
on Saturday at his studio home on Rocky Neck.

"Ned Rogers can pick you up," Kroll said.
"He's already bringing Guy. You know them,
right?"

Ed said yes, and asked if he might bring Jo
Nivison.

"More, the merrier," Kroll said.

So it was that later, after sunset that Saturday,
Ned Rogers in his jalopy, a Model T with an ah-

oogah klaxon horn, which he used freely, was driving three other artists, Ed, Guy and Jo, to Leon's party.

"Gloucester drivers," Ned said in disgust every few minutes, tooting his horn and gesturing profanely when someone cut him off or swerved without signaling.

"Sorry, Jo," Ned said.

"I saw nothing," Jo said.

As Ned drove and dealt with the other alleged drivers, the artists talked. Guy craned his neck to speak to Ed, in the backseat a proper distance from Jo, whom Ned had picked up first.

"You're both here to paint the ocean, are you?"

Ed waved a hand for Jo to speak first.

"I really prefer to sketch and to paint the beaches, the waves, the children. Anything colorful and lively, the way summer is in my feelings."

Now they were talking about art, and nothing got his engine going better than art, taking wings, Ed said, "I sometimes spot a formation of rocks by the ocean and that makes an interesting contrast, Guy. But I get a lot more when I just walk around this place."

"Ah, you lousy—" Ned shouted, with a string of profanity. "Sorry, Jo."

"I heard nothing," Jo said.

"Gloucester drivers, you know," Ned said.

Ed felt buoyant now, in good company, artists on their way to a party. He realized how much he had missed Leon Kroll; they had shared many a beer in discussing art into the small hours of the night in many night spots in New York.

"Maybe we should have taken the streetcar," Guy said.

"I heard that," Ned said.

"But they charge," Guy said.

"And I won't?" Ned asked, laughing in a way reminiscent of a hyena. After that, Ned asked, "Hey, has everybody here been to Gloucester before, or should I take the scenic route and give a tour?"

"You won't charge extra for the tour, will you?" Ed asked, triggering the hyena.

"Ed and I were here before the War but not since," Jo told Ned. And, right beside her, he had blossomed into a regular talking man.

Ned said, "Well, it won't take much time to show you the changes. Smells the same, though."

He made a few quick turns to get to Main Street, where the storefronts were like a line of toys. After the Hotel Gloucester, the police station and district courthouse, a granite bank was followed by a clothing store, its mannequins in cloche hats and svelte, short dresses, a jewelry store, newsstand, shoes, hardware, fabrics, Nick's Pool Room, Kennedy's butter and eggs, O'Connor's soda fountain, the five and dime, then Italian bakeries, small restaurants, coffee shops, and then swept along the waterfront by way of Rogers Street, past a hill atop which was "The Stone Jug," which Ned pointed out had once been home to the painter Fitz Hugh Lane but was lately (he said in a stage whisper) "a house of ill fame." The smell of salt air and fish came up as they putted past warehouse after warehouse, long wooden cod drying racks, a noisy power plant, all evidence of Gloucester's main employer, the Gorton-Pew Fisheries. The company owned and operated a navy-sized fleet of vessels from rowboats on up to the largest and most powerful trawlers in the country, hundreds of ships, thousands of employees. Ned and the trio next drove past laundries, butcher shops, a shipyard, a paint and varnish store, a gas stations and one an-

tique gallery. Taking an uphill right, Ned passed a
few garages and car dealerships, assorted maritime
goods merchants and fish stores, and more shipyards. He pointed out a sub chaser from the War,
now rotting in the Inner Harbor. Finally, they
reached the right turn to Rocky Neck, passing over
a breakwater to the core of the Gloucester art
colony, a cluster of cottages, galleries, studios, and
restaurants that catered to the artists here for
longer or shorter durations.

They arrived fashionably late at Leon Kroll's
party of artists, bohemians, and flappers. Bootleg
gin and cold cuts on Italian bread. A ukulele and a
sax player making music of an amateur sort, some
couples dancing.

Ed went over to the host, whom he thought
might not know Jo.

"Leon Kroll," he said. "Please meet my friend,
Jo Nivison, from New York."

"Second Avenue, nu?" Kroll asked Jo.

"Greenwich Village, actually, but now of
Brooklyn."

"I was close," Kroll said, shaking her hand.
"I'm so very glad to see you both and—Guy, I am
honored by your critical presence. I feel humbled."

"To know is not to do, Leon. I cannot paint as
well as I can criticize. Lovely studio, wonderful
paintings. Do you live here all year?"

"Now, yes, but I was originally from New
York."

"He paints nudes, as you see," Ed said. "And if
I ask him how the nude business is doing, he'll
say—"

"It's taking off," Kroll said.

Acting the straight man again, Ed said, "Leon
painted Diedre turning into a tree, in several shades
of green, a bit busy but brilliant."

"I called it 'Tree's a crowd,'" Kroll said.

Warming to the theme of the unclothed, Guy asked, "Am I alone in liking Matisse, and his odalisques?"

"I think we all think highly of Matisse and his odalisques," Kroll said, deflecting a lecture as everybody nodded, "but don't let's forget that this is a party, and over there, you see, is a table of drinkables and eatables. The knishes are homemade."

Leon unobtrusively held Ed back as Guy and Jo went over to the table.

"Does she model for you?" Leon asked.

"No."

"Jo promised to model for me in New York, she's obviously forgotten. She modeled for Henri, clothed, of course. Time flies but she is still one fetching woman. But a nice girl."

"That she is, Leon," Ed said.

"I thought so."

"You thought what, Leon?"

"You are in love again, Ed."

"I'm past that, Leon. Unless art counts."

"I hear you rescued her cat."

"Word travels, apparently."

"How are you doing, Ed? I saw somewhere that you had some things on exhibition, etchings."

"You keep close watch. Sure, but the last painting I sold was still at the Armory Exhibition."

"I remember. You beat me. I sold nothing, and anybody and everybody could sell the worst junk at the Armory show. But not me."

"You made up for it since, kiddo."

"Have a good time, pal, and don't tell anybody but the punchbowl is full of wine."

"My lips are sealed," Ed said, shaking hands with his good friend and mentor. He knew of nobody who disliked Leon Kroll.

Jo held a seat open beside her on the sofa for Ed as Guy mingled.

"Well, young miss, may I sit beside you?" he asked, pretending to be a stranger, if not a cad. He felt in an odd mood, open to new experiences, happy to be among artists, old friends—and this one, Jo.

"You may."

"Is it possible that I have ever seen you before on canvas in a museum?" he asked as he indulged in his glass of punch. It had a kick. Leon was right.

"Not me, some other girl."

"Ah, it comes back to me now. You were in Gloucester many years ago, in a blue bathing suit."

She laughed.

"You actually remember that, Ed?"

"With the flouncy collar up around your shoulders," he said.

"It was. What a memory you have."

"I had more hair back then, parted in the middle."

"You remain recognizable. I remember how you always painted in the shade."

"Not to be affected by the glare. But now I prefer the light, as intense and bright as possible. To burn away the details that are visible and by black shadows make the rest disappear."

"You talk more than you did after the movie."

"We had better things to do than talk after the movie."

"Fresh," she said.

"You haven't touched your drink."

"I'm intoxicated by my company."

"Are you? Guess what I paint, Jo."

"Fair ladies?"

"Nope."

"Churches?"

"Nope."

"Rocks, sea and sky?"

"Nope."

"What then?"

"The cows in Dogtown Common."

"You're joking."

"I am. There are no cows in Dogtown. I'm here to paint the redwoods."

"But there are no redwoods in Gloucester."

"I was misinformed."

"Oh, Eddie. You paint houses," she said, rewarding herself with a drink of punch for the correct answer.

"Not really, but I do stare at them. Gloucester's houses are different, Jo. Gloucester is a town of bold faces. *Faccia dura* the Italians call it."

"We are assaulted with right angles everywhere."

"Roofs here are very bold."

Jo said, "I suppose they are—" here she paused to make a Mussolini upraised, frowning chin— "bold. *Faccia dura*. That sounds dark."

"The dormers cast very positive shadows."

"Dormers."

"The cornices are exceptional. Houses built for sea captains, Jo, everything in Gloucester is tight and bold, ready for storms."

"I've never seen you so excited, Eddie. I don't suppose you like beaches."

"I don't know."

"Ever go?"

"I never swim."

"Good Harbor has waves. You could sketch. I sketch."

"I only have a few weeks, and some of the days will be rainy."

"The sun shines every day, Eddie. Only some days we can't see it."

"My God, you're an optimist."

"My God, you're talkative, Eddie. Are you all right? Eddie, how old are you?"

"Forty. How old are you?"

"Younger. Ever married?"

"No, not even one little time."

"Did you ever, ah, (sounding like Mae West, risqué) cast your shadow in a cornice?"

"Why, Jo," Ed said, taking a long swig of his drink.

She said, wagging her head, her bangs bouncing, "I'm bolder than a Gloucester roof. You have time, my friend, we all have the same twenty-four hours."

"In theory. But not of daylight. For the sun in Gloucester, you have to get up early."

"Do you?"

"Yes, Jo, and I do. Awfully damn early."

"So, you must go to bed awfully damn early."

"By ten o'clock. Unless there's a moon."

"Then you howl?"

"The shadows. In Paris when there's a full moon, its artists don't sleep."

"I'm a night owl myself, Eddie."

"Do you think it would work if I painted some? Could I shock with the mundane, do you think?"

"What?"

"In New York, late, people at a diner staring down at their coffees, nobody looking at anybody else. Would it make a painting, do you think?"

"Yes, a dreadful one. Sketch clammers if you like people looking down and not at each other."

"I like lighthouses."

"Well, I'm glad to hear that. I've seen two of them on bottles of soda here."

"Jo."

"Yes?"

"Nothing."

"You said my name."

"I did."

"*Pourquoi, monsieur?*"

"Maybe you could get up early tomorrow."

"Why?"

"To join me in sketching."

"Are you inviting me?"

"My God, this is tedious."

"You're an odd duck, if you don't mind my saying so."

"Quack."

"Quack back, yes, I'll sketch with you."

Chapter Fourteen

After Ned dropped them off in front of Mrs. Murphy's, when Jo gave him a certain look of interest and leaned her head to the right, staring up at her tall escort, Ed said he could use a walk to clear his head.

"Don't think I wouldn't walk with you, Ed," she said, gently.

"Don't think I'm asking you," Ed said. Without provocation, his mood had somehow soured.

Jo said, both hands clenched into fists at her side, "As I was saying before I was rudely interrupted—"

"I did not interrupt, you were done."

"I was not done," Jo said.

"You spoke, Jo, you paused, and I spoke."

"I spoke. I paused. You interrupted." Was she in the presence of Jekyll and Hyde?

"Around me, people pause at their own peril."

"Then I ought not to pause. I ought to do what others do and run away from you as far and as fast as I can."

"You—" Ed started.

"You, too," Jo said.

"That's not a complete sentence. You paused.

And I am not interrupting. I am commenting." Ed was beginning to walk now, and Jo stayed by his side, walking, too.

"Aren't you the puzzle solver?" she asked.

"Better than some. I found your cat," Ed said, emphasizing each of the last four words distinctly.

Jo told him instantly, "Who found who is a matter of doubt. Didn't he come up to you, meowing, pressing up against your pants and curling his tail? All you did was bend down and pick him up, after he found you."

"He told you this, your cat? I was there. You weren't."

"I know you both. Ed Hopper does not find and rescue stray cats."

"I may not be known for it, but I have more skills than you think."

"Do tell. Have you ever tried watercolors?"

"Kid stuff."

"Winslow Homer."

"Yes, Winslow Homer along with anybody else who can paint in watercolor on a par with the great Homer. A very select group. Jo, if I could paint like Winslow Homer, I'd never work again. My only decision would be to play with oils or watercolors today."

Jo laughed and told Ed that he was very funny.

"I think I see the light and you see the dark. That's our difference," she told him.

"Vive la différence. Can't you keep up with me?"

He took such large strides. Being over six feet tall, and she barely over five, she had to run to keep up, but she did, saying, "No woman faster."

"Women's shoes slow them down."

"Not me. Nope."

"Are you mocking me, Jo?"

"Not me. Nope."

"You've got my voice, my tone, you comedian."

"Yes. I remember. Cornices, dark shadows, bold roofs. Houses."

Ed stopped walking and turned to Jo. He opened his arms to embrace her, saying as he did, "You're fun, Jo."

"Not me. Nope," she said, not moving toward him.

"I have to apologize to hug you?"

She leaned her head to the right and looked at him with that certain look.

"All right, Jo. I'm sorry."

"Thank you."

They hugged and kissed as they walked—slowly —back, until they arrived at Mrs. Murphy's door.

"What time tomorrow?" she asked.

"Monday."

"You said tomorrow."

"I see the moon. I'll be up late. When do you eat breakfast on Monday?" he asked.

"Whenever I want."

"How about six?" he asked, an impatience in his tone now.

"Six it is."

"Seriously, I'll be here," he said, then asked, "You aren't kidding, are you?"

"Not me. Nope."

"You really will be awake and ready that early?"

"In Gloucester I awake no later than five. Every hour is precious to me here."

"Six o'clock then."

"Monday, just when the cornice casts its longest shadow."

"Cornice time Monday then, adieu."

On the threshold, they did not hug or kiss. He

bowed stiffly without smiling. She opened the door and went in without looking back at him. No one would have taken them for lovers, or even for especially close friends.

"That's six o'clock, remember," he said before she closed the door. "Monday."

He walked the streets of Gloucester, stopping to stare at the sights of moonlit shadows, nodding to himself, murmuring, and thinking how his old Parisian colleagues would have lapped this town up like a cat at the cream dish. Finally arriving at Mrs. Post's after two o'clock, it took a long time for Ed to fall asleep. Jo's face and expressions came to mind, along with one of his first paintings. Henri had praised it, an oil of a nude crawling into bed, her backside prominent. He could not do faces so he cheated by putting her head in the shadows, an indistinct dark mass, but for her legs, he dropped dollops of unmixed yellow and red and ochre, then mashed and stroked them into an unsettling, moving, almost writhing impression of fleshy legs, most of all her thighs and buttocks. Although Ed's perspective was no more accurate than El Greco's, Henri was impressed and said that the figure looked "natural." Ed fell asleep thinking, seeing, imagining thighs and buttocks in motion.

Chapter Fifteen

Having cooled down in a few days and gotten enough sleep, on Monday morning after breakfast in their respective guest houses, Ed knocked at Mrs. Murphy's door at six sharp and found Jo ready.

"We just missed the trolley," Ed said, "but let's get out and blow the stink off."

"Wherever did you hear that?" Jo asked.

"I overheard somebody the other day. It's a local thing."

"Aren't Gloucester people interesting?"

As they walked to the trolley stop and waited with their art supplies, they talked. Jo began by asking Ed, "Why did you come to Gloucester?"

Ed lied, "To see you again."

"Bunk. Check your nose, Pinocchio."

"I just knew you were coming, Jo."

"Really?"

"Not exactly, but I hoped."

His coy answer displeased her, and she shifted the conversation aiming to guide him in that art. She said, "Well, besides Arthur, who likes fresh fish, I came for the sea and the beaches, not that you asked. I like to sketch children playing and mothers. Fishing boats also. Not that you asked, Eddie. Aren't you interested in seascapes?"

"Not very much."

"People live in those houses you sketch, Eddie."

"I sketch them empty. My editors always want people waving their arms. Not me."

"You really are here for the houses?"

"Houses, empty houses. I'm not like you."

"I feel your way sometimes."

"Not as often as I do."

"Well, often enough."

"What do you do then?"

"Oh, I play with my cat. Or I draw or paint. Sometimes I read. I make an apple pie. Do you read?"

"In Gloucester? God, no. Too much to do."

"Not even a historical novel?"

"Jo, I wouldn't even read a based-on-fact novel about two goofy artists who meet and fall in love in Gloucester. Nobody reads historical novels. You either read history or you read a novel. History is solid, go for the solid."

"Do you like rocks? How about rocks?"

"Red granite."

"Oh, isn't red granite the best? What do you want to do, Eddie?"

"I want to paint sunlight on the side of a house."

"I meant, this morning. Where are we sketching?"

But Ed was off on the houses, houses he saw in his mind's eye, houses in rows and in ranks, a parade of houses, and he could speak of nothing else. He said, "The houses here are built close together, and they empty out each morning. Just when the houses are unoccupied, I feel their draw. One place with great houses is called Portagee Hill. Do you know it?"

She knew, not only because she had been consulting her guidebook, but also, as she said, "I've walked through on my way to the harbor."

"I love to place a house in a day specific to that day's sunshine and wind and clouds, the house of that day and no other day."

"You work fast, set up and paint outside," Jo said, certain of his technique.

"I do. I work from fact, *plein air*."

"Let me play the seer," she said, closing her eyes. "I see that you love the white of your paper."

"I would paint sunlight on a white wall if I could."

"But what about shadows, Ed? They begin at sunrise and grow longer and longer until everything is dark. Like your moods."

Hopper's eyes, which were not small at any time, seemed to enlarge and affix themselves to her as he said, "Jo, are you a kindred spirit, after all?"

"Can't tell yet, Eddie."

"You're leaving me in the dark."

"I say that we all live in the dark. Before the War, we knew all the answers. Now, everything is up in the air. Every day I have to decide whether to bob my hair, shorten my dress, smoke, drink, or use make up."

"How do you decide?" Ed asked.

"Mostly, I ask what Lorelei Lee would do."

"You do not."

"I do, too. Anita Loos is a very smart and forward-thinking woman, and she explains our options through her character in her Lorelei stories."

"Well, then, at least you don't face your questions alone. You have Lorelei."

Jo, feeling her forty years, painfully unmarried

and taunted for reading about a confident flapper stared at his wide eyes. Ed stared back. Breaking off their prolonged eye contact but certain of some electricity Jo asked, "India ink? Shall we sketch in black and white, pen and ink?"

"You don't need much color, but you need some. Winslow Homer painted Gloucester in drabby colors that are just wonderful."

"Drabby. I like that."

"I see the trolley. Slow just when you want it on time."

"Homer did seascapes, not houses."

"That's where I come in. Homer already covered the waterfront."

"You're funny."

"Not only funny. I'm awkward and clumsy. I have sharp edges and no couths, Lorelei. As a bonus, dear, I lumber. Like the trolley. It stopped now. Did it hit a dog or something?"

"A dog?"

"Just kidding."

"Don't kid about animals. I want to see you as an angel of light. You were born with a gift, Ed."

"Work with me long enough and I'll show you something else I was born with."

"Now look at who's not shy."

"Jo, I am too old to play the games of a blushing virgin. Is that okay with you?"

"I'm not as fast a girl as you may imagine, just because I'm an artist."

"Artist's model, I heard?"

"Who told you?"

"Leon said you modelled for Bob."

"For Bob and favored friends only."

"This trolley is taking forever."

"At least you're in good company."

"Would you favor me?"

"Somehow that sounds very salacious."

Ed ostentatiously eyed her from different angles.

"Don't do that, you're taking my clothes off."

"Only in the dark. I can't see anything. You're very fine, though."

"Do you like my cornices or my shadows best?"

"Woman, I told you, I'm too old to hide my interest. Did you learn that kind of talk from Lorelei?"

"I thought your interest was houses."

"Houses and you."

"In that order, why, I'm flattered to come in second, knowing how much you think of houses. But is this just because I'm available, in Gloucester?"

"Jo, I entertain, shall we say, secret hopes."

"Aren't we too old for 'secret hopes,' Ed? Why not let me hear them."

"Painting houses."

"That's no secret."

"Here's our trolley."

They boarded, paid their dimes and were silent during their breezy, bouncing ride to Lanesville, where Ed was finally going to explore Lane's Cove, in company, no less. He almost said that the summer was going by fast, but then one thing would have led to another, gabble the whole ride. Best use his eyes. She, too, stared, though, he thought, not with his intensity. And yet—their eyes had met, hadn't they?

Chapter Sixteen

Garrulous Leonard Craske to Floyd the Clammer spanned a great contrast. Floyd was as chary of speech as Craske was generous and Don's editor forewarned him that he might have to write Floyd's story with only twenty quoted words. Giving Don a relative's name and address as first contact, Garret told Don that Floyd was representative of a Gloucester type, the paradigm of man at the shore. In any of the cities and towns of the East Coast, in particular from the islands and shore of Cape Cod on up through to Newburyport, clammers were independent, first and foremost, fiercely so. What they wore, whether they shaved or washed, how they lived, nothing about them was given or set. They might dwell in a cave or a hut in Ravenswood, or they might take shelter under a porch, or make do with an abandoned cellar hole. Their social lives were diverse, but none boasted of whatever they did. As many clammers were bachelors as were married, and not a few had children by more than one woman.

"Get photos, and be descriptive," his editor, Garret Bean, told Don. "See what you can find out about him from others, too, the dealer he sells his

clams to, or the supplier of his clam fork and bas-
ket. Speak to his cousin first. I don't think anything
we run is ever more interesting to our tourists than
the clammers. Last year we sold more issues than
any other time when we ran a story about Clam
Miller of Clam Alley. Lots of them clipped the
story and sent it home."

"Why not interview Clam again?" Don asked.

"Clam's fame has gone to his head. Unwisely, I
shared the information with him that I just told
you. Now, he says he'll only be interviewed if we
pay him."

Bean advised Don, "Keep track of the tides.
Don't expect to find Floyd on the streets or talking
with you at leisure at low tide. Low tide is his office
hours, his work schedule. You'll catch him at high
tide."

In mid-July, 1923 the high tides came in mid-
day. Don found Floyd in the shady fringes of the
Annisquam River marshes past the Cut bridge. He
was at rest under sumacs, a frame that made him
look like the king of a tropical paradise.

"Hi, Floyd, I'm Don Nash," Don said to the
grizzled veteran of all the worst weather, cold and
heat that afflicted Cape Ann for decades. As they
shook hands, Don took a furtive sniff. Floyd
smelled natural, salty, somewhat of humus, but not
bad. He wondered about weaving smell into his
story.

"The reporter?" Floyd asked.

"Your cousin told you, right?"

"He said you could be trusted."

"Well, whatever you tell me, I'll have to comb
through. Anything you say I might use, but I won't
use everything you tell me."

"Can I tell you something not to print?"

"Off the record, we call it. Sure, you can."

"I'm more than a clammer."

"Are you?"

"I'm doing some government work for the Treasury Department."

"Oh, I see," Don said, wondering what information Floyd could ever possess that the government could use.

"I know about Dr. Blythe's other house, down in Bay View."

"He lives up on Portagee Hill."

"Everybody knows that, but he bought another house from a guy I know, right on Hodgkins Cove. You get the picture?"

"He wanted a summer place next to the water?"

"No, Don, he wanted a place to keep his shipments, or to hold shipments for the big guns that come into the cove."

"Oh," Don said. Dawn broke on Marblehead. "You know their schedule?"

"They wait for a midnight high tide, to get right in close to the shore, and a moonless night or bad weather, rain is fine with them."

Don had no doubt that advance knowledge of big deliveries in Hodgkins Cove on moonless nights when the tide is high was pretty useful information for the Treasury agents.

Don said, "Good for you, Floyd."

"Don't say nothing. Agreed?"

"I already said yes, and I won't say anything or write a word. But now I have my own questions. Are you ready for them?"

"Good. I just wanted to get that off my chest right away or it would bother me. Oh, and one more thing."

"What's that?"

"I asked the police who found the body."

"Which body?"

"You know, the Gloucester fisherman, Bag o' rocks."

"Birkelder?"

"Yeah, they told me who found the body. Or claimed to. Made me suspect something funny was going on. Naturally, they brought the corpse to Dr. Blythe."

Floyd rambled on to Don about how it was the key, who found the body, and that Bag o' rocks was not the type to take chances or fall over the side of a boat. The details were a stream that did not mean anything to Don, though, who started instead to get background for an article by asking his birth date, which Floyd did not know, his birthplace, ditto, schooling, in Gloucester up to the third grade. He dropped out of school at age nine to go clamming with his cousin, who now ran a bait store. Floyd remembered New Year's Day in 1900, when he "got good and drunk," treated "at all the bars by everybody in town, back in the day that Gloucester was wet as a hurricane."

The result was anti-clamatic. Garret Bean found nothing of interest in the article Don came up with, but he did run a quarter-page photo of the grizzled man, styled "a portrait of a rustic clammer familiar to residents and tourists of Gloucester alike" which sold more papers than any other that summer.

Chapter Seventeen

On their way to Lane's Cove, Ed and Jo reverted to being silent observers. The trolley sped past the Addison Gilbert Hospital, around the Mills, up Meeting House Hill, down through the Willows, across the sparkling waters of Goose Cove on either side of the stone bridge, through the hills of Annisquam—Ed spoke, saying to Jo that they ought to see the Annisquam Players before the end of summer—past the Bay View fire station and the Bradstreet Elementary School, its students off for the summer, a gray clapboard building with white trim, its unusually tall windows aligned. To Ed, the tall school building was in contention to be worked up, but the trolley raced by the school, affording him too little time to be certain.

They went down and then up from Hodgkins Cove, and over the trestles of Plum Cove. Just across the street from Hildonen's Market, summer realized itself most openly at the corner where Tucker Street sloped down toward Washington Street where that long road crested before, to the left, drivers swooped over to Lane's Cove, instead of bearing right up and into a curve past the Lane School, quarries, woods, and a string of houses, built by Finns. In 1900, no city boasted more Finns than Gloucester and those Finns all lived in Lanesville.

Ed pulled the cord and rang the bell, then rose and in true gentlemanly fashion took Jo by her arm. Once off the trolley, the two artists, each carrying large but thin sketch pads, began to talk, Jo first. Predictably.

Jo asked Ed, "Do you remember what Professor Henri said were the three most important things about painting?"

"Only to see, only to see, only to see."

Jo laughed.

"What is funny?" Ed asked.

"The way you said it, so sarcastic."

"I never realized my feelings were so evident. I did think it was cheap advice. If one cannot see, one cannot be an artist.

"What do you think are the three most important things about painting?" Jo asked Ed, while words were coming out of his mouth.

"There aren't three. There are just two: what to leave out and, second, closely related, maybe even the same thing, judging when your painting is complete."

"What to leave out, and when you're done," Jo said, trying them out aloud as she considered. "I think you have something there, Ed. Have you ever considered becoming a teacher?"

"No more than I have considered taking up barnstorming or singing and dancing on Broadway."

She laughed again. He smiled, "Or writing a historical novel."

She said, "You are so funny."

"A laugh a minute," he said. "How is Arthur?"

"Oh, he is over his diarrhea."

"Is he? I missed that episode entirely."

"I knew to leave it out."

Ed laughed now at her wit.

"Mrs. Murphy wants extra for cleaning."

"I do not blame her. How does one negotiate over price?"

"We reached an agreement by the day not by the incident."

"Seems fairer to you than to her."

"She likes Arthur."

"Well, there are two sides to Arthur."

"Aren't you the lucky one to travel alone?" Jo said.

She wanted him to counter that remark in some way, but he was moved in another direction. He replied, if reply it could be termed, with tales of his own childhood, including that day in third grade when he arrived early and the school building itself so fascinated him.

"Did you notice the school?"

"The tall one? Yes. Gray clapboard, I thought you were staring at it."

As they talked, they walked, and he found her flow of oddities and *non sequiturs* charming, surprising, and fun.

"Are we sketching together or apart?" she asked.

"Maybe both."

"That's no answer," Jo said. Within minutes, they were at Lane's Cove, facing the breakwater and to move forward, they had to maneuver in and among anchors, lobster pots and dories ashore.

"Everybody trusts everybody here," Ed said, noting oars, small motors and tools lying about unattended.

"It's nice," Jo said, gesturing in the direction of houses nearby, "I bet not a door is locked."

"On the other hand, who would steal an anchor? And who could steal a lobster pot? And there are eyes everywhere."

The cove, though not crowded, included a half-dozen children leaping from the breakwater into the water, and here and there an owner painted his boat while two men with eyes peeled smoked pipes in front of one of the cove's several shacks.

"I should like to sketch those shacks," Ed said, pointing at three in a row on the right, hugging the rocky part of the cove. He added, "Houses built on rock."

The windowless shacks were all taller with roofs more steeply peaked than one might expect. Ed imagined some sort of lofts for sails, nets, and other fishing equipment. Or for the snow to slide off easier. Gloucestermen were canny builders. And realists. Someone had nailed or otherwise affixed the jaws of several sharks to the side of the first shed, apparently trophies but reflecting an undercurrent of savagery in the marine world not far beyond the breakwater from which children occasionally whooped and jumped.

"It's quiet here," she said during an interval that one only heard lapping waves beside the granite wharf. "And I love the flowers—it's too late for lilacs and too early for heather, Ed, but just you look at the calliopsis, the beds of salvia and those purple cornflowers."

"Well, you draw the blossoms while I work on the sheds."

So it was answered at last, they each set up separately to take in the varying beauties of this sheltered bit of coast, where many working people kept an eye out on weather, exchanged news on occurrences offshore, whether fish were plentiful and, if so, where. They were pitched here exactly between the land and the water, between the people who had a foot in each, the lobstermen, the fishermen and, lately, the rum runners and their untouchable adversaries of the United States Treasury Department.

This was an artist's theme, Ed thought, although no artist was at work capturing the day here before it went away. How many artists in New York would curse themselves that they were in bed and not at Lane's Cove on this day. If Ed did not take on the passing scene, it would not be remembered in a month, let alone in a hundred years.

Building not for the day but for centuries, he turned toward houses in the distance. They addressed his condition exactly. They stood like hungry dogs, looking at someone not in the picture, seeking attention that they were not being given. The jokey title "Gloucester Mansions" came to mind. These houses were mansions-in-training, wishful mansions, envious haunts of broken dreams.

This was the prey he was stalking. Lanesville would live. The houses looking forlorn at the cove and the greater world, perched together like barnacles, would be his painting.

After the houses and their clotheslines, the shacks. He set to work. After executing eight increasingly original manifestations on paper of the fishing shacks of Lane's Cove, Ed was almost delirious. He had faith that from these sketches in New York he would wrest watercolors of the shacks of Lane's Cove that would all but leap up off the surface in near three dimensions, such lines and contrasts. He noted colors in his abbreviations, "brn," "dk brn," "lt brn," brown, dark brown, light brown. Touches of "nr or," near orange, and "rd?" some shade of red salted and peppered his sketches. The medley of these harlequins was completely a celebration of the sun god. They did not stand, they danced, and as an artist Ed felt that he but danced with them, his hand out to take part in the spinning and whirling at Lane's Cove that morning. It was immensely satisfying. He was in a good mood as he strode across the cove, past the tall fringe of grass, back to Jo.

"Success?" he asked.

She smiled and held up her sketch pad and flipped pages to reveal several closeup views, impressions and essays of a flower in full bloom on paper.

"Nice," he said, involuntarily flinching, thinking of saying the same to Carol.

Her eyebrows creased, and she asked, "Why did you wince?"

"Did I?"

"You did, just now. Don't you like my sketch?"

"I said 'nice', and they are nice, they just aren't finished."

"That is why you winced?"

"I don't know, maybe a nervous tic."

She was silent as she wrapped up her portable stool and gathered her equipment.

"I had a good morning," Ed said, sensing that he could by no means articulate even to his fellow artist in words what he had felt and what he had seen and done minutes ago. It was likewise impossible to imagine holding up his sketches of shacks to show her.

"Good," she said. Then, Jo being Jo, she shifted gear, looked him in the eye and said, "No, really, good. I'm glad. This cove is kind of magic, isn't it?"

Feeling licensed to talk freely after that, both of them giggling and hitting high notes, they made their way merrily uphill to catch the trolley back.

Neither of them knew the schedule or the time, but neither wanted to eat, neither wanted anything at all but to be with one another, to relax under the sun, and to do this together again and again as long as they were in Gloucester.

Once on the trolley, Ed was still speaking. To Jo's suspicious amazement, he was bubbling on in reminiscence about finding Arthur and taking him on the trolley to Mrs. Murphy's. It was a funny story but the longer he talked, the more the intuitive woman wondered: was there someone else? Had he met another woman in Gloucester?

Jo was innocent but not naïve. She could not live for years in New York without observing the edges of the underworld even as she stayed above it. This seaboard city was not New York but, even so, a diverse group of women lived here or were passing through, single women who hoped to find a soulmate, exotic raven-haired Italian and Portuguese beauties, blond and blue-eyed Finns, along with ubiquitous flappers who smoked and drank, while a few rouged tarts in short skirts furtively roamed and patrolled as they had for hundreds of years in these parts.

But no, he was with her now and he was talking about Arthur. Who could really resist reminiscing about Arthur, once having taken him up into their arms and finding his bewhiskered face rubbing one's chest or his alert eyes looking up under his large ears, tuned like ear-horns to hear whatever you might say to him? Ed was simply human and, being human, caught up in Arthur, the most remarkable of felines, the king of cats. One day she must write a book about Arthur, illustrated if, in his old age, he would ever stand still long enough for her to sketch the boy.

She and he got off the trolley at Mrs. Murphy's,

and he walked her to the door, but when she asked if he cared to visit with Arthur, he declined. He wanted to go home, shower and nap, he said. Miffed by his brusque dismissal of an audience with Arthur, she turned and entered the guest house only pausing long enough to say, "Well, I hope we may do this again soon, Ed."

Ed walked off at a slow saunter, pondering what he may have done wrong. Women were more mysterious than the stars and planets and subject to fewer laws. Nothing was static. He had not resigned himself to a changing world but felt in his hands the power to stop motion, however briefly. He might yet contrive to paint an alternate world that not only satisfied him but also would draw buyers into his vision.

Was Gloucester the door to that world and to those buyers?

It was pretty to think so, but on this mixed day of flowers and shacks, tension, and laughter, perhaps love and perhaps not, the artist on holiday nodded at Joan of Arc and resolved to take a cold, bracing shower.

Chapter Eighteen

Mrs. Murphy invited Jo to sit and have tea. Jo intuited that Mrs. Murphy did not so much care for tea as for company. When her chores were done, and she faced no laundry or cooking, Mrs. Murphy sat and sewed or knit but without appearing to be content. Jo agreed to tea.

"You are quite talented, Jo," Mrs. Murphy said, providing two cups of hot water and teabags along with shortbread squares which were still warm.

"Thanks, but I'm no Rembrandt."

"What do you lack that Rembrandt has?"

"Publicity. At galleries and exhibitions, art shows, Mrs. Murphy, whenever I have something on view, I have to blow my own horn."

"How, dear?"

"I talk, I say hello, I make new friends. Because I'm so short, they call me 'Napoleon.' I aim to conquer."

The way Jo said this made them both laugh.

"Are you self-taught?"

Jo froze a second. Did it seem that she was an amateur, who had never been instructed in painting? Then again, unless Mrs. Murphy had looked through her sketchbooks, her question was based on nothing more than curiosity or courtesy.

Jo inhaled and told her, "I went to classes at Chase, the professionals' art school in New York. I learned to paint in colors as red as my hair, lime green for contrast and I can usually work in a bright shade of lemon yellow. Somebody told me it is as if storms swept over my canvases, especially my watercolors."

"Do you live with your family?"

"Oh, that's a longer story than you have time to hear."

"Tell me, please."

"Well, I've washed dishes in hash houses, clerked at the five and dime, and at a phonograph store, my favorite job, and I posed for selected artists, good ones. I have developed a habit of having buyers of anything that I painted write their names and addresses into a little black notebook."

"How clever. You have a following."

"Not yet, but my paintings were hung last year near Modigliani, Man Ray and Picasso."

"Is that good?"

"Good for attention. One critic said that he approached my work 'always warily, with my hands at the ready to shield my eyes.' I have now been invited to submit six—six—paintings for the fall exhibition at the Brooklyn Museum."

"Isn't that wonderful."

"But tell me about your life," Jo said, reaching for a piece of shortbread. Prime the pump of this nice woman. What was Jo's father's saying? He taught a generation of children to play the piano, always saying, and repeating, "What is well begun is half done."

"Well, Mr. Murphy died almost twelve years ago, lost at sea. You must know how that is the hazard around here. Even now, I look at the sky trying to tell if a storm is brewing, if the wind is breezing up, or if we'll have fair weather for a time at least."

She sighed.

"It was calm in Gloucester, that's what strikes me. It was calm, and only a bit of cloud. But at sea it was a different story, a deadly storm, high winds, high waves, and the boat he signed on for this trip was old. It broke apart, they think, and sank quickly. All of them perished at once, five men."

"I'm so sorry."

"Aye," she said, shaking her head. Jo saw in Mrs. Murphy the woman who still looked up at the sky to tell the weather even after her husband had left off of any need for weather, fair or foul.

"Anyhow, I had the house here and it was paid for, but Mike was never one for repairs. If I was going to make a go of a guest house, well, I needed some money. I went to the bank."

"Brave of you."

"My bravery came later, after the banker said that he saw in me the possibility of success, but I would have to mortgage this place. That was taking a risk with all that I had left in the world, and I did not sleep so well as I had. Well, I signed the papers and had some money, but the house was mortgaged. I guessed that I should put advertisements in Boston newspapers, then in New York. You know, you saw one."

"I did."

"I made no money that first year, just enough came in to cover the mortgage. Lean times, you know about them yourself."

"I do."

"Anyhow, it was easier the next year, and the next. I even had guests from France and from

Canada. This was a busy place. Sometimes all
three rooms all booked. And some of them come
back, I'm pleased to say. I hope that you will come
back."

"I hope so, too. You've been so kind to Arthur."

"Oh, Arthur," Mrs. Murphy said before they
spent five minutes identifying and anatomizing
Arthur's many good points and cleverness, beyond
any cat before him.

Jo asked, "Am I the only guest at present? I
never see anybody but—"

Her landlady said, "Sometimes the bathroom
appears to have been used, I know, the toilet seat
up. Mr. Haywood from Vermont. He comes for the
ocean air and to work on his book."

"What book, Mrs. Murphy?"

"He is writing a biography of Franklin Pierce.
He says that it is his life's ambition to do justice to
Franklin Pierce. He told me, Jo, that the only one to
write a life of Franklin Pierce was Nathaniel
Hawthorne."

"He's writing a biography that was already
written by Nathaniel Hawthorne?"

"He says that there is always room for another
biography. He rents two rooms, one to sleep in and
where he has me bring his meals up, and the other
where he writes, and reads his research. Two trunks
full of books and papers."

"Is he mad?"

"I wouldn't rent to a madman, Jo. No, he's only
a biographer, that's all. They make up invisible
friends and talk to them."

"He talks to himself?"

"Not himself, dear. I hear him, 'Well, Senator
Davis, I say this with no intent to offend and
leaning upon our long friendship, sir,' and then
soothing someone over the loss of a child, a boy,

killed in an accident. From the life of the other man, I suppose, his 'subject' he calls him. Like he was a king."

Jo pondered how close she herself was to madness as an artist who painted flowers. Who but a mad woman could not be satisfied with real and natural flowers? Who else would take such pains to strive to imitate flowers on paper or on canvas?

"I should like to meet Mr. Haywood someday. What does he look like?"

"Oh, he's beyond middle-aged, dear, and rather stout, and he wears these enormous owl-eyed spectacles."

"How does he have the funds to travel, I wonder?"

"I don't know. He has wealthy friends but no local references. What he gave me, on fine stationery, monogramed and all, was from a man in New York, a veteran of the War, odd name, Gatsby, who said that he was awarded a medal by Monaco or some other country Over There. Of course, without a Gloucester reference I asked for rent in advance. Anyway, no matter, Haywood seems to be all right. I don't ask him to pay in advance anymore."

"I'd like to meet him. I was going to be a nurse in the War myself, Mrs. Murphy, but I ended up so sick immediately that the nurses nursed me. I was no help at all."

"He's not the veteran, that was Gatsby."

"I'd like to meet Mr. Haywood in any case."

"I'm not sure he will entertain your wish. He is devoted to his task. Keeps private. All I know is that for these past three years, two weeks every July, he arrives, takes two rooms, and leaves no happier than when he came. I don't suppose that I understand biographers. How long does it take to write a biography?"

"I don't know."

"How long does a painting take?"

"It varies. Hours, days, weeks, sometimes years, oil paintings that you keep scraping away at and adding to or changing."

"Then I suppose that I am realistic to think that Mr. Haywood will not be done with Franklin Pierce this year."

Jo was unable to do anything but smile at her guileless landlady's focus on the likelihood of a reliable renter who might take two rooms in July again next year.

With that, Mrs. Murphy rose to gather up the residue of their refreshments. If Jo ran into this mysterious Mr. Haywood, she must remember to ask him about Franklin Pierce. Although questions about Franklin Pierce had rarely stirred her earlier, now she had to know—who was Senator Davis, and did Pierce really lose his son to an accident? And—did Mr. Haywood *know* that Pierce consoled his wife, or only *guess*? Did biographers often make guesses? Jo counted on Mr. Haywood to share. Surely, a man who was devoting his own life to re-counting the life of another man would be happy to share whatever he knew. But she must be precise in her questions. She did not wish to endure a lecture about Franklin Pierce, especially not a lecture by somebody who thought that they must outdo Nathaniel Hawthorne. Why, that would be like seeking to outdo Winslow Homer. Altogether ridiculous. Nobody had surpassed that master's watercolors, or ever would, not even the friend for whom she wished the best in the world, Ed Hopper.

Chapter Nineteen

One afternoon soon afterward, Ed was told that he had a visitor and, upon going downstairs, found Guy puffing and spouting words as he did when he was upset or angry.

"Where have you been?"

"I've been around," Ed said.

"You usually don't move so much or so fast. I could not find you and your landlady had no idea. You've been missing meals."

"Are you my keeper now, Guy?"

"Eddie, are you in love?"

Ed stared without a word of reply.

"Eddie, are you not at liberty to say?"

Ed remained silent.

"It's not a crime. I've been there on occasion myself. It's a good feeling."

Ed continued close mouthed.

"Look, lover boy, I've got news. Do you know who is in Gloucester?"

"President Harding?"

"No, our old pal, Tim Tolman."

Now, that was a surprise, and Ed wanted to follow through. Guy had been right to try hunt Ed down. With Ed's immediate approval, Guy took Ed to meet up with Tim, an off-and-on art patron, stockbroker, partner in the Shifting Sands art gallery in lower Manhattan and a fair but only semi-professional artist in his own right, who worked in oils, primarily foggy landscapes. According to Guy, Tim was in the last day of his two-week visit to Gloucester, where he had a couple of clients who summered in second houses in East Gloucester. Guy and Tim were set to meet at the snug little Depauw Café but Ed was welcome to make it three.

The Depauw Café on Cod Street was one of the city's secret treasures, a sort of calm before the storm, white linen and candles, two waiters and a French chef. Nobody left the Depauw Café hungry. Here, among ship models and fine paintings of Gloucester schooners going back many decades, Tim had staked out a table every day for dinner. As soon as they greeted and got seated, Tim spoke.

"I've wondered about you, Ed," Tim said, lighting up and puffing at his cigar. "You carrying a torch for someone?"

Ed looked at Guy, his eyes glinting, "Guy say something?"

"No, I'm Sherlock Holmes, elementary deduction. Ed Hopper is a creature of habit and, well, Ed Hopper off track is either crazy or in love. And since you are up walking on your own and not glassy eyed, I figure it's just the old Cupid's arrow."

Ed shook his head, really shaking away further questions. Tim had no more to say on the subject than he already had.

"Jake," Tim said as he inhaled his cigar.

Ed thought that Tim's advice would be too valuable to miss by asking him in vain not to smoke; he would endure the stink rather than be diverted.

Tim told Ed, "I've admired your work, on the El, in magazines. You have quite an eye and you've got almost a John Held grasp of our times. I've wondered why the spark has not jumped the gap yet, from illustrating to fine art. I'm sure that you could paint cheerful themes."

The word "cheerful" threw Ed off, made Guy stifle a snicker, and Ed followed up immediately.

"Cheerful, really?"

"You know, the Winslow Homer stuff, sentimental, nice, warm, children at play on the beach, or boating—he has one called 'Breezing Up' that he painted and repainted—schoolhouse daydreams, you know. Engravings or in color. The schooners at sunset, the sky aflame and the sailing craft small."

Ed countered, vehemently, "He did ships at sea, people in distress, not every day was sunny."

"But what sold were his bright watercolors, colorful life, happy folk. You could make a good living on themes like that. People go to comedies more than to tragedies."

"I don't prefer the bright colors."

"What do you prefer?"

"Cross examination by critics like me," Guy said, weighing in to shift the conversation toward levity. He was unsuccessful and ignored by the other two.

Ed said without hesitation, "Sunlight on a white wall."

A waiter came by for their orders, but after that business they resumed the conversation on color, Tim telling Ed, "I know that white is your favorite color, titanium white. You must see it in your dreams. For people dressed in white, well, there are bridal portraits, I suppose, but the field is limited, Ed."

"I don't paint people."

"Ed's illustrations are filled with faces, and people. Aren't they?" Tim asked Guy, moving to Ed's sore point, commercial art as if Ed could not be trusted to answer directly.

"They are. Ed exaggerates his weakness on this point. His figures are severe but not unnatural. They are not dolls."

Ed said, "They are dolls. I only sketch in people if I am forced. I can tap into what I've learned but it's not easy, it's not my strength. I took life painting with Henri. I attended some open sessions in Paris. But I know enough to know that I am not in the higher ranks of portraitists. And you know that, too, Tim."

Guy asked Tim to get to the point so that when their meals arrived, they would have been done with work talk and ready for fun. With that encouragement by Guy, Tim told Ed, "People won't buy paintings of empty houses. Or, if you do a house, avoid the darker shades. Inject color. Robin's egg blue instead of rust, red instead of cyanine blue, yellow, my God, lemon yellow over mauve or burnt umber any day of the week. That market is solid."

"In the end, I am painting for myself," Ed said.

The meals began to arrive. Guy and Ed had fresh, broiled haddock with fried potatoes and steaming buttered asparagus while Tim had a slab of prime rib, a baked potato, and a side dish of green beans.

"You know Joe Kennedy?" he asked them both. They did not. As they ate their fish, Tim gave them tips. As he smoked his cigar, exhaling clouds and his face lit up from the candle flickering on the center of their table, his face appeared satanic.

"Joe managed the Fore River shipyard during the War. He knows whoever one ought to know, the

Roosevelts and the Saltonstalls, you know. Almost killed a couple years back in the Wall Street bombing. It went off, he was at the corner, just far enough away not to be killed. Anyhoo, this year he's going to open his own investment house. I think—word to the wise, boys—get on the elevator going up. You catch my drift? He shorts stocks. I think he's in on Canadian whiskey, nothing illegal. That's what you call a hedge play for the repeal of Prohibition. I'm with him. Anyhow, I was going to say, Joe eats the same meal every night, steak, a baked potato, green beans, and he says it keeps him fit and trim. Besides, it's delicious, not that fish isn't delicious, but you catch my drift."

Guy asked him how his gallery was doing.

Looking at Ed instead, Tim said, "Paint for yourself and starve. Paint for others and thrive, Ed. The bright sky is the limit if you bring joy down on paper, something cheerful. Have you considered that red lobster shack in Rockport harbor? With all the buoys on its walls?"

"Guy and I both agreed that nobody would wish to paint that garish shack," Ed said.

"We did," Guy confirmed.

"Well, I can lead a painter to a theme, but I can't make him paint, can I? Eat up, boys, while it's hot. The chef here knows what he's doing. You never leave the Depauw Café hungry."

"Agreed," Guy said, having been chewing and swallowing with gusto for several minutes. "Let us eat."

"I'll bear your advice in mind, Tim," Ed said. He did not add what he thought, which was "if I ever want to sell my soul."

Tim snuffed out his cigar, but his exhaust fumes had already permeated Ed's clothes and he was sure that he would be smelling smoke tomorrow.

Cheerful subjects be damned. He was not that poor or that much in love yet.

"Either of you guys seen France since the War?" Tim asked.

While Ed shook his head and got busy cutting his haddock, Guy said, "I'm moving to Paris next year."

"You and thirty thousand other Americans," Tim said. "And they all live on the Left Bank. Paris must get a hundred thousand American tourists a year now, and, believe me, the French welcome every American dollar they see. I keep going there myself, I was to Paris last spring and this past winter both. Most modern city in the whole world, everything new in art and literature is coming out of Paris. I bought a Picasso, 'Two Women Running on the Beach,' had it in my gallery ten minutes, doubled my coin. Last trip, I brought over ten copies of Joyce's book, you know the blue cover?"

"The scandal."

"Right, old sport. You can't buy it here. The post office and customs burn any copies they find. But I bought them at Shakespeare and Company, the twenty-dollar premium edition, for $ 150 because I was buying ten. Passed through Customs, 'nothing to declare.' They don't check VIP's luggage so I'm good to go. Sold them books for triple. Paid for my ticket. Everything's cheap in France, boys. Delicious food, beautiful girls. A whole community of American expats are in Paris living well on next to nothing."

"You read the book?"

"Flipped through it, kind of confusing writer. Not a classic if that's what you're wondering. You know, like historical novels, not anything anybody will remember next year. I couldn't wait to unload my ten while they were hot."

Tim detailed other bargain prices, including those of the *demimonde* and alcohol and meals at bistros, as well as other business deals that made him richer after his trip than when he left.

"I leave for a pleasure trip and find out when I get home that I was away on business," Tim said, laughing with a snort. Then he said, "Oh, and I almost forgot. I was in Paris for Sarah Bernhardt's funeral. What a day. It was like Yankee Stadium packed on game day, but it was in the streets between the church, I forget the name."

"Saint Francoise de Sales," Guy said.

"Yes, the Saint Francis de, and we walked, well, the crowd of about fifty thousand moved and took me with them to Pere Lachaise, you know, the cemetery."

Guy said, "They stopped in front of her theater for a moment of silence."

"I was too far back to notice, kiddo. All I know is that I was there, and I can tell my grandchildren, if I have any, what it was like. They must eat garlic for breakfast."

For his part, Ed could not wait to finish his haddock, which was hot, flaky, and perfectly seasoned. When the waiter asked if they would like dessert or coffee, Guy and Tim ordered while Ed begged off.

"I have to meet someone," he said. pled a necessity to meet someone.

"Some one or some body?" Tim said, rolling his eyes in an exaggerated way. "Guy, our Eddie has a promise. Late night tonight spooning, eh, old sport?"

Ed asked what he owed, Tim said that it was nothing, that his tax man saw to it that the government paid for everything. Good nights followed, handshakes and see-you-around-New- Yorks were exchanged as Ed felt his feet moving faster than usual. The hell with this infernal place. After the summer, his soles might have to be replaced, if not the heels. Perhaps he could paint his old shoes for Tim to sell in his gallery, an *homage* to Van Gogh. Fat chance.

Joe Kennedy, shorts, making money, selling paintings and books, trips to Paris, *bon soir, ma'mselle*, was steak-eating, cigar-chomping Tim, right? Did he really know everything and everybody? Right now, Tim, appearing nightly as King of the Depauw Café, seemed to have luck under his arm in a locked box to which he alone possessed the key.

Once in the bracing cool outside air, Ed resolved never to cross the threshold of the Depauw Café again. He felt, despite the excellence of its cuisine and his usual fascination with eating places, it was forever the tempting doorway to another life than the one he wanted to live. And Guy could have his Paris, too. What exactly was wrong with the United States, he'd like to know. If Gloucester wasn't the cat's pajamas, what city was?

Chapter Twenty

Ed and Jo went together next to Good Harbor Beach, next to Long Beach, the beaches of Cape Ann most noted for its large waves. From Good Harbor one had a good, clear view of the Atlantic, of Salt Island and of Twin Lights. They were about five years too late to see fog part and reveal a Presidential ship. Up a hill at its terminus was Bass Rocks, where a house perched in which T.S. Eliot had summered during his Harvard years. From up atop that hill, the sea-scoured, raw beach resembled a vast waste land. In the waters beyond the beach lay an unsung crossroads of recent naval history. In February, 1919, President Wilson, returning on the troop carrier USS George Washington from the Peace Conference at Versailles, encountered thick fog when headed for Boston. The ship was imperiled and nearly came up onto Good Harbor Beach but because the mists cleared in time, and the ship did not stray from deep water, that doleful event never became a part of Gloucester's history. The crush of waves made for the background noise as Ed and Jo talked, she on a blanket, he on a towel, both with sketch pads.

"I have never really talked here at Good Harbor, Ed," she said.

"Nobody to talk to, I suppose," Ed said.

It sounded funny enough to laugh, and they both did, although neither could have said just why, and they were dry laughs. Jo's remarks in a gush thereafter were the kinds of remarks and the sorts of questions people ask upon a first meeting. It seemed that they were forever starting and restarting their relationship from scratch. They did not know one another well yet. They had much of one another to explore. She spoke of herself in her twenties and her father as being then "people who shared the same house and some of their meals, without intruding upon one another too closely."

"We chose not to crowd. I work best in solitude."

"I, as well," Ed said, holding up his end of the conversation.

Her mother was closer, Jo said, a parent who rooted for her children's liberation from the time they could walk. Unless they were bleeding, she was a "hands off" disciplinarian. She could and did hug and kiss her children, and show them picture books, but she made clear signals that none of them ought to cling to her skirts.

"We were expected to mend our own clothes and shop for our own shoes and do a number of things that all children eventually do but which we were pushed to do younger."

"Sink or swim," Ed said, gazing out at the big waves of Good Harbor.

"We swam," Jo said.

Jo knew that people were their families and wondered about Ed's family, but the man was an absolute stone.

"My mother told me during our longest talk,

when I turned thirteen, about intimate matters but the one remark of all I remember she spoken in such seriousness. It was 'You are not marrying a man, you are marrying his family, too, and you must know all that you can about his family.'"

Ed continued to stare at the incoming tide and Jo felt foolish, having brought up the topic of marriage.

"Your mother was a wise woman," Ed said.

She did not go on to tell Ed how she had asked her mother how she would know who was the right one for her, to which her mother said not to worry, she would know. Her mother was plainly better at giving advice than in fielding questions. From both parents, Jo had squirreled away many nineteenth century tips for better living.

"Ed, did you ever try watercolors?"

Ed shook his head as if his hair were wet and dripping, then said, gesturing dismissively with one hand, "I am an oil painter. Watercolors are for set ups, trying to see how a commercial design would work, like a study for a magazine cover."

"I love watercolors."

"I know you do. I don't."

"I know you don't. I think if you *tried* watercolors in *Gloucester*, with the light here, you might like them. I mean, really. I could help you out and loan you mine."

"You are using them, my dear."

"I want to see how you feel about watercolors after you try using them here, my dear."

He asked if she had them with her in her big basketweave carryall, which she did. Within a few minutes, he was at the ready with borrowed materials to paint in watercolors at Good Harbor beach.

"I need a model," he said.

"Well, I have modeled," Jo said, smiling.

"Sit right there, as you are," Ed said.

As Jo was, she was sitting on the sand in an old light blue bathing suit, sun-faded and blossoming happily haphazardly in whimsical shades, as she sketched, too, her pug-nosed face and gorgeous red hair completely concealed under a large conical "Chinese" hat.

With a sketch pad on his knees and a stable canning jar of water beside him, half buried in the sand, its glass lid upturned next to it, Ed selected a brush but, before dipping it into water, said to Jo, "You know, I haven't sold a painting in ten years. Not a single damned one."

She turned and, as they looked into one another's eyes for the first long time just then, said, "I was going to ask. Not since the Armory Show?"

"Yes," Ed sighed, feeling shame, saying next what all of the artists they knew said, *verbatim* and in the same mocking way that they all said it, "At the Armory Show even Kandinsky sold something for five-hundred dollars."

Jo was going to say that she heard it was a thousand, but Ed's face was sad, and she held her tongue. The Armory Show was legendary and was still talked about, the grand and exciting show at which everything was selling, where anybody could sell anything because everybody was buying, the show that falsely promised a prosperous future for the artists of any school. Then came the War. The Armory Show stood alone. Profits were exaggerated as in any myth and the Armory Show became envied by the misinformed who were not part of it.

She wondered whether to question Ed. What did he paint? What did he try to sell? Had he spoken with any gallery owners? Wasn't Tim Tolman a friend of his? She decided to limit herself to her own experience and to advise him by hint-ing. She said, "I sold five of my paintings before I left New York. Five. Bright colors sell."

"I don't know," he said. Kandinsky's colors, some of them pastels, pulsing curves and energetic neon blobs came into his head against his will. If he were illustrating a children's book, Kandinsky's palette would serve handily. Goddam Kandinsky.

On the beach that morning, Ed worked fast. In part, he was driven to do so by the heat, as the paint was drying instantly. Painting on dry paper, he also was feverish to capture a fleeting moment in another artist's creative life, and he paid particular attention to Jo's hands and fingers. The strokes he made with speed simply suggested them by way of slight blurs of pink-and-mauve, hands in motion, enough to reflect life. When he was done, he told her, "This is the bee's knees, kid."

She moved from her pose and held out her hands to hold what he had made of her, sitting on Good Harbor beach and sketching.

"With my hat and wrapped up in my large bathing suit, you have painted me as a mysterious personage," she said.

"You are a mystery, Jo, inviting me out here and talking about your family. Then, do I have it right, you planned all along to loan me your watercolors and have me feel the power of that medium in this town?"

"I did have a plan, and it was watercolors for you. I want to help you to get ahead. My family talk was unplanned."

Ed mulled and said no more. Jo said, "Well, if that is all for our day at the beach, I should change, and we ought to go back on the trolley."

"Yes, Moofy awaits," Ed grumbled.

There was a public bathhouse in which Jo showered—screaming at the cold water—and changed into her carryall wardrobe of her most flamboyant orange dress and cerise silk scarf ensemble. They walked back together, down the sand and paved parking lot, past the few cars parked there on a weekday, Model T's and Packards, a shiny red-and-chrome Stutz Bearcat and various other makes. Ed's eye fixed on one or two of the cars with a commercial artist's vision, involuntarily seeing the automobile advertisement or billboard that he could make of this one or that one. He must do something of a street scene in Gloucester, which included some cars. Their spare tires on the back were especially enticing and curious shapes.

Watercolors required discipline to suggest and not to overdo in detail, especially the elements that appealed to him. But that was the challenge. Watercolors lived suspended in that challenge between the suggestion and the defined. Too much definition spoiled everything, too little left an abstract fog in part or in whole. Abstraction was fine for Jo, to whom garish and contrasting colors were the core of her art. Ed's heart beat for viewers. He wanted people to stand before any painting of his and see what he originally saw and captured in a medium, starkly, plainly, clearly. Already, in Gloucester that summer Ed felt that he had achieved the first part; it was Act Two that was the tough nut to crack. Were there no second acts in American artists' lives?

Chapter Twenty-One

The caravan of ten brown, boxy trucks, each one painted on its side "UNITED STATES POST OFFICE," was ready. The trucks were fueled up and all working fine.

"What can go wrong?" Sharpie asked.

"Nothing now," Tuna said.

The signal to go, and truck number one, two, three each peeled off and away down Whale Avenue, then the next three, and the next, to the last truck of a line of nine, in which Sharpie drove and Tuna rode shotgun.

It was almost midnight, time enough to believe that nobody was out on the roads, no accidents were likely, no cops were alert, even if awake. The plan was not to exceed the speed limit, to amble along at fifteen or twenty miles an hour and get to Saugus for delivery. Who was going to stop a mail truck?

Then, just as the first truck got into Essex, a flashlight, two flashlights were waving, and there were whistles and shouts to stop. In the first vehicle, panic reigned in case it was a hijacking by rivals, which could mean fatal news for drivers and others aboard.

By the time the tenth truck drove up, though, it was obvious that it was no hijacking. Uniformed local police and Feds were all around, conspicuously armed, and someone was taking photographs, popping flashes to get images as the drivers were being handcuffed and moved, one by one, into one of the three patrol cars standing by. The man in charge was Agent Wittgenstein. Don approached him to say a few words, maybe get an interview.

Don said, "Agent Wittgenstein?"

"A logical conclusion, young man."

"What a night, what a story."

"You covering it for the *Times*?"

"I am. I need names. Does anybody have a list?"

"They give fake names a lot of times, so best wait until court, when their identifications are made."

"How about give me numbers and ages then, descriptions, scars, missing legs, firearms, anything for color. You know, were they Irish or Italian?"

"Finns."

"Finns?"

"Just kidding. But Finns do drink a lot, don't they?"

"So I hear."

"What's your name, kid?"

"Don Nash."

"The Granite Cove mystery?"

"Yes, I wrote those articles."

"Good series, just like riding alongside the detectives."

"I had cooperation," Don said, looking expectantly at his new friend and admirer.

"Okay, Don. Here's the deal, it was an Italian gang, Manga Campagna's. But don't quote me, just say 'a reliable source' because I am."

"Agreed. Mail trucks, who would have guessed? What an idea."

"They think of everything eventually except informants."

"Dangerous job, informant."

"Damn right. See who disappears in the next month. You follow me?"

"What are you saying?"

"Somebody is working on that angle as we speak, I'm sure. They look at each other and think, 'Was it you? Was it *you*?' but really they can't tell the sheep from the goats. And if they could, it would be somebody else next time. Rival gang wars bring us the best information. Mark my words, Don. See who disappears."

Don wrote up what little he had but the head-line would be bigger than his story.

"Off the record, you think Prohibition will last?" Don asked.

"Off the record, I think it won't. Too much of a gift to the criminal element. I mean when Mr. and Mrs. America will still buy booze and go out to speakeasies, break the law, the government can't win. We'll win battles, like tonight, but not the war. We'll all be back to drinking legally in another five, outside ten years."

"We've never repealed a Constitutional amendment."

"Tell it to Rockefeller. He's putting his money on repeal. Look it up. When a Baptist won't sup-port Prohibition, Prohibition is not working."

Don wondered what would happen then to all of the rum runners and the speedboats, and even the Coast Guard unit on Ten Pound Island. Would the seaplane hangar become obsolete? Would

Rogers Street's speakeasies turn into legal bars? But that was speculation. Tonight, he was covering a successful raid in which the Feds triumphed. He watched them break open barrels of beer and pour away boxloads of bottles of whiskey. The street flowed with liquor, which ran down the drains. A lot of rats were going to get ossified tonight.

But would someone disappear? Really?

Chapter Twenty-Two

The earth rotated around the sun the same twenty-four-hour spin that it always did, and yet for one of the inhabitants of the spinning planet, time ran leadenly slow as he waited to meet up with Jo. They were to rendezvous here in a grassy ball field on the end of the Boulevard at high noon. Ed arrived at eleven. He had enjoyed their day at Good Harbor, and his initial portrait of her, but he was certain—and Jo agreed—that she knew more about using watercolors than he did.

"You teach art back in Brooklyn, don't you?" he asked her.

"Yes, I do."

"Well, then, teach me watercolors," Ed said, finding it easier to say than he thought. He was waiting to learn more from her.

Gloucester time had never run so slowly for the crew of the Dorchester Company. Back in 1623, they were, rather, constantly watching the sun anxiously as it simply sped, aiming to split and salt and lay out the cod before sunset and darkness, when they could do no more than cover themselves with blankets or wrapped inside sailcloth and attempt some sleep ashore, hearing animals, fearing Indi-

ans, awakening often and getting truly little sleep
before it was dawn again and time to move, move,
move.

Some of Gloucester's later days were burned
more vividly into the memories of its residents, the
flashes of British cannon from ships offshore, the
hurtling cannonball that smashed into the church
steeple. That day endured vividly until all who had
witnessed it were in their graves.

At least, Ed needed not wait longer than he had
to. Jo appeared. She was on time. But not early.
Women. Ed stood and smiled unusually broadly.

"Are you ready for watercolors?" she asked,
looking up at him as he stooped down to kiss her
on the forehead.

"I feel like a boy in school," he said.

"Well, I'm just the teacher for you, boy."

"I believe you are."

It would be best if they had no particular object
in sight for the lesson, she said.

"These rocks and trees will do," she said, gesturing to the rocks and trees on the fringe of the
ball field in which they stood.

She said, "First lesson, go slowly. Your paint is
molasses. Your farms are underwater. Everything is
as in a dream. Get it?"

"Got…it," he said slowly.

She had him use the broad brush to sweep over
the sheet on his easel, coating its surface with a
sheen of moisture. He was, she said, to paint "wet
on wet" before trying a dry surface. Next, he wet a
brush as she instructed and dipped it into a blue
paint. She nodded approval as he swung his arm
toward a thick linen-like paper and slid—slowly—
into a long, thin curve, much like a single hair.

"Good," she said.

They both watched as the filament feathered

and bled into the wet around it, making a blue cloud, a vapor with a backbone. She had him dab yellow around it, dots that dissolved, replaced by globes of varying shades of yellow and green, a sort of miniature colorful Milky Way with suns about a blue void.

"Well, what do you think?" she asked.

"So far, it is mesmerizing. So little can bring out so much so quickly, I can understand going slow and stopping, resting, and reflecting. Is that how *you* paint, Jo?"

"You anticipate me, that was my next class, stopping and looking, letting the painting talk back to you."

"Which color next?" he asked.

"I'm handing over the baton to you now, student. You find what cries out to you. There is no democracy of colors, but each one in its time steps up and commands priority. Or, because you are the king, perhaps mix up some royal purple."

Ed studied what he had painted, which had covered less than a tenth of the sheet, and decided that what it needed was company: more blue and more yellow. Not mixing up royal purple, he slowly, changing brushes, developed an abstract of colors until he was satisfied that he had reached a balance between a dreamy vision of the bushes and rocks nearby and untouched paper. He opted to leave a third of the paper, its top, a colorless sky, as it were.

"Not Winslow Homer, is it, Jo?"

Jo smiled and told him, "You are Winslow Homer in training. Which Professor Henri would only say in anger."

"I remember, he wanted us to explore."

"What does exploration mean to you?"

"I work at the atomic level, Jo. The Greeks imagined splitting until there was no more to split, which they called an 'a-tom,' an un-splittable. I work by subtraction. I explore the minimum."

"Do you have any questions?"

As he painted, Ed spoke slowly and philosophically, saying, "The question is how much less a human being can have and still be a human being. You know, take away reason, that way madness lies. Take away sight, that is blindness. I do not deal with gulfs that large. But really, how much can we do without? Can we live for ourselves alone?"

"I don't think so, and neither does Arthur."

As he seemed to be making the paints form a building in fog, she asked if it was a house.

"This is a secret I entrust only to you, Jo. The houses that I paint are arks, Noah's vessels, landed boats, moored now but battened down, shelters in case of storm."

"Stranded boats," she said.

"And always empty."

"But what about gingerbread and turrets, Victorian porches?"

Ed stared at her as if he was having a vision.

"You have something there. I should explore them in watercolors."

"I find flowers wonderful subjects, and we don't need flowers to live, do we? But they are life incarnate, the blooming and exultant, colorful flower, life. They are life redeemed by the quality of its moments. Professor Henri told me that my paintings offset life's evils. Quite a compliment, don't you think?"

"He always tended toward the mystical, but he never said anything like that to me."

"What did he tell you, Ed?"

"When he passed, he would suggest, you know, add white here, mess it up there, smudge."

"Smudge, really?"

"Nothing is flatter or deader than a clear and detailed oil, the thought."

"But you remind me, he told me not to be afraid to avoid specificity."

"You see? Our Henri contradicted himself."

"I had you try wet on wet for more fog, less rigidity."

Ed stared at Jo again.

"You may be right, Jo, possibly that's why I haven't sold a painting in a long time. Too on the nose."

"Sometimes I back off and squint, you know, at my arrangement of flowers, to see the blur that I want to capture."

"To see the blur, that's good."

"Shall we try applying watercolor to a dry surface next?"

"A challenge. Blurs will be much harder with a dry surface. A dry surface will be full of traps to draw out my careful attention to detail."

"And I'm going to be at your side watching you defeat these temptations, each one, making a smudge instead, *a la* Professor Henri. The right bit of paint fog to evoke the subject without bringing it out too loudly. Suggest, don't show."

"Now?"

"Now. Pack up your easel and let's walk."

The two proceeded and discussed where and what to eat and how they both admired the compact utilitarian neatness of the Blynman Bridge, which a bridgetender in a check raised and lowered for high-masted boats to pass through this last stretch of the Annisquam River, before they entered a small sweetshop with a view of the harbor, at which they had fresh-baked, still-warm pastries and tea.

Chapter Twenty-Three

Jo could not sleep. Silence was unsettling. In her childhood, she had never been alone and the absence of sound in this house was constant, not like the creak of the floorboards of her old house or the noise of doors or windows and the tinkling of her father downstairs on the piano, even with the door to the parlor closed, not to mention her mother, who kept no schedule and might bake a cake at 2 in the morning as easily as 2 in the afternoon, the splash of water in the sink, the clink of glassware, sometimes the top of a tin cannister that would drop. Or her sister might awaken and whisper a conversation with Jo for a half-hour. The cat, Mac, whom she loved and who loved her, would come in and sleep across the end of her bed.

This hardly changed in her adulthood. After schoolrooms full of pupils and the smell of paint or plaster, depending on the projects, the buzz of voices, often excited, as they worked and admired one another's drawings or other creations, Jo went home to roommates. Roommates who, like her, were up late reading, brewing tea, curling hair, sewing dresses, writing letters, and in the night still awake, tossing or turning, or snoring in a virtual cacophony.

Her entry into the Red Cross, barracks living, the infirmary months so sick, day and night indistinguishably noisy and active times, breathing engine oil on ships over and back, the incessantly droning engines, wave sounds, echoes.

Next, when she landed in a church, in a bed on the side of the nave, in a church never locked to permit midnight prayers, early morning visits, even sleeping by homeless on pews, the company and the noises of her church were strangely comforting.

Now independent, still unmarried, in an apartment of her own, she heard traffic night and day, roisterers until dawn, in a city that never sleeps. By day, not only teaching but teaching well, a more skillful and earnest pedagogue than her casual father ever was, she was a passionate artist who fanned the wisps of any youngster's talent into flame. By night, after supper and her chores, reading alone and keeping a diary, and a cat, what bothered her most was the absence of anybody to talk with, and, even when she talked, the impossibility of much to share with virtual strangers upon whom she imposed herself. She found her greatest comfort in art classes, and in art galleries. She knew and grew intensely attached to several artists in New York, having lost contact with the members of her earlier theater troupes. Had she been asked in confessional to articulate her distress, she might have said, "I lack family."

As the branch is bent, so grows the tree, her mother said, who was no arborist or gardener, who knew an apple from a pear but never tried an artichoke and eeked at spiders and ants alike. She grew no plants. They were "troublesome," she said to Jo, "unless you have a green thumb, which I lack and you as well." Jo rebelled and edged green plants to bloom in pots. She was a dutiful plant mother. For her mother nothing green was good unless it was in her kitchen, she had seen it before, and she was preparing it for cooking. By contrast, green became a focal color in many of Jo's paintings, the connector, and flowers were her most typical theme. She told Professor Henri that she liked their "regular irregularity," which brought out his rare laughter.

Her mother stood tall in the kitchen, Jo granted, a creative and fabulous cook, the very queen of a hundred ways to make an apple amazing, and modest about it. She was not so much reluctant to share recipes as a cook who cooked extemporaneously. She maintained that Jo would learn to cook "in her own way on her own time" but, by several repeated classes, she did teach Jo to bake an apple pie and, although hers never came out as good as her mother's, it reliably filled wherever Jo lived with the bite of bubbling cinnamon and spices, melted butter and sugar, rising dough smells. A slice of Jo's, when served, especially if still warm, delighted one's tongue down to the tonsils, with cheddar cheese even more so. In fact, her mother cooked intuitively, encouraging the precipitation of meals, never knowing what to expect but experimenting. Food happened.

In 1923, her father was dead, her mother was prematurely aging and had difficulties both in hearing and in understanding what Jo said when she visited. Her mother no longer cooked but had a cousin helping her. For all of her difficulties, her mother was jolly. She was blessed by a certain blindness of the bad parts of life. Jo sought out family beyond her home. Theater groups had formed Jo's second families for a while, joyful and merry bands though they were, gradually, each of the troupes, disintegrated, leaving not a rack behind. As a novice she had thrown herself into relating with these acquaintances as friends forever, and was disappointed. She had ever since resisted forming quick attachments or indulging in immediate affection. "Love at first sight" was alien to her adult world by her own cold *fiat*.

Jo enjoyed the company of men before and after cultural events, and usually in the form of two couples, a foursome making the rounds of bars, or walking to some New York sight on a lark, or riding together on the Elevated. She knew infatuations but did not explore them very far. "Leave at first sight" might have served as her model, along with Lorelei Lee's "Smile, smile, smile." Although she had been a nude model for art classes and artists approved by Robert Henri, she did not so much as bare her bosom to any of her male admirers. Their regular departures suggested that she was out of tune with the times in 1923. She enjoyed parties, she did not mind a drink or boisterous singing, she was no prude, but she had a starchiness about what was right and right meant loving one man in a commitment for life. This man she had yet to find, or had she?

Put together, her aching solitude, the many cumulative miseries of aloneness, and an unsatisfied but intense determination to find the right man and so become part of a devoted and married couple provided her with exactly the same problems that she brought with her when she arrived in Gloucester, and exactly the same consolation, her cat.

As if to say that she was not alone, Arthur picked this exact moment to leap up onto the bed and stretch his long form out on top of her blanket, his head within easy reach for her to scratch him just behind the ears. She did, he purred, and Jo managed a smile before she went to sleep.

"What are you saying, moofy? Don't worry about Ed, you've got me?"

With that remark and a laugh, she fell asleep quickly.

Chapter Twenty-Four

Dr. Blythe looked up and down Main Street before he ducked down Duncan and knocked on an unpainted door that was level with the sidewalk. It was habitual for him to be cautious, entangled as he had become with a lucrative but illegal relationship with the underworld. Not many would know him here so near the working waterfront.

"Yeah?" a voice said from within.

"Piping plover," Dr. Blythe said.

Before opening the door, a man in a thick wool gray sweater and two-day beard appeared at the porthole on the door to say, "Five bucks."

Dr. Blythe flashed his badge up to porthole, which unbattened the hatches. Suddenly, bolts and locks were snapping and cracking as the same voice said in a new and ingratiating tone, "Come on in, officer. I'm sorry. I'll have to memorize your face. No charge, of course. The law is always welcome here."

As the law, and as welcome, Dr. Blythe entered. The smoke was stagnant and stifling. Although he wanted a good drink and, as word reached the bartender that he was "the law," he would be given a good glass of the real stuff, he did not enjoy wading through smoke. He was not one of the hypocritical doctors who told their patients not to smoke, or to cut down, but who smoked himself. Tobacco was a stink in his nostrils, but where else was he going to get a slug of scotch and be found by one of the flapper girls out for fun?

"What'll it be, sir?"

"Got scotch? Aged scotch?"

"Imported direct from Ireland, the best yellow spot."

"That'll do."

Dr. Blythe had a lieutenant's badge from the chief of police because he was summoned to accidents and the patrolmen were not happy about taking orders from a civilian, to stop traffic or to move a man by police car and siren. With a rank of lieutenant, Dr. Blythe was able to give orders to anyone on the scene but Lieutenant Conrad.

When the drink came back on a tray, he found himself joined at his table, as he hoped he might be. He ordered a drink, but he wanted a woman.

"Out keeping Gloucester safe, Dr. Blythe?"

"Keep your voice down, please."

"I'm Carol," she said, bending low and in a stage whisper.

"Nice to meet you. Carol."

"We met. Last year. For a blood test."

"I don't—"

"You wouldn't remember, I was going to get married, we both took the test, no clap, and then we pulled a license for a priest to announce the banns."

She stopped with that.

Dr. Blythe asked, "Was there more?"

"Yeah, he turned up dead. You did the autopsy."

"I do a lot of autopsies, Carol."

"Young guy, my age, barrel-chested, hair on his chest, a real man, curly black hair, big but muscular. By the name of Birkelder."

"Drowned?" Dr. Blythe asked.

"So you concluded."

"I'm sorry."

"Think how sorry I was, Doctor," she said without emotion. After a pause, she went on, "You know, Baggy worked the waterfront all of his life, went out fishing starting thirteen, he never fell overboard, never nothing. He wasn't clumsy. Baggy was big but he was graceful, light on his feet, danced like a friggin' moonbeam on the harbor. Then, I hear he's doing the dixie on a clear day and hitting the water so hard that he forgot how to swim. Funny, you know?"

"I think he had a head bruise."

"Yeah, I think so, too, Doctor."

"An accident."

"So I understand."

"I feel badly about your loss."

"I guess my loss is your gain tonight."

He stared at her. She smiled and gave him that look, staring him down.

"Don't you like what you see? I'm like a widow without no pension," she said, kinking her head and squinting as if to judge her image from whatever he seemed to be seeing.

"I just came by for a drink."

"I know you and your wife are separated. It must be," she paused, then said with a wink, "hard."

He swallowed the last of the scotch, and felt different. Maybe not enough oxygen, too much smoke, maybe the drink, maybe just Carol. He stood up.

"I, uh, have had enough."

"You want to leave separately or together?"

"Separately."

"Meet you in front of the Five and Dime."

He said nothing. Would he meet her? What was her game? Still, she had told him who she was. If she had wanted to stab him or shoot him, she had her chance here. Although that would have been in front of witnesses, she obviously knew them better than he did. Any secret of hers would be safe with them. Was he going to take a chance elsewhere? She looked…good. Not in the sense of virtue, but in the sense of lithe and sleek. He thought about taking her to his home up on Portagee Hill. It was dark and it was late.

On the other hand, watching the neighbors was the big hobby on the Hill. People looked through their curtains on hearing an engine. Moreover, lately he was sure that somebody did not like him because they rubbed off half his name from the mailbox. A sign but not a good sign, being rubbed out. Still, a hotel in Gloucester would be impossible, he would be recognized, and he did not want to drive down the line.

Should he take Carol on trust and go to her place? Such were his thoughts as he stopped, standing in front of the Five and Ten. He was there first, staring at posters in the window but thinking of her body without even the flapper dress she had donned that did not reach her turned-down hose. Quickly, in minutes, Carol was coming down Main Street and easily saw him, although the awning cast a dark shadow over its door, its windows, and Dr. Blythe.

"What's on sale this week?" Carol asked, in case anyone was in earshot.

Dr. Blythe read from a poster, "They've got two

for one on lipsticks, and a free comb with any purchase. Some selected song sheets are half price."

"Yeah, last year's. Who wants 'The Sheik of Araby' or 'Way Down Yonder in New Orleans' this year?"

Dr. Blythe chuckled, his wife being a trained classical pianist and fastidious about the best in music, worshiping Beethoven, Bach and Brahms. Here, he was going to probe the depths of quite a different ear.

"My place or yours, sailor?" Carol asked.

Dr. Blythe saw her take a cigarette out of a pack in her pocketbook.

"Your place, but would you not smoke?"

"All rightee. Your wish is my apple pie, kid."

"I'll take my car. Do you have one also?"

"Yeah, but let's leave it parked, and come back to it after we get to know one another better. All right by you, big boy?"

"I'm fine with that. Is your home far? You don't share it with anyone, do you?"

"Just off East Gloucester Square. And no, not since I lost my fiancé."

She wrapped her arms around Dr. Blythe and gave him a memorable and extended kiss. She tasted like cigars, having been hanging around that speakeasy long before he arrived, or she had dredged up something from the waiter she tipped. What a life. Dr. Blythe stiffened, as if for that moment unwilling to be seen in such company, at least kissing it. She relaxed her grip and smiled, asking, "Nice?"

He, too, relaxed and whispered, "Oh, you kid."

He had found his woman for tonight. They walked off arm in arm, Carol's sequined pocketbook swinging.

Chapter Twenty-Five

Ed and Jo had been in life classes—in which their Professor Henri harassed students who would not see the light and shadows to see and to sketch them, and the planes, as well as the concave and the convex inherent in a body—and which Ed attended after early instances of blushing, staring only in attenuated bursts at the unclothed woman —while Jo had had no problem—until everybody in class was seeing a body as an object, as they had not seen bodies before. In Henri's large studio classroom, Henri, standing and orating while an unapologetically nude woman reclined on pillows or stood holding a pole in the background, told his students of varying ages but mostly younger than Ed and Jo, fifty times if he did once that "Not the subject but what you feel about the subject counts," and that they must forget about fine art subjects altogether and "paint pictures of what interests *you*." If they did, Henri promised them, they would make a stir in the world.

Ed, who read and re-read Ralph Waldo Emerson, was impressed by philosophers. Jo, who had not, was not. Jo was practical. She understood what interested ordinary people, and what would sell.

Life paintings would sell. Henri painted and sold
life paintings more often than he was able to peddle
his depictions of ashcans in alleys. Jo painted and
in recent years readily sold flowers, still lifes and
landscapes, very bright landscapes from which their
creator's joy emanated.

Ed was one of America's most outstanding
loners within whom a creator's joy too rarely
burned. He felt a misfit and, reaching forty, thought
about how many years he might be destined to live
a long and complaining life—eighty-four was his
guess—before he was released from the torture.
The seeming irony behind why he chose to live in
the most populous city in the country and, this
summer, to head to a city guaranteed to be
crowded and frenetic, he ought to have explained
to save us from having to guess, but he did not.

One thing for sure: he did not come to
Gloucester for the waters. Although waters there
are in Gloucester, in 1923 Ed painted barely a drop
of Gloucester's famous waters. Nor had the waters
interested him ten years earlier, when he had summered in Gloucester in 1912, worrying about his
father, who was ill that year and died the next. His
father was only 61 but he was bored. He had
nothing to occupy him, nothing to hold him. Ed
thought that he would have lived longer had he
kept his store, had his son joined him in keeping his
store.

His parents had been good to him. The mar-
velous thing about his parents was—and he did not
know if they were both equally involved—that they
filled the parlor with a constant and renewed flow
of illustrated books for children, instructional art
brochures, art magazines, colorful catalogs, and art
books. At first, Ed only enjoyed the pictures of soldiers, battles, ships at sea and such exotic fare. Only

in his teen years did he find himself uninterested in
these themes, or in landscapes, or in scenes of people, and find himself looking, staring at and
studying the way artists had constructed the buildings, the stores, the houses.

By his twenties, he stared at houses, streets,
buildings, automobiles, sky and clouds, and telephone poles. At age thirty, in Gloucester, tacking
back from a seascape to squat Squam Light, adding
people, his picture and images of people did not
please him during the making or when complete.
One painting, "Sailing," that sold for $ 250 in
1913, his last success, his Armory Show triumph.
He had painted it over a used canvas that had been
an unsmiling self-portrait. In fact, he had painted it
over twice. First, the sailboat was going to star-
board, then he redid it as a sailboat going to port.
The sail half-covered and shadowed the faces of its
two passengers, as he hesitated to deal with faces at
any distance. The proportions and ratios of the
sailboat and sail (without masts or ropes) would
have satisfied no boatsman. Ed had outgrown
meticulousness in designing boats. It was a sailboat
on canvas only, one that was not seaworthy—but
this wretched marine theme, of all things, had
proved salable. Once.

In Gloucester, Ed, over six feet tall and wearing
an oversized homburg hat, bearing his battered
wooden box of paints and brushes, his old easel,
and a canvas, would nod wordlessly toward a telephone pole and say, "Good morning." The only
thing he liked better than one telephone pole was
two telephone poles. He was in that sense bipolar.

Unhappy in his own way, as all unhappy artists
are, he demurred to mix with Gloucester's past. By
contrast, Jo was a past maven. She could not get
enough of the past. She was afloat in Gloucester in

all that happened since 1623, reading articles reminding every event since the first codfish was slapped down to dry on the Fort stage rock. She went to see the Cape Ann Museum's exhibits about the civil war.

"Were there no slaves in Gloucester, ever?" Jo asked.

"No," a docent told her.

"But wasn't it legal to keep slaves?"

"Only in the South."

Jo was no expert, but it made sense to her that if wealthy shipowners in Gloucester found a way to make money in trade, they would, and she had read that not every rich man has scruples. She meant to ask My. Haywood about Franklin Pierce, and whatever he knew, but he went back to Vermont before she could.

"Have you seen Howard Blackburn's boats?" the docent then asked Jo. When Jo said she had not, and that she knew nothing about Howard Blackburn, the docent said, "You must see the boats and, I hope, you might meet the man. He lives in Gloucester near here and is always out walking, a tall, white-haired, sturdy man you will recognize by his hands."

"How?" Jo asked.

"No fingers. He lost his fingers when—well, let me tell you the story alongside of his boats, which he gave to the museum."

They moved to look over the "Great Republic," a 25-foot sailboat in which Blackburn made it from Gloucester to Portugal in 39 days, and the sailing dory he named "America." Beside them, the docent continued:

"Howard Blackburn was just another Gloucester fisherman when caught in a storm out on George's Banks, separated from his ship in a dory in a thick fog. With no way to find his ship, he and his dorymate began to row for the nearest land, night and day for five days without water, without foot, without sleep."

"You would think he would die."

"The dorymate did, poor boy, the second day. The weather was freezing, and it sometimes snowed. Blackburn lost his mittens, so he just hooked his hands and fingers to freeze around the oars. When Blackburn hit land, it was Newfoundland and the folks there, poor as they were, took him in, of course."

"But he lost his fingers, you said?"

"They had to be cut off, frostbitten. And some of his toes, and half of each thumb. He was touch-and-go between life and death for a month, from exposure and dehydration and all he'd endured, but he survived."

"In his twenties?"

"Twenty-four, poor man. But when he returned to Gloucester, he was not one to sit. He opened a bar well-patronized by the fishermen, you can imagine. He made money. He went up to Alaska to try his luck finding gold. Along the way, he built a tavern, you can see it today, a brick building down the lower end of Main Street, with 'Blackburn 1900' overhead. And he decided he would like to travel."

"He took trips?"

"He, with no fingers, made solo voyages sailing across the Atlantic, once to England and once to Portugal, and another trip down the Mississippi and up the Eastern seaboard. Alone. Can you imagine?"

When Jo admitted she could not imagine, the docent emphasized, "But—it all actually happened.

Part of Gloucester history made by one stubborn fisherman."

Blackburn personally made history, but Jo was coming to sense that history as often moved nationally and then moved into Gloucester. The seaplane circling the harbor could be tracked back to the Wright brothers. Anywhere she looked, if she saw gangsters, flappers, red hot mamas, movies, air mail, air mattresses, ice boxes, cat's whiskers and crystal radio sets, jazz, new words, new dances, new companies, new stocks, what she saw coincided with the end of 300 years—tick tick—of Gloucester history.

Chapter Twenty-Six

After her visit to the museum and hearing the docent, Jo seemed to know as much about Howard Blackburn as she did about Ed. These things Jo knew about Ed: that he was aloof, that he was aloof and that he was aloof. His eyes were beady and glaring, not usually directed at her, not that she cared. He seemed to vary inexplicably between lively and lifeless, grieving some invisible wounds or losses. He was most certainly not married, a bachelor who picked out his own tasteless clothes. She could not even imagine him with a cat. His sketches were balanced. She had used her watercolors once with near abandon but by nature he muted his colors sinfully, drifting toward the waste of raw umber by default.

She did not know that he was off sketching by himself, and exulting in success.

Before a selected house today, within twenty minutes Ed was satisfied that he had begun. It was not that his outline was finished. To pursue completion of a sketch, or of a painting was a fool's errand. Henri taught that, wise old bird that he was. "Your sketch is never finished," he said. "Repeat." His students in ragged unison repeated, "Our

sketches are never finished." After that he said,
"You only know when to quit. Then you do what?"
he asked. The students knew what to say in chorus:
"Then we quit."

It was more of a cool and willful abandonment
to the iron laws of creation than a warm or tickling
sense of satisfaction that moved him next. You
must steel yourself to abandon a still-warm sketch
and to move on to the next. You had to leave behind your regrets, to hell with the feelings that
nagged at you to stall, to keep trying. You had to
tell yourself that you were not going to improve on
what you already did, so stop, fool.

"Then we quit," the cranky loner said to himself under his breath. Ed smiled for the first time
that day. One word made him smirk. *We*, indeed.

Ed had whispered but he needed not to have
been so quiet. No one near heard him. Some days
—and this made him avoid the usual sights of the
city, like the Harbor or Lane's Cove or, God bless
us, Rockport anywhere—a group of adults or
even children would stand by or behind him,
asking questions of him or talking among themselves. Not here, not this morning, not in front of
this forlorn house. Jo was not even by, distracting
him.

Unknown to Jo who wondered what Ed was doing, the house Ed selected was yielding, an obedient
dog turning tricks for a beloved master, allowing Ed
to take it up in his two hands without too much of
what he saw leaking and escaping through his fingers, though some of his starting vision would always drip off and an artist had to live with a
broken heart for that reason, as all of his paintings
were, in part, paintings that got away. A fisherman
casts a net and hauls in—nothing. It happens.
Sometimes the vision perishes before the hands can

sketch. But not today. The fisherman's net was filled to bursting.

The two New Yorkers at Mrs. Post's were still resident, and at it on boats every fair day to fish. How were they doing out at sea on their charter boat of the day? He did not care if they caught a whale, he had beaten them. His vacation had begun in earnest. This house was a great haul. He was in Gloucester for this. Some artists would die, or at least trade their puny souls to paint such sketches as he had going. These lines versus eternal damnation? Ed himself might have to think a long time before deciding. They felt that good.

He continued to add to his collection of views, sketching the cornices over and over, a frolic and detour away from the main frame but of interest on their own. A veritable assortment of cornices filled a page like balls in the air over a juggler's head. The shadows, if examined closely, told the minutes he had been at work on them, as the angle changed, as the sun moved along on its arc.

Ed loved shadows and could not get enough of them into his sketchbook. Few houses would have offered him more, even the lines of clapboards, lines that gave him pause, reminded him of a washboard, or the ripples of waves coming into shore. The whole was dynamic, a light-and-shadow show performed daily but unseen except for this morning, when he was all eyes to pick up details with hungry eyes.

His hand and fingers moved as fast as a pianist in the midst of a concert's crescendo. Flick, tick, nick, sweep, a long broad stroke, a dot, two, three, a light shadow he indicated by smudging with a folded nubbin of thin, crumpled paper.

Ed was lost in his task. He surrendered to this function and could hardly feel the pencil, so unified was his arm to his instrument, hovering then striking over the paper battleground as he, with a general's eyes over a war map, examined the positions of the enemy he loved, his objective, this house. He would not let perspective defeat him, nor the moving sun above. He set his pencil to paper and barely lifted it as he kept at a connected but circuitous line to outline the house front and its roof.

Deep down, he knew that he could never really tell if the sketches were as good as he thought they were until later. Until they cooled off in a drawer, until he calmed down enough to look at them through more objective eyes, but today they seemed to be the bubbling best work he had ever done. Key up Beethoven's "Ode to Joy." Ed Hopper felt positively reborn.

Chapter Twenty-Seven

Before St. Peter's Day, June 29, the confessionals were full for weeks, even more than before Easter. Late June was the local high tide of religious ritual. Nothing else came close. The Fiesta itself began on June 29 at mid-day with a procession of a selected fishermen. The dozen men, both old and young, were identically clad in white shirts, black pants, and red embroidered vests "like in the old country."

Their faces ran a spectrum from bland and clear, pale teens to swarthy, weather-beaten wrinkled men who had been long at sea, and their expressions ran from the side-glances, stifled grins and winks of the young through the somber, thoughtful visages of men who had seen too much to laugh too readily. They bore the silk ribbon-bedecked statue of Saint Peter shoulder-high on trestles beginning at Our Lady of Good Voyage Church. They proceeded through cheering crowds through the winding streets of Gloucester's cow-paths to the land's edge near the Fort section. There St. Peter—to cries of "*Viva San Pietro*"—was set down in the center of an open-air altar built by the devoutly faithful Portuguese and Italians of Gloucester's tight-knit fleet.

Dancing in the Fort followed with music by local bands, all of whom offered lively vintage tunes of Italy and Portugal. Ed and Jo watched and listened, Jo clapping in time and thoroughly surrendering herself to sway and move to the music. She could not understand Ed just standing, watching, and he could not understand her.

The following Sunday morning at the outdoor Mass, Ed and Jo found two spaces among family groups, who nonetheless smiled in a welcoming way and nodded to them, everyone in finery, everyone so dressed up. It struck Ed, drifting to morbid thoughts, that the man beside him in a conservative black suit was wearing what he would wear in his coffin, if he did not die at sea. To Ed, every adult male in Gloucester was a fisherman. Jo was agog at all of the flowers, how the women of the church had somehow found or loaned vases in every niche or surface and how the air now smelled not of salt and fish but more like a garden. She was moved because she had only known such heady incense and candle wax from her time living in church in Greenwich Village.

People parted for the Cardinal and priests to come through, flanked by altar boys, two swinging incense, the others singing in Latin. She and Ed imitated what everybody else did, standing, kneeling, genuflecting, getting a workout. They did everything but head up to the communion rail to take part in that ritual.

The Latin was astonishingly effective in evoking another world. The Cardinal made the most of every syllable as he raised the host. His voice was a deep bass, notable as a cantor's might be, carried aloft and afar by the sea breezes of this sabbath day. His sermon always included verses like "I will make you a fisher of men," allusions to the disciples called to follow by leaving their nets and boats, and Jesus's walk across stormy waters. Gloucester Catholics felt their greatest and most forgivable pride on the Sunday of the outdoor Mass at St. Peter's Fiesta and 1923 was no exception. "*Pax vobiscum*," and the response, "*Et cum spirituo tuo*," flowed into "*Ite Missa est*," and the Mass was over.

The greasy pole event that afternoon was another thing altogether. Slathered up with engine grease from stem to stern, a telephone pole stuck out from a ladder over Gloucester Harbor as a taunt and a test to of grit and determination. The young men of Gloucester were eligible to make the attempt, and many a son of a fisherman valiantly fell before, finally, some lucky lad managed to make it, either inch by inch sideways, or running much of the length and grabbing the flag just when plunging off the end into the air and down into the harbor.

The Cardinal then blessed the seemingly endless fleet numbering hundreds of vessels, all of the ships passing by him one by one and then out into the harbor.

Chapter Twenty-Eight

The beginning of Ed's beginnings was and will always be his first day in the third-grade class in the elementary school in Nyack, New York. For two years, he had walked to school with an older neighbor, Elias, but Elias and his family had moved that summer and he had not gotten a new friend. The neighboring houses' daughters were both younger and he was in no way going to walk with the mothers and daughters as the boy who went to school with them. The mothers had asked, his mother had happily accepted without consulting with him, and then had to (she said) "humiliate herself for such a fussbudget" and say that Edward preferred to walk alone.

"I do prefer to walk alone," he shouted back at her. His father stepped forward and suggested, quietly but with clenched teeth, that he lower his voice and apologize to his mother, which he did in a grudging tone while looking at the grains of wood in the floor and, seeing it, thinking it was surprisingly beautiful and he had been missing something all of his life to this moment. He found his eyes.

On the first day in third grade, Ed found himself in the schoolyard too early, alone and awaiting any familiar face. It was as if he were in a deserted and abandoned town, someplace he used to live, bereft of residents. Ed noticed as he otherwise might have missed how the rising run's rays on the red shingled schoolhouse made a glare that masked almost any of the red, turning it into something gray and filmy like brackish water, with which he was familiar, which Ed loved for its natural muddy scent and heaviness compared to the center of the stream when Elias and he used to go rowing in his father's boat.

Ed would have stared at the sides of the school-house in sunlight and shade for a longer time but other students in knickers began to arrive, shouting, all of whom much closer than he had heard, so intensely had he been studying as he began to learn about seeing, being and beauty. Had Elias not moved away, Ed doubted that he would have ever begun to see and feel such things so early as that first day of third grade.

Elias's absence removed the beam from his eyes, as it were. Ed saw Elias himself from time to time on a few Old Home Days in Nyack, and he was invited to visit, as in those days they lived only twenty miles apart, but their hearts no longer beat to the same drummer. Elias was growing up to farm, alongside his father, and he hunted and fished. He did not study a duck for its feathers. Ed did, in addition sketching the duck with care. The gap between them was too wide to bridge. Beginning in third grade, Ed needed to find a friend with eyes who cared about details. It took him a long time.

Chapter Twenty-Nine

Ed and Jo spent another sunny day at Good Harbor and, before they went out again at night, they ate Mrs. Murphy's haddock chowder with pilot crackers, and a dessert of blueberry cobbler. In the parlor, on the floor, rolling like a kid, Ed played with the sated and increasingly rotund Arthur, who played rough and drew lines that drew blood on the back of Ed's hands before fleeing and hiding under the sofa, only his tail visible and twitching.

Ed announced when Jo appeared dressed to leave, "We will be delayed while I wait here and lick my wounds."

"I'll see if Mrs. Murphy has some mercurochrome."

Mrs. Murphy instructed him to go upstairs to the bathroom, where she kept a well-stocked medicine cabinet. Besides bottles of Lydia Pinkham's Vegetable Compound and Carter's Little Liver Pills, she did have mercurochrome as well as band-aids, which she applied liberally over the scratches. He finally looked the victim of a great battle, which caused Jo to laugh when he came down.

"I am glad to be the source of so much merriment," Ed said to her.

Within an hour, they were sitting on the hot, white sand of Good Harbor beach, Jo having changed into her bathing suit although not yet swimming. She sketched children running about.

"I have been to Good Harbor many times," Jo said.

Ed waited, silent, surveying the expanse of eaves surging ashore, scanning from the twin lighthouses over on the Rockport side, past Salt Island, and over toward the hilltop houses that tempted him to approach them. Kids yelled on the right as they jumped from a narrow wooden bridge into a stream that ran alongside the beach back to the marshes. Ed still said nothing.

"I sketch a lot, of course. And I paint, but only if it's cloudy. I don't like to paint when there are too many people around," she said.

Ed nodded, then they made eye contact. Although neither could have said just why, it was as if they were meeting for the first time.

Jo thought of telling him the longest story she knew.

"Did you know that I lived in a church for a while?" she asked.

"That I had not expected. You? Where?"

"Well, I signed up with the Red Cross but then I had to return from Over There before I could help wounded soldiers due to bronchitis. I was fired *and* the job I had with New York City schools was gone. They did not hold it for me, and other jobs were not to be had, my parents were both dead, my sister was five states away, I could not burden another teacher and my theater friends were scattered, so I was evicted, jobless, sick and penniless, hauling my possessions through the streets—"

"I am so sorry."

"—until I ducked into a church to pray, the one church in Greenwich Village frequented by artists."

"The Church of the Ascension."

"Exactly, you know it. Well, I might have been overly loud in sobbing, or I fell asleep in the pew, but in any case, the sexton was suddenly beside me, talking. And, of course, I told everything about the Red Cross, the war, bronchitis, the school department, and my present poverty, which led this wonderful old man—his name was Ralph—to show me this tiny little room in back of the nave, already set up with a bed, one of two niches for the sexton to use. He used it by giving me the spot for my residence. Do you know, Ed, from that moment I have been blessed by an unending series of good luck cards?"

"How long did you stay?"

"The sexton cleared it with the rector the next day and I lived, as I like to say, without tears or rent for a year in the Church of the Ascension, smelling incense, candle wax and the varnish of pews, going through winter and summer, until the school department found a job for me after all."

"I only knew you were a teacher."

"Well, I was, and still am. It is a joy to teach children I do not have to live with all day and then do my own artwork, mainly each summer. Why are you in Gloucester?"

"To answer questions other artists ask," Ed said but, noting the way Jo's eyes sparked at that sort of humor, he backpedaled, saying, "especially if they are pretty."

Jo looked at him anew, but he was already backtracking from any romance.

Ed said, "To breathe fresh air. I hate cigarette smoke."

Jo said, in an overly hearty response, "Me, too."

"And, while I am breathing, to sketch and paint."

"What do you paint?"

Ed shuffled his feet without knowing that he did, saying, "Anything that interests me."

"What interests you?" Jo asked, feeling like a dentist pulling teeth.

"I'm not sure. The usual shuffling when nothing quite seems worthy and within my range. If it's worthy, I find I cannot do it. And what's in my range seems unworthy of any time or attention. Houses, perhaps."

"What about ships and the harbor, or lighthouses?"

"Not so much."

"An artist who is in Gloucester to paint houses is news. I should call a reporter."

"Nobody outside my family ever wanted to help me," Jo said suddenly, as if revealing a pent-up secret.

"My mother would help."

"I didn't mean my mother didn't help. It's everyone but my family and my father could not help me if he wanted to and he did not want to anyway, all he wanted to do was to play music. Piano. And teach urchins and old maids for a quarter a lesson. A piano teacher lived with us, not a father. His address was the same as ours, Eddie, but he lived in Musicland."

"Your mother—"

"My mother was a free spirit, she gave my younger brother and me an example but no breakfast, no manners, no discipline. We ran free."

"No help."

"On my own, I got a scholarship to Hunter and turned myself into a teacher while I acted in community plays and painted, and posed but when the war came, I signed up with the Red Cross to volunteer Over There."

"Did Henri paint you?"

"He did a miniature of me in a scarlet dress with my red hair prominent and wild. He gave me tight lips, as if I had just made up my mind about something. I liked that."

"Not nude?"

"He never asked. Why?"

"Sorry, just that if you, if he, before I saw you, you know, if he had seen you, all of you—"

"Jealous?"

Ed grunted.

"I ought to be flattered."

"What happened in the Red Cross?"

"I got sick. The Red Cross kept me on when I was so sick, but then when I was back on my feet, they let me go and the city had no teaching position for me. I could not pay rent, my theatrical contacts had vanished overnight. No job and no savings. Nobody to ask for help. When I lost my apartment, I just broke down. You know the church we artists go to in the Village?"

"The Church of the Ascension."

"My refuge from the storm. The elder helped me. And then everything turned around and I got help from all hands."

"Really? I must not go all summer here without attending church, then."

Ed was studying this gabby, bustling force barely contained in flesh before him. He was moved, and he asked a question he had never asked anybody.

"Will you help me?"

"I'm not that good or famous yet, Ed."

"You have a knack. Your paintings sell. The galleries—"

"They help me. You have to be willing, to accept—"

"Your stuff is going to be exhibited in Brooklyn this fall, isn't it?"

"Watercolors, they invited me to send some. How did you know?"

"I hear things, as much as I keep to myself."

"I can help you. But it's a watercolor show. And you don't do watercolors."

"I do but only for commercial jobs, on commission. My real artistic gift is for oils."

"Well, I suggest that you try watercolors."

Chapter Thirty

The night Ed had trouble falling asleep. As if in a fever dream, he kept seeing the same things over and over, in watercolors. Then the watercolors began to melt, to merge, to mix into a mud without distinction of color, all one dark brown, a spilled pudding. This loop of a movie (except in color) re-peated every minute or two. Ed kept turning, resting on one side, then the other, on his stomach, on his back. Nothing helped. He wondered if his landlady allowed midnight snacks. He considered getting dressed and going out into the night, whether to find something to do or simply for the night air to clear his head. It was impossible for him to escape the nightmare following him, hounding him, haunting him and keeping him awake.

Wait, perhaps the Muse might be soothed by assent.

"I accept. I shall use watercolors in Gloucester. I shall paint something eligible to enter in the Brooklyn Museum competition."

This statement he said aloud but not loudly, in something more than a whisper but inaudible in any room but his own, addressed to his inner Muse, his restless Muse.

Without realizing exactly when he drifted off, soon Ed was, indeed, asleep. He had appeased his Muse. He was going to do some watercolors in Gloucester.

Chapter Thirty-One

Before Ed came by to pick Jo up for their trip to Dogtown, Jo has asked Mrs. Murphy if she had anything she could read about the place.

"Oh, you don't want to go there, Jo. To Dogtown? No, it's haunted."

"By ghosts?"

"Spirits, day or night. I know a man who will never go back there, he told me that he saw a colonial man, you know, dressed like in the olden times, in the swamp. When the ghost looked at him, the man got shivers and chilled and could not run away fast enough."

At Jo's repeated request, though, Mrs. Murphy found a booklet about Dogtown in the bookshelves of her late husband. In giving it to Jo, Mrs. Murphy said, "Thank me by discussing this subject no further. Don't tell me anything more. I swear, when I opened this booklet, the first line I read was about *witches*. Please don't give it back. When you're done, burn it."

Thus, when Ed arrived, Jo knew more about Dogtown, its history, its size, and the people behind the "cellar holes" formerly occupied by cabins and huts of the early settlers of Gloucester, who had built so far from the shoreline and harbor—it was said—in order to evade pirate raids.

"It's a sad place that we're going to, Ed. Very sad, abandoned."

"It was settled long ago, though. By farmers, right?"

"Yes, artists and tourists came later. Ed, of course, farms, cows, sheep, goats, pigs, and poultry. In the late 1690s and into the 1700s before the Revolution about a hundred families supported themselves, visited, cared for one another when sick and all that. It was not Dogtown, it was Gloucester."

"They didn't like the harbor?"

"It was dangerous to live near water because of pirates and if there was a war in Europe against England, any foreign warships might bombard the town."

"So they dug in for defense, living far in the woods."

"Exactly. Then, after the Revolution, once the risks were less, the roads in and around the harbor were better, commercial shipping and fishing took off, business was all around the harbor."

"People moved."

"Moved and left nothing behind. Abandoned their houses to the dogs."

"Dogtown."

"That's the reason behind the name. Old women, widows living in these houses until their last days kept dogs. And people called them witches, Ed. You know, like in Salem."

"None of which matters because what we're looking for are rocks and trees."

The trolley only took them as far as the Riverdale Mills. After they got off, they faced a long walk up Reynard and Cherry Streets, then uphill and into the woods on an unpaved road that gradually became a rocky path ever narrower. They were deep in woods.

"We ought to leave breadcrumbs," Jo said.

"I can find our way," Ed said.

"No signposts, no lights."

"Stone walls, boulders, there's a magnolia tree. I'm keeping track."

Jo was keeping an eye out for flowers, small or large. She was the first to find a theme she wanted to stop and sketch. As she sketched, Ed came up behind her and embraced her and nuzzled her neck, and that was all of the sketching they did that day.

Chapter Thirty-Two

The morning was chilly from the breeze off the ocean at Good Harbor Beach. Kendall, the studio's plump advance man, was wrapped in an Icelandic sweater with a turtleneck and still held his hands to hug himself. The camera, crew and actors had yet to appear. Garret had assigned Don to interview anybody he could and write up an article.

"Cold morning," Don said.

"Ah-he-whew-ah," Kendall said, in the breath that people make when they shiver, although he was not shivering. "I'm used to California."

"It'll warm up soon, going into the eighties to-day," Don said.

Kendall acted as if his vocal cords were frozen.

"Where's everybody else?" Don asked.

"The truck will pull in and—it's nearly high tide, right?"

Looking at the shoreline, Don agreed that it was.

"They have to go over to the island, but they've got a rowboat," Kendall said, indicating Salt Island, where a crew of carpenters had already started to put together a stucco, plaster, and wood Moorish *hacienda*.

"Today the day you burn it down?" Don asked. He had heard about a spectacular *finalé* in which Hollywood put the torch to its buildings, mostly plywood fronts.

"Yes. When does it get to eighty degrees?"

"A couple hours. When do the actors arrive?"

"About now, and the camera crew, and the director."

"You like your job?"

"What are you, being funny? Of course, I like my job. Mostly, I'm in Hollywood and I'm warm and I don't stand around on a freezing beach waiting for the tide to come in. You? You like your job?"

"Every day is different," Don said.

"Oh, here come the clowns. That truck driver would drive into the ocean if he did not have company to guide him. He can't function until noon most days."

Kendall mimed drinking, bottoms up.

So much for Prohibition, Don thought.

Kendall pointed toward Salt Island and the truck ground its way through beach sand to the flats and across to park next to the island, on a sand bar. They began taking out props and costumes.

"When do the swimmers arrive?" Kendall asked.

"Mostly, they sleep late and really won't be here in force until noon, low tide when there's more beach."

"Good. This is supposed to be an island far-away from anybody, you know, on the Mediterranean, pirates, a Spanish lady hostage, the gallant gentleman to the rescue, blah, blah, blah."

"All the world's a stage. I want to interview the stars. When is the best time?"

"I think just you forget the idea. They're at

work when they arrive, getting into make-up and costumes, rehearsing, acting, after that they flop like flounders, tired, you know. Maybe catch up to them in town tonight. Then they can act like movie stars and talk to you."

Meanwhile, a couple began slogging through the beach.

"Who's that?" Kendall asked.

"Artists. I've seen them around before. They come to draw and paint."

"No kidding. Locals?"

"No, New Yorkers, I think."

"They're older than I'd expect. At least baldy is, but the short woman, with her sunglasses and that hat, I can't see her face, I can't tell. They married?"

"I don't know."

"See if they talk. If they're talking, they're not married. If they're not talking, then they're married."

Don wondered if they were husband and wife, a couple of sketching partners, or both at the same time. When they walked past Kendall and Don, they were both looking at the incoming waves and saying nothing.

"Married," Kendall said.

"Not talking anyway," Don said, unconvinced. They did not get close enough for him to see if they were wearing rings.

"They're too old to be lovers," Kendall argued.

"Well, don't say I didn't warn you, Kendall. This is Gloucester, where love is in the air."

Kendall smiled and shook his head.

"Only in the movies, Don," he said.

Chapter Thirty-Three

She was a judge. Jo agreed and then immediately regretted having committed herself to take part. She was one of three jurors in the Tricentennial Competition sponsored by the Gloucester Art Forum, but because she was not the type to go back on her word, she sat at the jurors' table on a platform above onlookers. Jo had faith in herself to be objective and aware of artistic standards, but she was without certainty about anything else.

She spotted Ed in the crowd. He should be up here instead of me, she thought. Who was that standing beside him, engaging in chatter? The dancer, Sabrina. How coincidental, or was it? She had no taste and no obvious reason to be present unless she was chasing Ed. Plus, she could not be thirty years old, while Ed was almost old enough to have been her father. What was he thinking? And she, did she imagine that he had money?

The jury discussion was tedious and slow. She had no patience with Arvel Coyle, the chair, and his insistence to his two co-jurors, "I urge you to pay the maximum possible attention to the figure on the left, which is exquisitely rendered. You see the delicate detail?"

In Jo's eyes, it was perfectly impossible to ignore that the structure of this painting of beachgoers was unbalanced. She said of Arvel's choice, "There is that figure on the left, yes, but with nothing on the right to offset or to complement it. That canvas, if divided into quarters, is also lopsided in terms of light and dark colors, as if a tray of oil had been tipped and all of the oil ran to the left."

"I am seeking that we take the time to—"

The other juror, Thaddeus Wisterby, interrupted to join Jo on point, "To talk drivel over wasted efforts, Arvel. This is intended as a juried show judging the submissions even-handedly and on merit. If we are going to judge by the best *fragment* in an awkwardly designed piece, by all means, let us do so and say that we are doing *that* rather than judging the work as a whole, so that I may resign in protest."

"I did not mean to look *only* at the painting's figure on the left," Arvel said.

Seizing the moment, Jo said, "Then do not urge us to look at it. Urge us to look at these works as a whole, in each instance. On that basis, I suggest that the most outstanding submission in this competition is by Leon Kroll."

"A nude," Arvel said.

"Have we never awarded top prize to an artist who painted a nude?" Thaddeus asked, twitting Arvel.

"Not in my memory. But, of course, that does not mean it is ineligible."

"Of course, it does not," prickly Thaddeus said, then turned on Jo, asking, "Are we fighting for the ashcan school?"

"A nude is not an ashcan."

"A marginal subject, Jo, dear. You might as well paint the carcass of a slaughtered cow. It is shocking but a nude today is not the best artwork in the world."

"What is?" Jo asked.

Arvel added, "Yes, what is?"

Thaddeus said, "The sea, the sea, the sea. Over there, framed in dark wood, breakers on the back shore. Do I make myself clear?"

Facing a humdrum theme done in a competent enough but perfectly pedestrian manner, Jo said, "I quit. Do I make myself clear? You two decide."

She left the panel and fled, seeking Ed's comfort.

"Who would have thought? Leon Kroll in Gloucester, a prophet is not honored in his own land. I thought his painting was outstanding but they're going for waves pounding rocks."

"We both know what great paintings are," Ed said, hugging her.

"How do you view mine?"

"You ought to have entered."

"I was not eligible. I am not a member or a resident."

In the background, Arvel announced the winner—a tie between the painting of breaking waves and the multi-figure beach crowd—to applause as Jo said to Ed, "You are good."

"We were talking about great."

"In your works as a whole, the marks of greatness are increasingly predominant."

"I am good to great, with gusts to sixty, am I?"

"No, you are already good. And you will reach greatness, Jo."

"Like you. I will never be the artist you already are. You can draw more emotion from shades of brown than I can with my rainbow spectrum. I lack your sharp eye for the telling detail, your license to omit, to twist a detail up or down in intensity and emphasis. The canvases you are painting this summer are extraordinary."

"Extraordinary for me," Ed said.

"Extraordinary in the history of American art."

"How so?"

"From humble, ordinary houses, trees, telephone poles, the cars in the street your compositions are a brew of magic. Not a moment but several moments overlapping, the breeze is moving leaves beside Adam's House."

"You never told me."

"You never asked."

They walked back to Mrs. Murphy's together, after dawdling a bit at the cemetery beside her house, where they could be together, both undistracted and unobserved.

Chapter Thirty-Four

Meanwhile, in Bay View, between Annisquam and Lanesville, a high tide at midnight on a moonless night seemed to offer everything that a rum runner could ask for in his prayers. The sole offsetting disadvantage of these factors, in fact, was a clammer named Floyd who tipped off the Feds to expect an incoming shipment of liquor at just such a time and place, the cargo headed for storage in a vacant dwelling owned by one Dr. Adam Blythe. The authorities were thus forewarned and forearmed on the night that the trawler *St. Catherine* chugged into the arms of Hodgkins Cove. They listened as the boat shut off its engines and set down its anchor. Two small speedboats manned by well-versed members of the syndicate then left the dock. Boarding the boat anchored offshore, they began the process of unloading boxes.

To see all the action, Don had wanted to travel with the Coast Guard as they ran around the waters of Cape Ann with armed Treasury agents. The pursuit of Federal lawbreakers on the seas would have been the height of what he desired, an embedded journalist in a rank tabloid journalist's stunt. Not even his editor could reject an article that recounted his personal experiences as an eye-witness, but the Coast Guard put the kibosh on that idea.

Don spotted his old friend, Agent Wittgenstein, and explained his problem.

"I have to get out there," Don said. "Like you said when I covered the mystery of Granite Cove, I want to be alongside."

"That was different. The Coast Guard is right. You could get killed."

"I'll take my chances."

"Don't think about it. You a veteran?"

"Yes."

"Well, you didn't stick your head up Over There, you learned that, right?"

"That was different."

"You cover it from shore, we'll bring the booze to you. Plenty of time for notes and pictures. Big story, all glory without dodging bullets."

"But—"

"Wittgenstein has spoken."

It was true. Sometimes the gangsters were better armed than the Feds, Thomson submachine guns and long-range rifles with superior sights.

Foreclosed by sea, Don took up a post on the lee side of the cove and hunkered down beside the sea wall under two blankets and a hip flask of warming liquid. Prohibition had closed the bars, but not with a neat click. Don knew the "blind pigs" that police and locals—and Feds, so far—had let alone. His preferred speakeasy had never been raided, possibly out of friendship for its popular owner, possibly because of the owner's generosity to his friends. Business was booming and Glouces-ter, a port with a big harbor and a lot of coves, was a conduit for liquor. The success of the Feds on this occasion in Hodgkins Cove would not reduce the river by many drops, but it would make ink flow at the *Times*.

The issue for Don would be the name of Dr. Blythe. It was public record: Dr. Blythe owned the real estate to which the shipments were headed. That was from Floyd the Clammer, though. If the Feds seized the booze at sea, before any of it was stowed away in the vacant house, well, the house was simply one of many dotting the shore around Hodgkins Cove. Even if the booze were taken up to the house with a brass band playing Don guessed that his editor would allow nothing more specific than "a vacant house on the shore of the cove."

As things happened, searchlight glared at sea, no gun battle ensued, arrests were made, speed-boats revved up, the mother ship and cargo were seized. It was another successful raid. Wittgenstein had one of the Treasury agents give Don a list of the crew arrested that night. One name leaped out at Don: Manga Campagna. The actual chief had been overseeing this one. Wittgenstein was right on the money, naming the same mug as the master-mind of the post office trucks parade. The link be-tween Manga and Dr. Blythe's autopsy of Bag o' rocks Birkelder was almost coming to light. He wondered if the Feds had informants besides Floyd. Rumor had it that Carol, Birkelder's disconsolate fiancé, was a Federal contact. She had supposedly trailed a New York guy who was acting suspicious, casing joints all around the city after midnight. Could she have given something to the authorities? Had she made it inside Dr. Blythe's office or home?

More was unknown than was known, but there was plenty to think about. That happy night at the cove Don little knew or guessed that the good doctor had trusted the wrong people, people who would blame and tag anybody but themselves for

unprofitable transactions, people who would
convey to Dr. Blythe a demand for remuneration,
faulting him for a problem in secrecy. The mob
chief had been arrested and embarrassed. Unaware of Floyd the Clammer, they guessed that it
was Dr. Blythe who had blabbed, and sentenced
him to cover their losses. Refusing to pay on a point
of principle, being innocent as charged, Dr. Blythe
went missing before month's end while Floyd the
Clammer continued to clam.

Chapter Thirty-Five

The day came at last. On the Fourth of July, the day of the great concert by the United States Marine Corps band, Guy and Ed, at Guy's behest, were determined to enjoy a sauna first, "a real Finn sauna," while they were in Gloucester. Mrs. Post was well informed on this point. Through her, they found Jacobson's was recommended, on the edge of Lane's Cove. Fifty cents each Saturday included "clean towels" and the right to use their backyard shore land, leaping from secluded rocks into the cold Atlantic, bathing suits optional. Ed could swim, although he did not enjoy swimming in Gloucester any more than dancing with ice blocks. Nonetheless, the exhilarating possibility of a rush from the heat of a steamy sauna into immersion in an icy ocean was too sensational an activity to refuse.

Guy asked Ed as they rode together to Lanesville, "Did you know that Finland is like Fen Land, a land of swamps?"

"No."

"Suomi is the Finn word for their country, and it means swampland. They say, 'In the beginning, there was the swamp, a hoe and Jussi.'"

Ed took a guess, "And then Jussi cleared some of the swamp for a farm?"

"Just so," Guy said.

The two men pulled the cord and stopped the trolley opposite Hildonen's Market, after which they walked down and around Lane's Cove to Jacobson's.

"A grand day for a sauna," Guy said, as they both felt the northwest ocean breeze coming on strong, twenty to forty miles an hour, in their faces.

Ed spotted some rather derelict homes up on a hillside and thought about returning someday to capture them. He loved the crisscrossed clotheslines and the weathered sidings. He knew the title. It would be called "Gloucester mansions," another aspect of this odd island at the far northeastern tip of Massachusetts. How many types of people from all corners of the globe had ventured forth to settle here? In three centuries, this Gloucester had known enslaved Blacks, British tub-thumpers for their own independence and liberty, a diverse assortment of Germans, Swedes, Finns, Irish, Italians, Portuguese, and no end of Canadians, including French Canadians. Gloucester was the destination of many of the earliest settlers of North America. In the first census in 1790, Gloucester was the tenth most populous city in the country.

"I bet the Finns vote for Socialists," Guy said.

"You'll have to ask."

"I did. I asked the name of the hall up at the trolley stop at the head of the cove. You know what, it's the Finn Socialist Hall."

"News to me."

"They hold dances and concerts but the fellow I asked said they also have a 'workingman's library' and lectures. On economics, Ed."

"You should scout it out. Then you can tell Attorney General Palmer," Ed said, referring to the originator of the so-called "Palmer Raids," which led to the deportation of hundreds of politically active aliens, and not a few lawful citizens as well. Others behind the hysteria included J. Edgar Hoover. Thousands of volunteers stepped up to inform on any immigrant neighbors they did not like or of whom they were suspicious.

"I don't speak Finn," Guy said, as if he would scout if he could scout.

"The lectures are in Finn?"

"They are. And nobody but Finns can speak it. It's not like German or Spanish."

"What is it like, Guy?"

"It's all vowels and sing-song, like Italian spoken by a Japanese."

"It's a secret language."

"That's what I mean."

"Well, I hope they find other ways to make a living because from what I saw in the granite quarries, they work too hard."

It turned out that neither Guy nor Ed could stand ten full minutes in the heat of the sauna, which was intensified by pouring water by the ladle or bucket and sitting on the top bench. They ran out of the sauna and fled for the relief of cold salt water, shouting and diving into it like kids. Neither of them wanted a second sauna, although they had reserved time left. They waved on the group of four boys without swimsuits then waiting their time in the sauna, and dried off, dressed, and returned refreshed to the trolley stop for the next car through.

Downtown, they got off and joined crowds larger than usual, all headed for Stage Fort Park, the site of the concert.

"The locals are out in force, as well as tourists," Guy said.

"I see some veterans," Ed said, having noted the presence of young men who had lost an arm or a leg, or whose face was terribly scarred. The War was less than five years ago, and many walked the streets of Gloucester having been changed forever Over There. The concert, however, was dedicated to the veterans of an earlier war, the War of 1898, in which Gloucester had sent its Company G.

"Rum times we live in," Guy said, gesturing to a young man on crutches. How many had perished in the effort to repel the Hun from France. Guy and Ed had known France before the War, the France of *La Belle Epoque*. That France, their Paris, that life was gone now, never to come again. But the critic and the analyst in Guy made him expand on his comment, adding, "Would have been rummer had the Kaiser won."

Ed nodded.

Today was Company G's day, Company G, all volunteers, the local unit that marched off to fight overseas twenty-five years earlier. At the junction of Prospect and Pleasant Street a *bas relief* in bronze on granite stood in perpetual honor of their patriotic fervor.

"Ladies and gentlemen," the Mayor said, waving his hands for quiet. "I have the great honor of introducing to you the men of Gloucester's Company G."

The crowd, swarming like ants on a cupcake, rose to the occasion and cheered and cheered again as he announced each name in turn, beginning with "Captain James Centennial Nutt, born of the hundredth anniversary of American independence, on July 4, 1876." That patriotic accolade elicited over two minutes and, finally, three hearty cheers specifically for Captain Nutt. Few members of Company G were gray-haired although some had clearly added weight enough to place a strain on their blue uniforms.

The six-year-old grandson of one of the men of Company G then stood to recite a poem that he had memorized, the last few words of which he shouted:

> *O, dewy was the morning upon that day*
> *   in May*
> *And Dewey was the admiral down in*
> *   Manila Bay,*
> *And dewy were the Spaniards' eyes, them*
> *   orbs or gray and blue—*
> *And do we feel discouraged? I DO NOT*
> *   THINK WE DO!*

After the boy's poem, the crowd erupted into a full-throated cheer and great and prolonged applause. The Mayor then faced down a great rhetorical challenge because of the whimsical way the war wended, tossing men here and there without forethought. He described how it was that Company G boarded trains for Waltham in late April, days after Congress declared war on Spain. He noted with pride that they were the first to arrive and to bivouac at the departure point, and had been greeted by the Governor and his military aids. Nobody knew where or when they would ship out to next, which turned out to be near Atlanta by slow rail.

"Before our men got to Atlanta, Admiral Dewey had won the great victory in Manila Bay," the Mayor said, which led to applause and cheers for Admiral Dewey. "The Philippines had fallen. Spain's possessions in the Pacific came under the American flag." More cheers, and a few hats thrown up into the air.

"Throw your hat up, Guy," Ed said.

"Not me, brother, you throw yours away if you want, though."

The Mayor continued, "The Gloucester men arrived in Atlanta in time to find a raging typhoid epidemic in camp, which required quarantine under the sweltering conditions of Georgia, which was fatal for some of Gloucester's best young men, who died in fever. Meanwhile, Teddy Roosevelt and his Rough Riders charged up San Juan Hill, Santiago fell, and other Cuban cities and forts. Some high ups in the Army determined that a more northern climate might help the Gloucester men to recuperate or to stay well if they had not contracted fever yet. The company was ordered to Memphis, Tennessee. There, in fact, they broke ground and built their own temporary quarters."

The Mayor concluded, "By late July, as the gallant men of our company remained stranded in Tennessee, hostilities ended in Cuba, and a peace treaty was being negotiated in Europe, which was signed in mid-August. In sum, my friends, the war was over before Company G got to play its intended part. But such was their fate to suffer, some to sicken, some to die upon the altar of national sacrifice, without the public acclaim normal to those who survive wars. These, our honored veterans, who stepped forward at risk of life and limb for the liberation of Cuba, and the Philippines, and other parts of the then-global Spanish Empire, though they brought back no captured enemy flags nor tales of glory in combat, weathered the storm and, upon returning to home port, in good

Gloucester tradition need no more than that to be acclaimed by us, their fellow townsmen and women. Men of Company G, families of men of Company G, your city salutes you and says: well done."

Cheers followed as the Mayor yielded the red, white and blue platform to Captain James Centennial Nutt, who responded on behalf of Company G, told those assembled, "We humbly thank you for this great turn out. We offered to lay down our lives, and some of us never returned to this, our city, our home, Gloucester. But the fact is that when the Army sent us to Tennessee and I was set to work supervising the design and construction of latrines, I wrote to my sweetheart to say that we must set the date for our wedding. The war was over. My friends up here on the platform understand when I say that we wanted only to get home and get on with our lives. Enjoy the concert. Again, we thank you."

On the grassy knoll beside the old fort, a defense optimistically neglected or dismantled and then reconstructed in every war, which had protected Gloucester from enemies coming at the city by sea each war since the Revolution, the spit-and-polish Marines played rousing renditions of "El Capitan," "Stars and Stripes Forever," and the "Washington Post March." In honor of Captain Nutt and his wife, whose twenty-fifth anniversary was days away, the band played Johan Strauss's "Anniversary Waltz." Captain and his bride began that dance which, before it ended, embraced a hundred or two hundred misty-eyed couples.

Vicariously buoyed up on feelings that they felt were emanated from those dancing couples, Guy and Ed walked to their boarding houses. Guy said that he had only felt like this back in France, on the evening of Bastille Day, when people danced in the streets under the stars. It was that feeling. "Ocean-ic," Guy said.

"Imagine being named Centennial," Guy said next. "You'd have to learn to spell early in life on that ground only."

Ed said, "Could have been worse. In Gloucester today some poor kid is getting saddled with the middle name 'Tricentennial.'"

Chapter Thirty-Six

How Jo looked was fit matter for a doll faced portrait by Egon Schiele, wearing a broad head-band, a loose blouse of stripes and cotton, long black skirt over black stockings. She also stood as tall as she could on shoes with extra high heels, blocks in which she felt that she was walking awkwardly in wooden shoes strapped to the bottoms of her feet. She endured this because she did not wish Ed to think of her as a shrimp.

When the trolley came, they sat together, of course. He was beside her, his bodily warmth. Ed was sitting beside her, a man she really only knew by name and in the sketchiest sort of way, like a drawing half-begun and halted at midpoint for lack of adequate light.

"I think that we are on earth to help one another," Jo said. "What do you think, Ed?"

"You think that I can help others, do you?"

"At least one other."

"Really?"

"Really."

"You want me to say it first," Ed said in what was seemingly unlikely to start a fight, although it did.

Jo replied, "Some men do."

Ed said, "Find a man who does."

It hung in the air in a way that perhaps he had never intended, as a caddish rebuff to her, although they were both in a zone of emotion they had never more than briefly inhabited before this.

"I picked you," Jo said, each word distinctly separate, a second making each one ponderous. But they were not the three words that each had in their minds, unsaid.

Ed thought of something and said, "No, I picked you. After I found your goddam cat."

Jo kinked her head to one side and raised an eyebrow, not unlike an undecided viewer of an artwork that was striking but—did she like it or loathe it?

"You usually tell the story differently."

"How do you know?"

"Guy told me."

"Guy should keep his mouth shut."

"He told me that you said our relationship," Jo said, elongating the word as re-la-tion-ship, unpacking its syllables like a train passing by when you count the cars, "started with you saying, 'Oh, shit.'"

Ed actually laughed. He dared to laugh. Jo's cheeks reddened and she inhaled a sigh.

"Well, it did."

"You made it up."

"I did not. Our relationship *did* start with me saying, 'Oh, shit.' You had all these," here Ed gestured as if a guide at a museum in a room full of paintings, "little artsy posters up all over town, on telephone poles, on trees, screaming 'LOST CAT.' And I spotted that goddam lost cat next to a hedge and I said, 'Oh, shit' because now I—

Jo could be silent no longer. She said, "What?

Because now you had to take my cat on a long trolley ride along with your easel and your paint box, all to bring Moofy back to me."

Ed made a move with his mouth and lips as if he were tasting something bad, and said, "No. Because I had to decide which of two shitty days to have, the one trying to paint and break my heart (gestures gingerly) lifting the fragile membrane of sunlight that surrounds Gloucester and tease it up and out and onto my canvas, like that was going to happen, or the one taking your goddam cat on a trolley ride."

"Stop damning my poor cat."

Ed was silent now, as if he had done with speaking for the day.

Jo asked quietly, "Shall I stay?"

Ed nodded, "Please yourself."

Jo looked at the distance and, without turning her head back to her beau, said, "Well, we were happy."

Ed ought not to have asked her, "When?" even though he simply meant for her to give him her perspective on the moments of highest happiness that summer. She took it differently, as if he recalled no happiness.

"You're never happy," she said in a tone of frustration.

It moved him to sarcasm, unfortunately.

He said, "Oh, yes, yes. It all comes back to me now. When I found your cat and had a shitty day."

Jo said, "Hmmm. I thought I made you purr. Sometimes."

Ed was moved, in spite of himself.

"Shit, Jo, I was in love with you and with Gloucester, with Gloucester houses and sunlight. Jesus, it was pretty."

"Were? Was?" Jo asked.

Ed took a step back from her, then another.

"I don't want an argument."

"You are doing a poor job of satisfying your wants, mister."

"Why are you so upset?"

With that, Jo's gloves were off, and she went into rant.

"Mute no more, are you? Words now—to hurt me? You lout."

"Oh, Jo, don't let's—"

"I used to be young and stupid, now I am old and stupid."

Tears were flowing, she was going into sobs. He tried to embrace her but she retreated, a five-foot woman running from a hulking man well over six feet tall, who was looming over her reaching for her as she stepped back. If anybody had seen them from a distance, especially after Jo ranted and began to cry, they would have asked, "What are you doing to her? Are you all right, lady?"

"You're beautiful, not stupid. I'm the stupid one. I love you."

"Why didn't you say so?" Jo asked between sobs, her arms out for their embrace.

He hugged her and almost cried himself, but managed not to and only said softly, "I ought to have."

Chapter Thirty-Seven

Once burned, twice learned. What was the old saying? Jo was not Jeanne, but Jeanne was nonetheless the context of that summer in Gloucester. Jo followed Jeanne, and that made Ed very wary. He could not, he would not take anything on trust.

After all, Ed thought that he knew everything about pleasing a woman while he was with Jeanne. He felt above all of the troubles inherent in life for others. The War was over, he was loved, he had a place in the world of art in its center, New York City. Nobody could doubt Jeanne's beauty, her svelte body, her taste in clothes and charm. She spoke Parisian French with verve and a fetching, funny English, with malapropisms nobody else could make up but which he understood. She made him laugh. Who else ever had? She made him read poetry aloud *en français* and brought him to ecstasy.

He fooled himself, not Jeanne. It was not so much that he had loved and lost. He knew that was common. He had experienced heartbreak before, he recited names to Jeanne when she asked. He recalled now her oddly pleased expression as he ticked off his short list. But when it pleased her— she, his last hope, had left him.

At first, he denied the possibility. How foolish he looked and felt bringing flowers only to hear from a profane landlord that "the broad skipped out on the rent." The unshaven man in a dirty undershirt's profanity—for he swore like an expert—was wilting to her lover, now former lover, abandoned lover who held a bouquet and reeked of stupidity. He found a trash can for the flowers and "ash can school, ash can school" ran through his head for the next hour, and no other thoughts. Next, he expected that one day she would return, saying that she had to run out on her rent arrears, and had no choice. For weeks he convinced himself of her imminent contrite appearance at his door, reaching out, holding him tightly, kissing him furiously, weeping for lost moments, making up for his suffering.

Finally, when the postman delivered her letter, he was angry, angrier than the landlord had been, and even more profane when he realized that she would never return, that she truly had skipped town. Was she in the arms of another, an American, a successful man, a rich one? *Certament*, she was done with starving artists. It made him sick.

Then he decided it would be all right, well, after a certain amount of drinking. He had gotten along without Jeanne before, and he would do so again just fine. The delivery of a letter postmarked New Orleans changed nothing. He felt above opening anything she touched. She could say nothing that would please him. He was not interested in hearing it. He mounted it in his office with a thumbtack at first, on the wall, like a trophy. He finally demoted it to clutter on a side table. He thought about depositing it in a trash can without doing so. He forced himself from thinking about it at all.

Jo was arguing, he thought, trying to get head-first into his heart, to persuade him of some advantage in their connection. It was unsettling, how rational she was. Jeanne, at least, had made a show of being attracted to him as a woman to a man, in love with him. Jo seemed to lack the capacity for adoration. Except for adoring her goddam Arthur.

Chapter Thirty-Eight

Red, auburn, gold-tipped, whatever her color—and it varied by the light, indoors, outdoors, day and night—her long hair was her glory. She felt glorious, at least. She brushed it straight, then combed it back from a fringe of bangs, and tugged the rest tightly as she swirled an elastic around in back. She liked being a redhead. She would not have taken blonde of any shade in the spectrum, or any sort of brunette or even the most striking and shiny-silk raven black were God to offer it with money on the side. Beside her, on a rag rug, in the sunlight of early morning, Arthur was licking and bathing, his front paw constantly addressing his ears and face. She adored her time alone with him as she brushed and combed, and he licked.

"You understand, my man," Jo told her cat, and patted his shoulder.

He stopped instantly and glowered at her for interrupting his ablutions. Jo recognized her error and acknowledged it in a soothing tone.

"I'm sorry, Arthur. Do continue. I broke your concentration, didn't I? I know, honeybunny, I know."

Arthur resumed.

"Arthur, Ed and I had our first fight."

The cat looked at her as if he might jump off the bed.

"Don't you dare, Arthur. Listen to mama, she needs your consolation and advice."

He kinked his head sideways, then rolled on his back, paws up as if boxing.

"Tell you all about it? All right. I said something I probably should not have said."

The last few words came out grudgingly as if a phonograph player was running down.

"What I said, Arthur, was, 'Ed Hopper, you live in a world of your own.'"

Arthur began to wash his face, his tongue all over his paws.

"I know, it did not seem bad to me at the time either. But Ed said, instantly, 'You say that like it was a bad thing, Jo.' I knew from his tone, and using my name at the end, it was an angry reaction."

She held Arthur closer and indulged him by scratching behind his ears. He was purring in seconds.

"I wish I could make Ed purr. Anyhow, one thing led to another, all downhill until we both thought we should leave and go our separate ways. And now I'm not sure he will ever speak to me again."

She was misting up and sniffling, but stifled herself. She was a grown woman in 1923, and no kind of crybaby. She had nothing to apologize for, she had not insulted him or said anything untrue. He did live in a world of his own. He did. And he was sure fighting to keep it that way. She never felt a part of it. It was almost as if she was going to have to decide to let him go or to join him in his world. He was not leaving that world.

Jo had no confidence that Ed would talk to her soothingly or otherwise, or mention that she had such nice hair, so pretty. Not that she brushed and combed for him. It was a matter of self-respect and an obligation to her Creator God. Why would she be given red hair only to ignore it? Neglect of such hair would be as sinful as to bury one's talents. God gave talents to be used. She had the red hair that went with confidence.

Ed was altogether too silent. But God had not given him quick wit or a golden tongue. That was it. He would talk, with careful handling. One must simply find an ice pick. But where was the ice pick with which she could break the block open?

That day, walking up from Main Street to Prospect Street, on a jaunt of her own really, under her floppy broad-brimmed straw hat and wearing a loose pink top with a Mexican scarf swirled about her neck, her shorts pale blue, and her shoes the comfortable ones that nurses wear, she found her ice pick. It hit her like a shovel between the eyes. It was a wedding cake.

"I found a wedding cake, black and white, on top of a hill, a great subject for you, beyond my brush," Jo told Ed later that afternoon, as soon as she could locate him.

"Wedding cake? I cannot see myself too excited over painting a 'Wedding Cake House,'" Ed told her, shaking his head and smiling. Did it really look like a wedding cake or was she trying to tell him something? Perhaps both, but that was what the house resembled, atop a hill, amid the hedges, fences, and stairs themselves all pointing and cele-brating and headed to this pinnacle of Victorian architecture. He found this out later when he ap-proached it, but meanwhile he learned more from

Jo, who could always find the words. Why was he so mute?

"Gloucester in its glory. I found out that it's owned by the Haskells, Ed, an old Gloucester family. It is so precious, it's impossible. Old Gloucester is just written all over it. You could call it 'Haskell's House' or anything you want but I saw what was to be seen."

At that last, an echo of Henri, they both laughed.

"Let's go, then," Ed said, convinced and unable to add anything more to the conversation. With her watercolors in his hand, they set out to take a look at what was to be seen at that part of Washington Street near Our Lady of Good Voyage. The accusation did not quite form in his mind, the sights were far too distracting, but had he a better wordsmith inside of his skull, he would have told her outright that she was not very subtle. The hedges, the stairs, the fences, the streets here all led to the wedding cake when they did not lead to the church.

Chapter Thirty-Nine

We have come to the night when everything changed. It had been six weeks since Ed and Jo arrived in Gloucester. It had been five weeks since Ed found and returned the cat. Guy left for New York. It had been three weeks since Jo gave Ed instruction in the use of the watercolors he borrowed from her. Despite everything and even counting all of the words exchanged during her "demonstration" (as she called the lesson she taught, to mute its didactic stature), no more than a thousand words had passed between them, most from her to him, and little of it flirty or romantic. Tonight they both felt pressed, obliged by forces to speak. After staying on Good Harbor beach until its crowds of women and children and their umbrellas and blankets and towels left, Ed and Jo were the last two people on the strand of sand that remained warm from an exceptionally hot day. Soon, the sand would be cool, especially as the tide had turned and it was not coming in. Neither in beach attire, both clothed as if walking downtown, they lay back on their respective long towels. They looked up at the stars long enough that one might say they studied them.

"What do you want, Ed?"

She knew that she would have to prime the pump. He was never going to break silence otherwise. Or he would say, rising, "Well, time to go." The question she blurted was not premeditated. Did she intend that he say that he wanted her? She could not have said what her intention was. She possibly, actually, really and truly wanted to know what it was that Ed wanted. Period. No more than that. If so, she received what she intended to elicit.

"More time and more houses."

That was what Ed wanted. Not only this summer but for the rest of his life.

Jo felt flustered enough to inject something with a sarcasm that carried clearly in the otherwise utterly silent night air.

"And more titanium white."

"Comedian," Ed said, a little louder than he had intended.

"No, you're the comedian, Edward Hopper."

"I do not have a funny bone in my body, and you know it."

"I won't argue."

"You—" he started to say but stifled himself.

"What?"

He was silent for a full minute, then he said, in a doleful tone, "You don't laugh at me, do you, Jo?"

This was not Jo's first time talking with a man as they lay side by side, but it was the first time she had felt pity for Ed, and it was a new emotion for her to feel while on her back. She turned but he was not looking at her. He was on his back, his face directed toward the constellation known as the Big Bear. The stars were the first fiction. Stars scattered throughout the visible universe and at greatly varying differences in size and distance appeared like dots of light to mortals, who saw patterns and, as nights were long and life was hard, they invented what they wanted above them: a nightly show of gods in action, stories, literature.

Jo was resolved that, until Ed turned to look her in the eye, she would say nothing. He turned his head, his eyes met hers and then she spoke, articulating her reply in slow and serious words.

"No, Ed, I do not laugh at you. I do find your mannerisms strange and many of them make me smile. But fondly."

Her hand reached toward him, and her fingers touched his shoulder.

He laughed out loud and heartily.

"Now—that's funny," he said, precipitating in a fit of uninhibited laughter.

"I'm glad you find me so funny."

"No," Ed said, reaching and with his fingers touching her shoulder now, as if to detain someone to hear him out. "I find you a delight, Miss Nivison."

Then it struck him he was uncertain of that.

"You are not married, are you?"

Some women were married who vacationed alone, separated from partners, and no longer wearing rings, or biding time until a divorce. This was 1923, not 1823. Times had changed. Marriages were less impermeable, less eternal, though how and when this deterioration occurred no one could tell.

"I am not married, and never have been, Ed. You?"

It was odd to be asked, although he had just asked the same thing.

"Never," Ed said. He had lost a step, almost barred the door to imagining a serious relationship by his monosyllabic denial. He went on headlong and determined, recklessly really, taking on the curves of the course at high speed, risking a terrible crash, "Jo, you are an absolute beaut. If you are as fond of my mannerisms as I am of your woman-isms, there is no more to need. We may become a couple."

"A couple of comedians?" Jo asked, her eye-brows high, her eyes moist the way they got when she felt high emotions. Had he just proposed some-thing? Not marriage, certainly. A pairing? A cou-pling? A summertime fling?

"Commedia dell'Arte, shall we say? Artist co-medians?"

"I don't think that's what it means."

"It will mean that for us, my girl."

"Your girl? Am I?"

"On one condition."

"What?"

"That you will help me with my watercolors."

"Now—that's funny," she said, in a laughter as hearty as his laughter had been minutes before. In the distance, someone picked up on her laughter and mockingly imitated it even louder. Ed and Jo were then both quiet, but smiling. Ed reached to grasp her hand and squeeze it tight. They were one now. How had he put it? They were a couple of comedians.

Chapter Forty

Googie at the switchboard, nicknamed for "googly-eyes," was all over Don for where he was going in case the boss needed to know.

"I am on my way to call on a million dollars," Don said. That was one way to put it. "Roger Babson" was another. Clearing up any confusion by the latter, saying that famous local name, Don made his destination clear.

Roger Babson was one of the huge and extended Babson clan of Gloucester, all of whom had made good. One of them, John J. Babson, had written and published the first history of Gloucester after the Great Fire of 1860. The fear that history would be lost if it were not written down ignited in his mind, half of the history of Gloucester being a Babson family story, beginning with the midwife, Isabelle Babson, in a town with no physicians. Of all of the Babsons, Roger Babson had made out best of all financially. Roger was a born inventor who loved nature and history but, above all, math and graphs. When he applied his mind to the stock market, charting it as if it were a living creature, he found it subject to hibernation, fever spikes and all sorts of cyclical, even predictable twists and turns. On those predictions, he made himself and other people fortunes, accruing the title "The Wizard of Wall Street."

His home was a great old place with a grand porch and view of the harbor, but on the heights and far from the breaking waves that slapped over the Boulevard in storms. Set up there with his several servants, Roger was quite the lord of the manor, but soft-spoken, courteous and a wonderful listener. It was his custom once each year, near the first of April, to play a prank. He would ask for a *Times* reporter to hear about "something unusual," which he made up, which the reporter knew he made up, and which the public knew he made up. This spring he had claimed that his house was emanating pink spots. When Don said that he could see no pink spots, Roger told him that the "freak of nature" had passed, he was too late. "I see now that the pink spots do not persist after ten in the morning," Roger said, as Don quoted him in the article, run with a photo. Today, in June, Roger obviously had a serious news item to report.

"Will you not join me in some lemonade, Mr. Nash?" Roger asked.

In the ten weeks since they had first met, Don had forgotten how small Roger Babson was, short and proportionally petite in all of his limbs. White-blonde hair flourished on top of his head, as did over his lower face a moustache and goatee of the style popular among Kentucky colonels around the time of the Civil War. Moreover, he wore a white linen suit of the type that the late Mark Twain had favored. His overall appearance was dazzling. With horns, he could have played the Devil in a French farce.

"Don't mind if I do, Mr. Babson, very kind of you," Don said, feeling the rhythm and the bounce of a Southerner accepting hospitality. He was taken out of Gloucester, out of himself. Bodily, he was going to sit on a porch within the reach of a fresh breeze of Gloucester Harbor, in sight of boats of its fleet, but beside Roger Babson, an engine of commerce, a driver up or down of stock prices, the legendary local born with a Midas Touch.

After they were both seated in woven cord chairs and holding tall glasses of iced lemonade, Roger said, "I suppose you would like to know the news I called the newspaper to report, Mr. Nash."

"That I would like to hear, sir," Don said, regaling in the ambience of the place, a comfortable old-fashioned way of living. He imagined, inside, Roger Babson's library, lined with books on every wall except for a large window or series of windows for sunlight upon his large mahogany desk, upon which in neat order were the day's financial newspapers and the very latest journals from around the world, silver wire baskets for incoming and outgoing correspondence, and somewhere a large globe of the world.

"I have word from a friend that we are soon to see the end of air crashes."

"An invention?"

"The invention of the century. An antigraviton."

"A machine to do what?"

"A machine to counter gravity. The force of gravity is the mass of the earth, and the mass of the earth is primarily its iron deposits. I have engaged my friend to make a world map of all known iron deposits. The key to the effectiveness of the antigraviton is its setting, as every region of the world has its own variation of gravity."

"Gravity is not universal?"

"Gravity is universal as a force, but it varies by

iron content. You know that compasses point north for that reason, do you not?"

"I do," Don said, taking a slug of the cold, sweet, best lemonade he had ever tasted. It was not spiked, either. Roger was an outspoken member of the Prohibitionist Party.

"And have you any idea what it is that orients a homing pigeon?"

"I am going to guess that it is iron deposits."

"Regional variations in gravitational pull more specifically, but you have the general idea. Very good. Now, my friend is on the verge of developing an anti-graviton for anything flying in the air today. It means the end of crashes. That is the news."

Don was done with his drink, and placed it upon a woven cord table.

"How—I mean no offense, Mr. Babson, but how am I to be certain that people will not read this as actual news rather than belatedly as one of your April Fool's pranks?"

"But it is true. It is not a prank."

"But you always say that, even about seeing tiny pink spots on everything, some sort of sunspots hitting the earth. And the year before, when you said that you had purchased the bustle of the dress worn by Jefferson Davis when escaping the Yankees and in flight from Richmond."

"But those were true."

"The readers of the *Times* understood, and I am worried that an article about an anti-graviton quoting one of America's best-known and most widely-followed authorities on trends in the country's businesses, well, will be taken seriously."

"It should be. It is news, the invention of the century."

Don nodded and said, humoring the sage, "I will communicate your news to my editor, Mr. Babson, for his consideration of its appropriate placement in the *Times*."

"Tell him that I suggest his front page."

"I shall, Mr. Babson," Don said, thanking and bidding him a good day.

Chapter Forty-One

See what is to be seen. That is fine, Ed realized, but it is not enough to see. We must try and understand. He had looked at Mrs. Post but he had never really understood her.

On the other hand, he no longer had to ask for coffee with sugar. She saw him and understood. It was being poured, prepared, and stirred into one of her mugs before he took his seat—he now had his seat at the table, the one up against the window, his back to the sunlight, a claim respected by the other guests.

She understood his preference for silence and, accordingly, when Ed spoke, Mrs. Post, a thin reed of a woman, jolted a bit, startled to hear his voice.

"How are you this morning, Mrs. Post?"

Nobody was awake so early as he and Mrs. Post. It was past dawn on a sunny day. Mrs. Post adjusted her glasses, which were ironically thick, and spoke, "I'm just fine. And you, Mr. Hopper?"

"Sit?" he asked. He had never seen her sit, let alone with a guest.

"I suppose I might," she said, taking the edge of a chair. They were all high-backed brown wooden chairs, a type that he admired for simplicity. There were two such chairs in his room beside the bed.

"May I ask personal questions, Mrs. Post?"

"If you are interested, go on ahead."

"How is it that you run this guest house?"

"Well, some years ago I found myself in a fix, you see. My husband, Grant, died at sea. We had two young children and this house, on which we owed, of course. So I went to the bank to see about a loan and Mr. Hanley said he trusted me to see a guest house through, which was the only idea I could think of to pull us through as a family."

"I see. How noble of you."

After a pause, Mrs. Post looked at Ed through her thick glasses, and then said, "No, it was just practical, that's all. I did better each year—I'm open all year, you see, and lots of people travel at odd times, for holidays or the unexpected," her eyes drifted from his as if toward a past she could still see. "To be cooking and washing and cleaning, you know, takes your mind off just yourself and your troubles."

"I did not meet your children."

"Oh, they're off now, Mr. Hopper. My daughter teaches in Boston, and likely to marry, but when she does the law requires her to resign. No female married teachers, you know, who might find themselves in the family way. It's been a long courtship but that's for the best, I think, don't you? And my son is in dentistry school in New York. I don't know if he will come back to Gloucester or not, I hope so. But a dentist can set up anywhere, isn't it so, Mr. Hopper?"

"Yes. I'm so glad for you. You run a tight ship," Ed said.

"Are you apt to paint today, such a bright day?" she asked, looking at him.

"Do you know, I just may," Ed said, finishing his coffee.

After she asked and he declined more coffee, she volunteered, "I've seen you walking in big strides when the weather is cloudy, and hesitating, I'd say, when it is so bright."

Ed realized that his landlady was a close observer despite her vision problems.

"I hesitate, feeling challenged and wondering if I am up to it. Shadows are harder work," Ed said.

"Shadows are the hardest work, I'd say. I've had my share of shadows, Mr. Hopper, let me tell you," Mrs. Post said. Footsteps down the hallway signaled another guest's imminent presence. Mrs. Post rose and headed toward the stove but not before she added, "Painting must take as much as it gives."

She was greeting one of the New York fishermen as Ed put his mug in the sink to help her out, the widow who must have been terrified entering the bank on Main Street, worrying that they might not grant her a loan and then what would she do? Gloucester had many widows, all of whom needed help. From which parts of the community did that help come? What shadows she faced made his seem trivial.

Ed went to his room to get everything he would need for the day, thinking about the darker side of Gloucester's long rise on the sea. Not every soul that went out the Georges Bank returned. Mrs. Post's Grant did not. Ed wanted to see a house today as a fisherman might see his house, returning after the hazard of a storm. If he could do that, he would show the world what a Gloucester house looked like.

Chapter Forty-Two

In Gloucester, they say that "an expert is an out of towner who owns a briefcase." An expert was coming to town, a certain Dr. Biggs, a professor turned Federal employee whose project involved data gathering and sifting to tell how fishing was faring. It was his job to monitor the fish in the sea. He monitored stocks around and between New England and Canada.

Don was to monitor the monitor, at least while Dr. Biggs was in Gloucester. By his editor's assignment, Don sat in on a meeting of twenty or so "old salts." The editor explained to him that the Master Mariners Association was composed of "fishing boat captains" of Gloucester, but when Don arrived early and asked a man next to him, a French Canadian, to help him out by naming "the other captains" filing into the room, the man began by saying, "That's Brown and his friend, I call him Tom, I don't know his full name. You'll have to ask Captain Brown what ship he was ever the captain of, and I think Tom is just his drinking buddy. Not every captain in Gloucester is a captain."

The meeting was intended to update everyone present, captains all, certainly men of the sea, on the Federal government's claims that it was "here to help" the fishing industry to prosper. Lately, Federal agents at sea were not only policing rum runners but also tracking the movements of cod, pollock and haddock. These were being counted for charting from out of all other varieties of fish being caught in nets. Cod, pollock and haddock were segregated out, tagged and released back into the sea to go their way until caught again and reported to the Feds again by selected and subsidized fishermen.

"How else are you going to know where fish go than by asking a fish?" Dr. Biggs, a pleasant, plump expert told the Gloucestermen assembled before him. He wanted Gloucester fishermen's cooperation in a study that he would like to expand in 1923 and in the future. There was no immediate stampede.

"Those tagged fish are fish we sell, you know," one man said in turn, revealing by his tone a different concern than the scientific priorities that lured Dr. Biggs to the salt water. Dr. Biggs had an answer that seemed to satisfy not only him, and everyone present, however. He was not tagging and liberating fish in this stage of the project.

"You will lose no fish from what you market. All we want for the lab are a few flakes, just scrape off a few scales of the already-tagged fish and send them in an envelope along with the tag. We will do the rest in identifying the species, the gender, the age, the health of the fish."

Another man's question was whether the game was worth the candle. He asked, with a tone of surprise, "You can tell all of that from a scale?"

Dr. Biggs said with ebullience, "All that and more all of the time. Under a microscope, the scale reveals its owner almost back to the day of its being an egg."

Immediately after Dr. Biggs's confident presentation, Captain Arnet accepted a motion that the Master Mariners Association take a position in favor of locals taking part in the project planned by Dr. Biggs. Debate was short and, in a few minutes, the ayes had it. The captains' vote was unanimous. The Federal oversight of Gloucester's fisheries thus began in this way without dissent.

Back at the *Times* office, using his notes, Don wrote up a short article accurately reflecting hope and optimism while a bell rang in his head. He found himself thinking for some reason about the relationships he had undertaken with women. If "love at first sight" never lasted long or ended well, what of the bond so quickly forged between Dr. Biggs and the captains who heard him this night? By contrast, via dubious and gradual "baby step" friendships Don had more often entered slowly into relationships that lasted. Of these thoughts about his checkered relationships Don said nothing in his article but solely reported the facts. He was still fishing personally, and his study was incomplete.

The article he typed up appeared on page six over a half-page advertisement carrying news of a shipment of straw hats at discount and the arrival of new dress patterns at Brown's department store.

Chapter Forty-Three

A couple of productive days later, Ed was excited when he met up again with Jo. His eyes were wide, and he was saying in an unusually loud tone, "I saw something on Rocky Neck. There's a Mansard roof begging for my attention. I need to see how it looks in the daytime."

Jo needed no persuasion. She said that she would get dressed. Ed actually asked her to be quick. Daylight was passing. She said, "In two shakes of Moofy's tail," after which she wiggled. Each shake of the lamb's tail took twenty minutes. When she reappeared, Ed said, "I don't believe it."

"Ed, it's not even nine o'clock."

"The longest shadows are gone. It may cloud up any time. If we have coffee, I may miss this day altogether."

As they left Mrs. Murphy's, the sound of the trolley dinged at a distance.

"Out, out. I hear the trolley," Jo said.

"You're telling me. We lost an hour."

"We won't have coffee. Just paint, just paint."

After a trolley and a cab ride, they found it was breezy when they reached Rocky Neck. The house

Ed had targeted was flapping like a frenetic fledgling. The extravagant fabric hanging down under its curtained khaki canopies waved wildly at passersby.

"I'm glad it's windy," Ed said.

"Was it not windy when you saw it?"

"Nothing like this. Now the house is alive."

"Look," Jo said, as canopies reveled in their floppy looseness.

Curiously, the fabric snapped and fell. He seemed to hear the house calling him, with each gust and fall "Et-wat" repeating. The house wanted him to look and once he looked, he could not look away. It did not so much beckon as billow. This house sailed, distinct from all other houses. He had never drawn or painted a house like this. He had never even seen a house like this.

"I could watch this house all day," Jo said.

"If it stays windy, I shall have a great painting," Ed said.

"But it's too windy to paint," Jo said, speaking loudly over the wind.

"Don't you think I know? I'm going to sketch. I'll paint it back in New York."

With that, he set up his portable stool, sat crouched and sketched, holding down the edges of his tablet from flapping in chorus with the house before him. Robert Henri was right. Of course, Henri was always right. The painting will say more about you than it says about the subject, or you will have failed. To climb the mountain, you must touch your innermost soul and communicate with you feel in your core of cores.

This daffy mansard-roofed bizarre bazaar was a playground for Ed's muses, all of them, the lugubrious, the ludicrous, the baffled, the thoughtful, the Janus-faced muse that found beauty in ugliness and ugliness in beauty, his favorite of all of his muses.

They played; Ed worked. The taming of "The Mansard House" (for such its title would be) was no small task. It had to be broken down if this wild house was to be broken at all. Ed crammed the pages of his notebook with pieces of roof and window and stair and side, as he took in bits, as it seemed on paper to disintegrate, as it became no house at all but so many items in the air over a juggler's head. He would, he thought, assemble it later. He would retain, though, its eclectic stew of this and that, now and then, here and there. Nothing really matched but all bubbled and boiled in a white heat of this windy day, naming him as the artist anointed to weave its moving pieces into the glance of a moment, to grant the house life on canvas, a rest that the house had never in life known, nor ever would.

Jo seated herself on a stone wall near him as he was riveted until it got too dark.

"That's it but I must return."

"Why?"

"With watercolors, I must return on the next fair and breezeless day, early, to take on this dragon, this terror, this demon. Jo, I must stare it down. I must have its skin. On our next encounter, I take down this creature and render it into art. In New York I will paint its windy day partner. This is a house of dreams."

They went to the store to call for a cab. They walked arm in arm but wordlessly.

He could not cease thinking about how such an explosively angular structure, better suited for Maxfield Parrish than for Edward Hopper, happened to drop just here. Especially in wind, it was a fantasy, a cloud-capped castle from the mists and wisps of

Medieval Europe, reshaped, distorted, and dis-
guised as a Victorian mansion by the sea. The
house was a page—no, several pages—torn out of
several different books and authors and eras, not
the house that Jack built, but the house that Jack
and Jill and their children and their children's children dreamed up and brewed into existence over
many years of many nights. Nothing fit, nothing
matched, nothing sat still. It was wonderful. That
proverbial camel supposedly a horse designed by a
committee stood before Ed as a house, this house.
He could never have designed a better one than
"The Mansard House."

In the cab, Ed finally resumed speaking,
"Magic holds this house together, not gravity. It is
every few feet another house, look here, look there,
the infinitude made manifest as if someone said
that he must, or she must build the house of all
houses in Rocky Neck—a house that stands up to
flap and greet me by name."

"I've lost your love to a house," Jo said.

"Don't think that way. You helped me to see
how to capture this marvel. Do you see it as a collection of high brick chimneys, too many gables,
strewn balconies, madcap porches? And the
mansard roof, its towers like flames leaping, with
latticed porches between white columnar legs like
thick stockings adorning a modest maiden."

"And all that flapping," Jo said.

"Striving to cover something without in the
least succeeding, a crazy quilt of symmetry and
asymmetry on display. Jo, which nobody notices,
people, passersby, parades of wide-eyes, children
and adults, tourists from overseas, all of them as if
charmed, blundering by blindly, as if this striking
house, this lightning bolt made of wood, this ship

on shore with its flapping sails, were invisible. Only I saw it."

"True."

"I alone saw its cornices dance, its pediments rise up and rear back, hooves high, the trimmings, the brackets, the stair balustrades. Oh, Jo, that house is not a composition but a circus performing for me alone, for no one else saw the Mansard House, at least the Mansard House that I saw. Or they would be changed people, because I am changed."

"We both are."

The cab let them out at Mrs. Murphy's. Jo led Ed, still dazzled and wobbly, into the boarding house parlor. She said, smiling, "Let us just sit and find out the degree of delight that can be experienced by two people earnest at the task."

Ed nodded. It took some minutes before he was thinking normally again. Mrs. Murphy offered them supper, which they politely declined with thanks, and then left the couple be.

Ed, who never started conversations, asked Jo, "Will you answer my questions?"

"It depends on the questions."

"Personal questions."

"I trust your judgment."

"Do you have a beau?"

"No."

"I've seen you with many different men."

"I suppose you have. Couldn't you say that of any woman you know?"

"You know what I mean. Dining and dancing, laughing. A lot of times, laughing."

"You should try it sometime."

"Have you," Ed said, looking askance to be sure that nobody was in earshot, "experimented?"

"I don't cook. I experiment with colors on canvas."

"You know what I mean."

"That's awfully personal."

"Don't answer then."

"I said we should strive to please one another."

"It would please me if you answered."

"I'm not a flapper."

"Not."

"Not."

"Don't look at me like an, an investigator."

"You're nervous."

"Nervous with nothing to confess."

"You are untouched, aren't you?"

She stared at him.

Then Jo laughed.

"What's funny?"

"I think you would never be pursuing me if I were not, Edward Hopper. You find a virgin irresistible, don't you?"

Ed said, "A long time ago, in Paris—"

"That French woman?"

"Not her. *Belles de jour*. And models. A waitress."

"While I've focused on art. And Arthur."

"Arthur was not my question."

"I answered your question."

"I'll take you at your word, Josephine Nivison."

"Children are out of the question, though."

"Out of the question."

"Are you sure, Ed?"

"Sure."

"Women usually want children, but I had to decide already."

"I did, too."

"You did not," she said. He laughed and tried to tickle her, but she drew back, pointing and saying, "You're teasing me."

Then Jo said, "My students were my joy, but I did not have to worry about them except as future artists, some of them, and all of them having to find their own way in this big world of ours."

"You loved your kids, I think."

"Of course I did. You cannot just love one child, you either love children or you don't love any at all," Jo said, without adding anything more about her decision. She had decided as she did, that was all. Ed found children more annoying than adorable. He had his own fish to fry now, concerning love.

"You love me?" he asked Jo, adding, "My dear?"

The big question. And just like him to ask her first, before he said a thing about love. But Jo was up for it. This summer she had felt something for Ed, a chemistry that she had not experienced with any man before, especially not with Ed. She confessed.

"Lately, yes. Mostly."

Only half joking, Ed then went into his sales pitch.

"Good enough. My apartment, shared bath, has a view of Washington Square."

"Do you have an ice box?" Jo asked, teasing back, game for the challenge of talking terms, although Ed actually had her with "my dear."

"Of course I do."

"All right. Describe your place in more detail."

"A clean, well-lit place up four flights, you'd have to be fit. Heated by my stove."

"Wood or coal?"

"Coal. I haul buckets up all the time, and never spill."

"I trust you do. I mean, do not. Spill."

"People downstairs are quiet."

"Nice?"

"Quiet, keep to themselves."

"Good neighbors."

"Not bad neighbors."

"You ever help them?"

"How?"

"Any way."

"No. I don't think they need help. They never asked."

"Do you talk?"

"Just in passing, to say hello. I know their names, Jack and Julia Shea."

"Do they work?"

"I think he does. No, I do not know what he does or his boss's name and his wife's favorite flower. Before you ask. I told you, they keep to themselves. Jo, would my place suit you or not?"

Jo nodded and then, reaching out and holding his long head in both of her hands as if preparatory to kissing him, she said, "If you could stand me, I think that I could stand you."

Ed raised his right hand suddenly like a traffic cop, saying, "I forgot. Do you smoke, Jo?"

"No."

He paused, doubtless to tease her one last time. She remained motionless, her hands around his face, waiting forever if need be.

Ed then lowered his hand and told her with a definitive tone, "Then, you can bunk in with me when we are back in New York."

"Thank you," Jo said, kissing him with a depth that truly delighted them both. When their next interactions were over and she was lying on his chest, both of their heads pointing up at the skies, the stars, and the infinite over old Gloucester, she asked, "What else shall we talk about tonight?"

"Better avoid 'The Mansard House.'"

"Delightful idea. I must feed the cat. Can you be patient, dear?"

"Ed Hopper is nothing if he is not patient," he said as if swimming in self-pity, which led her to come back to give him another long hug and kisses. As she did, she sighed and murmured almost inaudibly, "Arthur will just have to wait."

Chapter Forty-Four

Garret wanted Don to write up a story about a family that included a young widow, four girls and two boys ranging in age from 2 up to thirteen, and a cousin visiting for an indefinite time. The numbers Don knew from his editor, as well as the fact that the sea had recently taken the father of the house, a fisherman. Gloucester was small and tight enough that neighbors knew everything, and word spread quickly.

Don asked, "Do we still need something in the newspaper? Everybody must already know what you heard."

"Well, Don, think: do we need something in the newspaper? How does Don Nash buy the gas to run the roadster, and pay his rent and eat without the *Gloucester Daily Times*?"

"I see," Don said. Yes, we need a newspaper.

But the editor was on a roll and extemporized further. He said, "By every demographic, this city cannot support us. The newspaper should be a weekly. The amount of news and the base of readers—do you know how few in Gloucester graduate from high school? Most of the children who begin school here drop out with no diploma."

"So how is it that there is a daily in Gloucester?"

"The teachers make sure everybody can read before they leave to work at the shoe factory in Lynn, or go out in a boat to George's Bank, or do whatever they do. They do not want to read books. They want to read about the people they know and events in Gloucester and on Cape Ann."

"Every day."

"Every day, yes. Honor their need. You are going to let them know, whether they are Italian or not, or if they never go out to sea, how it is with a widow and the family after the fisherman dies. That's the story. You will tell that story. A story like that is too fragile to get through on the grapevine. For stories like that they need a newspaper, and that paper needs Don Nash."

Don nodded, his head humbly downcast and pointed his roadster to the widow's house.

Don Nash sat quietly in the parlor of the house in mourning. It was down the Fort. He had passed through the kitchen, sweet with garlic and an undertone of baking bread. Tomatoes were ripening on the windowsill. A framed circular color engraving of Jesus, adorned with palms, was on one wall. A small figure of Saint Peter stood on the back of the stove. As he waited, Don could imagine that comfort had lived here and of awakening mornings in this neat and snug home. Rising to stand, Don noted the dark brown hair, dark eyes, and olive cheeks of the mother, over whom her two oldest, tall daughters loomed, as she came into the living room slowly, a woman in black in a room where the shades were drawn. The oldest girl, Maria, was going to translate.

"I am sorry about your husband, Vincenzo," Don said in the quietest and softest possible tone

The mother and now widow showed an expression of unfeigned and unmitigated grief as her daughter translated. She had no need to hear his words in Italian, his tone and the name "Vincenzo" told her what he meant.

The three of them took seats as Don explained, and Maria translated, that the *Times* wanted to publish an article in which the results of one fisherman's loss could be told.

"People should know the true cost of the fish they eat," Don said.

The mother said nothing as he went on. Her hands clasped together, she looked down at the floor, shaking her head.

He decided to ask Maria, "Is your mother too sad to answer questions?"

Maria took it as a suggestion that she ask her mother. In response, the widow, Antoinette, spoke up, stiffening, her back straight and her head held high, looking Don in the eyes.

In Italian translated by Maria, she said, "Why do you say 'loss' and only 'loss'? I can talk about Vincenzo because he remains with us, and he strengthens me."

Don got his pencil out and flipped open his notepad, explaining that he was going to make notes for an accurate story. He was sorry for any delays as he did his job this way.

"I am in no hurry, and neither is my Vincenzo."

It was impossible to do otherwise and be accurate: he could not (and he did not) emphasize *loss*. The children all understood and were dealing with the absence of a father who, God knew, had had to be absent from them many weeks of every year in the performance of his job. He had lived for his family, Don wrote, and he still lived in and through them.

"He told me that if he were to die before me, to be strong, and rely on our faith," Antoinette said, making a point with her forefinger, as if Vincenzo had gestured so to her. His legacy was real and present. Don wrote an article in which he celebrated the brief life of one of Gloucester's humble workers, a man with a big heart and a loving family who was braving the elements at sea when the indifferent ocean claimed another victim from among Gloucester's best.

"You did not do what I asked, you did better," his editor said, punctuating his words with profanities. He added, "We're putting it in as our entry in the competition. But we know it's good. Not only readers have come in to say how they were touched, Donny, you can do my obituary any time. You got the publisher and I to weep. In fact, I want it in my pocket when I go, so that they'll find it to work up something like it for me. You have the touch, Donny. You bring back the dead."

"I'll have to see how my touch works for Dr. Blythe," Don said, having written up the *Times*'s series of reports that the doctor was missing and that the worst was feared. But Dr. Blythe's obituary was never written. When the Probate Court declared him legally dead years later, it was judged not newsworthy. Dr. Blythe sank without leaving a trace, although his yellow house, as "Adam's House," became immortal.

Chapter Forty-Five

After honoring Jo's suggestion that he paint a yellow house, Ed did, but not in the bright lemon-yellow Jo favored, instead with a yellow drifting toward orange, and shadowed brown as the clapboards were outlined—he moved on decisively without a suggestion by her, entirely by his own logic, but nonetheless with a conscious intent to amuse, if not to please Jo. He headed toward the wharves. He was going to paint the sea, or a ship, something maritime.

He passed fishermen mending nets and jawing, the wooden fronts of buildings, warehouses, and processing plants. The air was astringent, less salt, and more fumes of the residue of fish out of water. He stood to look about, a panorama of water, Five Pound Island sailing craft of several sizes, dories as well. The gulls circling and crying their screams at one another overhead, the bursts of a loud engine starting up and protesting. Soon, the plane in flight, the Treasury plane taking off from its hangar on Ten Pound Island, mid-harbor. Said to have been bought from the Indians for the sum of ten pounds, but nobody truly knew. The blue, cloud-scudded skies above, the boats, high-masted, sails unfurled, the chugging of engines, all amounted to a busier seascape than he cared to grapple with today.

Apart from the rest, detached, seemingly stubbornly separate, two identical trawlers were tied up, unmoving but for a slight up and down with the waves. These, in their formidable refusal to kneel or do anything but stand, seemed to him right.

He set up and began to draw, first, the indifferent green wall-like high sides of the first trawler. It occupied more than a third of his canvas and, had he stopped with that, nobody could have guessed that it was part of a boat. The pilot houses, although windowed, revealed no figures, and were dark. Many parts of the vessel were obscured, behind, as the second trawler effectively hid behind the first, and that first trawler would not reveal itself behind its wall of a green side.

The sense a viewer had was one of an inert mass or, if one were liberally inclined, of two masses, trawlers only vaguely, more blobby, squatty shapes or lumps. Nothing suggested any imminence of trawling at sea. Nothing invited one to imagine grace in the actions of these vessels. They were Frankensteins, robots, the reverse of anthropomorphic. They were infused with Ed's own rejection of salt water and boats subjects. His painting was rather an indictment, a non-verbal accusation, a charge that these subjects were uncooperative when he questioned them, that hey skulked and hid themselves from exposure.

A man came by to stand beside Ed. He had the unkempt gray beard that many men of the sea favored "to keep their throats warm," wore thick clothes over high boots, smelled of fish and seemed to have a slight limp. He spoke up with unapologetic interest.

"What are you doing?"

"I am sketching," Ed said.

"Do you like it, or are you doing it for hire?"

"I like it."

"On vacation, are you?"

"I am."

"You don't fish or swim?"

"No. Mostly I sketch and paint."

The man stood by, obviously mulling over what Ed had said.

"You going to sell them sketches?"

"If I can."

"I see you don't put much of that ship into your sketch."

"No."

"Why don't you sketch the whole thing?"

Ed thought his question remarkably astute.

"I pick what I think stands for the ship without needing more."

The man said, "I don't see why you cut, when you could sketch it all."

"I want to focus on part. Like part of a fish, its eye or its silver scales."

The man stood by again.

Then he said, "My name is Henry Gould and I started out fishing but lost my leg, and replaced it with a wooden one. Now I am a fish cutter when I'm not a lifeguard down to Half Moon beach. So I've looked into the eyes of fish, living and dead and they gave me the creeps. But I think I am receiving you. Focus, you call it?"

"Focus, or knowing what to leave out," Ed said.

"Ah, knowing what to leave out. Now that is one of the arts of life."

Ed was startled by the poet beside him, speaking so lyrically.

"I wish I knew not to leave out my leg, eh, buddy?" the man said, raising a laugh that infected Ed, so brazen he was. "Don't blame a curious fellow who asks questions. It passes time pleasanter. Thank you for answering. I'll leave you be now."

"Thanks, any time," Ed said. They had exchanged only about a hundred words but nonetheless during their two minutes together explored a corner of the world they shared with close attention. It was as Ed intended, that his paintings be scrutinized, and as he walked back to Mrs. Post's he was also amused to recall the man's remark, "I don't see why you cut, when you could sketch it all."

He must tell that to Jo.

Chapter Forty-Six

Instead of sending him out on news assignments, Garret told Don that he wanted feature stories, colorful items, for example, to get as many interviews as he could of the "gifted people passing through here" who practiced any art.

"Now you tell me," Don said in a disgusted tone, "after Sabrina the Mystical Artistical Dancer has left our city for parts unknown."

"I remember her. The parts you were interested in covering are in the public domain, my boy," Garret said. "There is no story behind her behind. But Gloucester is full of real artists, they come in like grasshoppers and nobody asks them a goddam thing, you know? And then they go off and get famous and we have not covered the news, news being made in our streets every day. I want those artists."

Don discovered Ed painting as he drove up Prospect Street. It was simply a matter of slowing down and parking in front of the Armory. But would the artist talk? There were, Don had found from past experiences, two types of artists, those who talked, and those who chose not to. He could only find out which type this one was by approaching the man.

"Good morning, sir," Don said. He did not put out his hand to shake, as the artist, seated on his portable stool, was engaged in applying watercolors to paper on his easel.

"Good morning to you," Ed said, not shifting his eyes to look at Don.

"Will it bother you to answer a few questions for the *Times*?"

Ed hesitated, then smiled warily.

He told Don, looking at him, "I'll pause for a couple of minutes."

"Who are you and where are you from?"

"My name is Edward Hopper and I hail from New York."

"Are you a professional artist?"

"Well, good question. I am getting too old to be an illustrator. But I am probably good for nothing else. Let's say that I want to be a professional artist. I aspire to that, all right?"

"All right. How do you like Gloucester?"

"I won't give you a complete list of its appeals to me, but I like your city for its light, which is nearly Mediterranean. Radiant, it transfigures ordinary objects. And I feel like I can get around on foot or with a trolley ride. Even around the Cape. All of your beaches are only a few feet from the road."

"Thank you. I won't hold you up any further," Don said, scratching the last of a few notes in his stenographer's pad.

"Thank you for leaving me be," Ed said, his eyes returning to the row of houses and street that led up to the Lady of Good Voyage Church.

Don scanned the painting for a brief description and could hardly look away. The man was an

artist. He transformed Prospect Street. Don imagined that here was a happy man doing what he enjoyed best and doing it well.

"Do you know Mrs. Murphy's boarding
house?" Ed asked.

Don said that he did.

"If you go there and ask for Miss Nivison, Jo
Nivison, you might get a better interview. And she
is better known than I am, too, by far. New York
galleries sell her paintings. And her cat, Arthur, is
worth a line or two also."

"Arthur?" Don asked, probing Ed's seriousness.

"Arthur," Ed said with firmness. "Her remarkable cat. Get a picture."

Don thanked him and promised to pay a call at
Mrs. Murphy's.

After this, his first interview, Ed felt strongly
that he ought to have done more with his life. How
little he had to say after having reached forty
without prizes, wealth, or recognition. While he
wished Jo well—and hoped the *Times* would publi-
cize her—entangling himself just now with a
woman, which he had resisted so long, was not
likely a good career move. Why should he tie himself down? These days, women were open to a
man's advances quicker and easier than ever. As he
knew from experience, they sometimes made the
opening moves. Was he really so lonely that he
needed a woman to wake up to each morning?

He was almost done with Prospect Street and
wondered about doing another, or moving closer to
the church. He was making these decisions himself.
Without consulting with Jo or anybody else. After
all, art was not committee work or a group project.
Jo was used to collaboration, brought up in the theater, people welding themselves into functioning
groups of actors. The art show juries and gallery

openings on which she thrived were likewise not for
him. She was partying her way to fame and modest
fortune in New York but that was not the ticket for
Ed Hopper. He had enough trouble finding and
holding an audience of one on a slow day to ini-
tiate a commercial art commission. Here he was
trying to sell *money*, begging to be allowed to in-
crease the haul of an entrepreneur or businessman
and treading water at that game, while such as Tim
Tolman were succeeding brilliantly.

Jo, too. She was recognized. She had her win-
ning ways. She, not he, had been Robert Henri's
pet. Was it her hair aflame? Her red hair advertised
her temper. She was bossy. Nonetheless, Ed experienced waves of fun when out with her. She *was* different. She could make him laugh, the things she
said. But he was not Jo, and Jo was not him. Would
their coupling work outside of this peculiar town,
Gloucester? Or was theirs just one more of many
summer romances?

These thoughts were his as he walked along
Prospect Street after he folded up his easel and his
stool, and put his watercolor into the wooden case
with his art supplies. "Prospect Street" struck him
as funny, as he went over his prospects, Jo or no Jo,
this house or that house, one life or another. He
was sorting out his future on *Prospect* Street.

He paused. Almost across the street from him
was a sturdy red brick block of a building, the armory. A car with a spare tire on its back was parked
in front. The street wound its way past a series of
fabulous houses to Our Lady of Good Voyage
church. The irony struck him as he set up his easel
for another quick watercolor *en plein air.* He was
painting, on Prospect Street, the way to church.
Was Jo ever not going to be associated in his mind
with church? He thought that Freud described a

natural association between women and open en-
closures, pocketbooks, and churches.

As he sketched quickly in pencil, he figured the
proportion of sky, and made a high horizon. It
amused him that people had no idea how the first
decisions made by an artist, in each painting, were
the largest. It was a whole different picture depending upon looking up more or looking down
more. Too much of the street and houses, too little
sky, made it a different and busier, really a more
comfortable, upholstered painting. The rendering
he foresaw in beginning resembled the wriggle of a
butterfly out of its cocoon, three quarters embedded and fraught with a sense of entrapment,
but with the sky above beckoning and granting the
light of hope.

The twin church steeples, like upside-down
bluebell flowers, emphasized the sky from below,
less pointing than nudging the viewer's eyes up-
ward. It was a cloudless, blue-sky day but Ed was
going to whiten the heavens himself, a sort of airy
fogginess or mist that invited anyone to consider
that one's future is invisible, uncertain, without
form and to be announced later. What was here
was an automobile with a spare tire handy, if
needed, beside the stalwart armory, if needed, on a
street to the church, when needed.

Done with his sketch, satisfied with very few
touch ups that he had a composition that worked,
balancing the big old armory on one side against—
he made the street wider and more inviting than it
was in scale—the eclectic row of houses curled up
to the turn right to the church. He planned the sky
perfectly, he judged, in having just so much but no
more, and, as he left the paper for a white sky or
added a touch or two of titanium white, he could
always change his mind. The blue of the steeple

domes on the church, however, should be exactly enough. But he would keep an open mind.

Back in New York, he turned it into an oil painting, drained it of its blue. Even the iconic church domes he turned golden, and exercised that Midas touch all over the resulting oil, imbuing the canvas with autumn colors. The trees were not green, but amber and suggestive of September. He was so pleased with the car parked in front of the armory, with its wonderful spinning spare tire and a canvas top with an elongated oval window, that he lopped off the armory altogether and stopped the right-hand side with that automobile. He was excited enough to duplicate the same worthy car ahead, down the road, in shadow. It came out poorly, as if a fly had landed on the painting. He left the imperfection as a smudgy and too-small echo of the great motif of the car in front of the armory. So the composition had meaning, and its defect had a function, too.

When he looked at the completed oil painting, in New York, as snow fell, he was pleased to have wrought a golden day out of the "way to church" blue-toned watercolor. Further, as he exaggerated things, the way to church was circuitous. One veered sharply away from the church toward the left before finding an unseen turn to the right, the turn that led to the front of the church. Ed's way to church, to marriage, to Jo as the cornerstone of his future in art, had been so circuitous and he had turned sharply to the left before he turned grudgingly to the right. Prospect Street, where he had mulled over his prospects, looking again and again before he leaped.

Chapter Forty-Seven

By August Ed and Jo were able to be quiet together, a trick usually only accomplished by old married couples. They were, however, in their forties and had been bumped, if not bruised, in noisier relationships before.

"Are you a man of faith?" Jo asked.

"Faith in mortality," Ed said.

"What does that mean?"

"I believe that everybody will die and that nothing matters long."

"I have faith."

"Upon what do you base that, Jo?"

"On faith.'

"And where do you find a basis for your faith?"

"Ed, I once arrived in a church with nothing but prayer and so many good things happened. You cannot live in a church for a year without seeing other people find hope, led by nothing but faith."

Ed was silent.

Jo said, "Anyhow, we can talk about something else."

"Or nothing," Ed said.

"You do not want to talk?" Jo asked.

He shook his head.

She sighed, then said, "I don't want to argue. It's unpleasant."

"I'm not arguing, Jo. When I get my paintings right, they do not show men in Arrow shirts checking their tie and celluloid collars in the mirror. They show the bleak and empty world we actually inhabit."

"But you've lived in Paris and in New York, Ed."

"Ultimately, we are alone."

"If you don't count God."

"Or colors and rainbows or whatever Golden Calf *you* want to worship."

"Tell that to Gloucester, three hundred years of faith, farming rocky pastures, making the stormy Atlantic feed them and this country. They made something and so have you, in painting air and light. And what they created will last and your paintings will last, too."

"Josephine, do you have any idea when I sold my last painting?"

"A year or two does not mean anything."

"Ten years, Jo, ten. I sold a painting at the Armory Exhibit in 1913. Period. Full stop."

Jo was dumbstruck.

Ed said, "You have nothing to say, do you?"

"I think your paintings have been overlooked."

Ed laughed mirthlessly and when he spoke again, he sounded angry.

"Overlooked? My paintings are stamped on, tossed aside, in every way neglected and ignored in favor of any other artist. Walt Disney is better. Rudolph Dirks is better. Anybody is better."

"I do not think so."

"You are prejudiced and if you saw me as I am, you would see my paintings for what they are. Shit."

"I think we ought to be quiet."

"I am only just beginning. Wake up, Jo."

"I am not asleep, Ed."

"You are blind to reality, like your paintings. All tulip red and Dutch cheese yellow commemorating a vase of flowers that will soon wither and shrivel."

"Some people like what I do."

"I do not. I am done with play acting. Unlike you, I do not seek to charm anybody."

"Are you saying I am not being honest?"

"You are in love with love. At your age, it is a natural weakness."

She slapped his face.

Moving not a fraction of an inch, Ed said, "Good. The truth hurts, but it is the truth."

She was crying.

Then Ed walked out. He said nothing more as he shut the door.

Their first real fight, now probably their last contact. But what had they quarreled about? Faith? Art? A thought came to her that never failed to calm her. That simple thought was a simple question: What will it matter in a hundred years?

She then slept a deep and dreamless sleep. When she awoke, she found Mrs. Murphy in tears downstairs. She wondered how much of their conversation her landlady had overheard, and was taken aback at how much the poor woman seemed to care that she and Ed were at odds and separated. But she was wrong.

It was not Ed and Jo's woes that led to Mrs. Murphy's lachrymose display. It was bad news. Black-bordered Boston newspapers had come into Gloucester on the early train with headlines that the President, Warren Harding, had died suddenly and unexpectedly in San Francisco during the night. With one hand raised and the other on the old, worn family Bible, in the yellow, flickering light of a kerosene lamp, Vice President Calvin Coolidge had been installed as Harding's successor before dawn, his father himself administering the oath, being a Justice of the Peace. That scene took place on the farm where Coolidge in his youth had chopped wood and hauled water.

"The summer is over," Mrs. Murphy said as she wept and, although tearless all night, Jo could no longer help herself. She wept, too, bursting out into great, gasping sobs, though not only for President Harding.

Chapter Forty-Eight

On Middle Street, Ed lacked capacity to grieve properly over the nation's loss at the same time that he was facing the devastation of another love's collapse. Jo followed Jeanne. He was relearning what he forgot, or was too foolish to grasp, or too weak to apply, twice burned now: that no man can rely on any woman.

He went out for a walk carrying all of his equipment. Over there, the angle of the roof, the stabbing shingle high in the air, no, not high enough, and no bold façade to make manifest in strokes of paint, the house cloaked in shadow many tones too dark, and without a stark telephone pole and wires to exemplify the feeble vanity of connection. Communication, as limited as tin cans and string, with children bellowing. Oh, Ed could just howl into his tin can, had he one, down the string to God's end, if He was listening. It was a veritable crucifixion to straddle the sidewalk, his arms constricted, contorted into the heft and hauling of the box and the easel and the two framed canvases he had the day before, when he had still been in love and light-hearted, optimistically tied together with coarse twine, aiming for a rich harvest of light and shadows. Planning ahead was as presumptuous as cooking up what the Red Sox would do at Fenway in the fifth inning—although he *could* predict that they would be in mourning as well, wearing black armbands.

Bleak, muted colors seethed in his head. Lately, it was both burnt sienna and raw umber, like the fading sepia photographs in family albums, colors that he loved with the degree of passion poor Saint Vincent Van Gogh reserved for yellow, which he would taste and eat if he could. Yellow realized its destiny, its *raison d'etre*, on Van Gogh's canvas. Could he tease brown to climb, to ascend to the heights of high art, in his canvases this morning? Or would the house that struck him be one of the maiden whites of Gloucester, the fleckless brides so grim and tall peaked, over which he would drain his tube of titanium white dry?

It tickled him inside much as when he left his barren apartment in Greenwich Village to drink at a bar but actually with a woman in mind, a stranger with whom to make intimate connection. He was going to be the intermediary between worlds. The fecund, fairyland of Gloucester this summer's day he was going to translate with his mere humble hands and simple tools, so that another set of eyes than his today could look and see and say, "Ah, yes," and take in what he took in.

Through him would run an electric current. He was to be the wire that connected the jolting volts of A GLOUCESTER MORNING IN SUN IN 1923 to future days and nights, to be resurrected, alive and thrashing like a just-caught mackerel in his paintings.

Ah, there it was, the house he had found the first day in Gloucester, the one that got away. He spotted the partly obliterated mailbox, ADAM.

Probably it had been ADAMS when new. But Adam fit this garden of Eden. This would do, thank you very much, Adam. "Adam's House" was in play now on this dazzling day, a house afire, its whitewash ablaze with the light that Ed craved. He would mount to heaven on Adam's house. This backdoor to Paradise was his no matter whose name was on the deed, no matter what a judge and jury would say about ownership, relying on the ridiculously thin evidence of a document conveying title. Ed, the artist licensed this day by the Creator God, stood in the sunlight looking at the house that he was to claim for all time.

He would call it "Adam's House" but it was— they all were—"Hopper's House." Adam's house would pass away. Hopper's would withstand centuries. As Gloucester itself of 1923 went down for the count, along with the 300th, what Ed did this day would survive and would endure to the 400th and to the 500th and more.

He set up his easel. He propped his canvas. Some days he had to use string and tie the canvas not to be blown by the wind but today was blessedly calm, the boats in the harbor languished, sails furled, putting on their engines, he heard the bevy of mechanical beasts in motion. Closer, he could have smelled the fumes of spent gasoline. As it was, high on Portagee Hill, Ed's widened nostrils smelled fresh, smart, salt air. His nose approved. He inhaled deeply and recalled, with a smug smile, that he was here to escape the stink of the bars and to chase girls. The stink he had defeated but the women he had yet to find and follow and flounder about. Flappers, dames, skirts, broads, where are you? If you had to choose a man who owned Adam's house or a man who owned a painting of Adam's house, which would you choose?

He spent a few minutes, reluctantly, because he felt the minutes as if they were a small bank account that he was spending at an awful rate, an account that would be gone before he put brush to paint. But it was necessary and his method, and he loved it more than any other part of the process of painting: looking at, taking in the subject, filling his eyes, enjoying the nuances and challenges, identifying the difficulties as quickly as possible, to be especially wary in sketching and in painting that there the bodies were buried, there were the details in which the Devil lived, there were the spoilers of an otherwise masterpiece.

He savored Adam's house, there was no better word for it. He tasted it with his eyes, he licked it visually all over as a happy puppy licks its master's hand. Nothing like Adams's house ever existed before, ever appeared on any canvas, ever startled the world. How mundane, when Adams came out of his front door and went out walking without giving his house a backward glance or, had he, he would have seen only where the sides might use a bit of paint, where it was peeling.

It does not need paint, Mr. Adam, it needs to be painted, and by a master, by someone like me. Ed began, not much less reluctantly than he paused, regretting the lack of more leisure to revel in the sight, to bask in the warm sun, to listen to the throb of boats and now and then birdsong, to lean left, lean right, see from a different perspective. He was not satisfied by the tastes, but his appetite had been whetted. He would dive into the feast that was Adam's house, its cornices—and those overlong, extended formidable picket fences. He would devour it, slice by slice, taking it up out of thin air and reviving it, live, on his canvas, until it was to its very soul on canvas, and extinguished as a Gloucester house, reborn in Artland.

By quick work in an hour, Adam's house, with some infusion of Ed himself, some imaginative give and take, some negotiation with the hand he was dealt, giving a card back, drawing another, had become the sketch, the good start of a house where Adam would dwell in the House of the Lord forever and ever. Amen.

Then a tree caught his eye. It was a geyser, an explosion, an ideal volcanic eruption beside Adam's house, the flaming green sword of the angel. The Tree of Life. I live for this, Ed thought as he sketched quickly, finding the house easier and more portable than he feared, then the tree as well.

Given more time, tiny corrections, little changes, brushed up, the frame of the building fairly danced, levitated onto his two-dimensional surface. *I was born to do this*, he thought, thinking ahead to the color combination and touch of blue that he would hope to mix just right, neither too thick nor too thin, not too light nor too dark, in covering that section between the roof and the front of the house. *I should paint sunlight on a white wall*, he thought.

The telephone pole like the cross on Calvary, with its wires off to—where? It made the painting, and if he leaned it just a bit, the pole guided one's eyes to the tower of City Hall, the fig leaf with which man dignified his fall from grace and Paradise. Those who dwell in Adam's house need governance and a tower with a chiming clock lest they run wild and unregulated. Just here, on this hill, at the crest of the heights, where telephone poles would convey one's utterances, if allowed, to California, Ed was communing with the core of humanity that was inherent in his flesh.

By early afternoon, he was done. Watercolors dry fast. Titanium white brightened his colors to Gloucester degree, and his shadows were sharper than any he had done in New York. Painted from a low vantage, this house had a dominance it would have lacked at eye level. He was exhilarated. You could not have told anything from his poker face, his expression was blank, but inside he danced: the hunter had bagged his game. This painting was finished.

He could cover it in a cotton cloth that he had for the purpose, then tie it in twine to the virgin canvas yet untouched. Would he, could he dare to take on another at this time of day? After such a wonderful experience? He imagined that he felt as a sultan feels looking over a harem after having had a memorable and intimate connection with one of the sweeter wives. So Rembrandt must have felt with upon the finishing touches of the "Night Watch." Such feelings are rare and to be held sacred and apart, and generated holy days to be celebrated ten or twenty years later.

As he walked back to Mrs. Post's, he said to himself, "I'm sorry that you died, Warren, old boy, but life goes on and Adam's house won't hurt you."

Chapter Forty-Nine

Jo and Ed had been in Gloucester during Gloucester's Tricentennial, but they never thought of it at all until that day at Stage Fort Park. Then it greatly mattered.

Mrs. Murphy was setting out a bowl for oatmeal and a cup and saucer for coffee, along with silverware for Jo, whom she knew would be the first of her guests awake. The two were far beyond talking about weather, cats, and various bits of Gloucester geography and lore, or New York City, in which Mrs. Murphy had a great interest because her late father had lived his first twenty years in New York City, more specifically, in Brooklyn. They had shared their deepest fears and highest hopes, their regrets and, in Jo's case, more than hints about her fondness for her fellow artist, Ed.

After Jo and Mrs. Murphy exchanged good mornings, Mrs. Murphy said, "I'm going to miss you. And Arthur."

Jo reciprocated with the same remark. She looked at her landlady now to see her better, in this kitchen, with her circumscribed functions, narrow hopes, limited travel, and then every now and then, usually in summers, the guests who offered her something of a window on the larger world. Jo stirred her spoon in hot oatmeal and maple syrup but did not eat.

"Jo, are you feeling unsettled?" Mrs. Murphy asked in a concerned tone.

"No, why?"

"Frankly, you look sickly, dear, since yesterday and you're stirring your food rather than eating."

"I'm not especially hungry."

"You may have picked up something, out late. Have you a fever?"

Mrs. Murphy stood and asked if she might test Jo's forehead. It was a mother's touch, the back of the hand lightly applied. Mrs. Murphy frowned and shook her head.

"You are warm. I'd like you to see my doctor."

"I'm all right."

After a pause, Mrs. Murphy said, "No, dear, I don't think so. You're not eating, you're warm, and apparently not sleeping, are you? Your eyes are red. Take it from me, you are not entirely well, and my doctor is the wisest man in the city, possibly in the country."

So it was that Doctor Morris Pett came to Mrs. Murphy's on a house call that afternoon, his big black bag with him. Before he arrived, Mrs. Murphy told Jo, "He won't send you a bill. If you say that you only have a painting to give him, a painting will do. I have had his help for a crocheted blanket, and a padded quilt. He knows all about women's problems, and he has delivered half of the babies in Gloucester, far more than anybody else. If a woman needs more time off her feet in the hospital, Dr. Pett is the one to prescribe it."

Dr. Pett, a tall, slim man with an athlete's grace —he had been a football star, awarded an athletic scholarship by Tufts—was a doctor with an office on Middle Street at Lowe's old stagecoach station. His observant eyes, youthful good looks, and jet-black hair belied years of experience in the most serious matters of life and death in Gloucester. Many fishermen with raging fever due to gurry poisoning were drawn back to life and health by Dr. Pett's skillful administration of a battery of medications to treat their infection. Few civilians were welcome at card games held by fishermen in back tables at the city's taverns. Polish-born Dr. Pett was one of the few.

"I feel foolish, but Mrs. Murphy insisted," Jo said, as Dr. Pett got his stethoscope in place to hear her heart. Once done with that, he worked on her medical history, quickly found out that both of her parents had died, as had her two brothers, and one of her cousins was her closest confidante. In between pleasantries about her visit and the summer, he listened to her tell him, in her own words, about quarreling with Ed.

"That's why I didn't sleep, and my eyes are red from crying. So, you see, it is not medical," Jo said. "I cried more when President Harding died."

Dr. Pett, who had quickly and efficiently gathered Jo's medical history, looked her in the red eyes and said, "We both know that you've been very ill in the past, Miss Nivison. During the War, when you hardly took time enough to recuperate, I think, and your nutrition was poor for years afterward. Without money, you've not been kind to your body. Without family near to warn you, you've pushed yourself beyond your limits."

"You think I am ill?"

"I think that you are among the people for whom other people are as necessary as bread. You were drawn to theater, to school and lately to art galleries and fellow artrists."

"I have my cat."

"True, but I think that you must attend tonight's activities. For your health. You ought to refresh yourself and get out of this house, as pleasant as Mrs. Murphy's is. You can leave your cat alone for a few hours, can't you?"

Dr. Pett left without having prescribed an aspirin, only leaving Jo with "doctor's orders" to take part in the evening's activities (for which he, after protesting "no charge," had accepted a painting of flowers of Lane's Cove, which he said showed that she had a good eye and a steady hand).

Now, to go or not to go? It was not like she had lost anything she had. Why grieve or fret? Theirs was obviously a summer romance, a traditional rise-and-fall romance in two acts, up and down. End of story.

Although it had been educational. Their time together had been instructive. In the past, she had kept no regular schedule. Lots of days she was too busy, other days not busy enough. She saw how differently Ed lived. He was as close to rigid as a mortal could get, the same apartment, the same routine, regular hours, set mealtimes. He was up early each day: unlike Jo, he needed no alarm clock. He washed and shaved and had his coffee. Was she not better off without him and he without her? But she would now start a schedule, and keep more regular work hours in New York, wouldn't she?

The loss was his, not hers. For Ed she would have been an accommodating and trained model, and the good head she had for business, having managed her own modest gifts into an optimum of exhibitions, awards, fame, and sales, was obvious. Paired up with an artist more gifted, like Ed, she could make waves.

But it was not to be. So what? Jo hugged her cat and told Arthur, her voice hoarse, "It will be all right. We will soon enough be back to normal in New York. I know you miss your friends there, Moofy. I'm sorry to have taken you away from them. But now we will go back, and everything will be as it was."

She put Arthur down on the floor, partly covered by circular woven rag rugs. "I helped him out, Arthur. He was in such a fix. I think he knows about watercolors now. But I could have done more for him if he would only let me. I have connections. Ed is so aloof, too aloof for his own good."

A few minutes after that, she went downstairs and told Mrs. Murphy that she was going out that evening. Mrs. Murphy was ecstatic.

"Heavens, girl, good choice. Think of it, both of you artists, good ones, both from New York."

"I'm just going out to the celebration."

"Of course you are. On doctor's orders. But, Jo, you have a gentleness about you, and no temper at all."

"You would be surprised."

"Even without your patience, I found Mr. Murphy. You'll do fine."

"I'm just going for the celebration," Jo said, recalling that Ed talked about patience on the night that they had first engaged so closely. The word from Mrs. Murphy's lips seemed like an omen, and a good one.

"May I fix you a lunch before you have to leave?"

"Just something for Arthur, please."

"I've boiled a flounder for Arthur. His favorite, I think. Bot nothing for you? You had no breakfast."

She declined Mrs. Murphy's offer, thanking her

kindly. She then fasted until afternoon, after which she applied a subtle rouge just under her cheek-bones and a bit of gray eye shadow. Having studied her face and found it acceptable for a public appearance, she dressed in a celebratory, a light orange dress which barely came down to her knees. Tossing a cerise silk scarf around her neck and down her back to set ff her auburn hair, finally donning a broad-brimmed summer hat, thinking that it would be the last time she would wear it in Gloucester, she felt that she looked her best when she went out to join the crowds.

Chapter Fifty

The historical pageant and choruses were assembling at Stage Fort Park. Jo heard the hubbub ahead, including first graders rehearsing "America the Beautiful," repeating "From sea to shining sea" in their shrill, high young voices. Dr. Pett's words ran through her mind to steel her determination:

"I think that you are among the people for whom other people are as necessary as bread."

"I think you must attend tonight's activities. For your health. You ought to refresh yourself and get out of this house, as pleasant as Mrs. Murphy's is."

So here she was. She would be all right. Arthur would be all right at Mrs. Murphy's. The atmosphere would doubtless be festive, people of all ages would be alive with excitement, especially the children, which would especially bring her joy to see. It was no good sitting almost alone in her room beside Arthur when she could flaunt her glad rags and enjoy herself. If there was dancing, she just might take to dancing on the grass under the stars as the bands played. She had no reputation to care about losing among people she would never see again, did she?

Meanwhile, back on Middle Street, as he

passed by Dr. Pett unaware, Ed felt that it was safe now to admire Gloucester on display, to stand in place and see the city go by. The experience at Stage Fort Park he expected to be much like one he had had in New York four years previously when the "Fighting 69th" and other ranks and files of men marched by in the thousands, military bands blasting. They were coming back from war, returning from Over There, and how the people cheered. All ages rejoiced as one that day. The War was over, perhaps all wars ever. The boys were back, flags flying. He did not usually like crowds, or the smallest group of people if they were not artists, but this event was history as art. The pageant and the crowds tonight would be just the type of show to engage him, with much going on every minute, moments of light and shadow unique, transient and— only to be observed once in a century. He did not expect to see Jo. Each unaware of the other's plans, however, they had left their respective boarding houses and headed for the same place, Stage Fort Park, in mid-afternoon.

Chapter Fifty-One

It was the long-awaited day, Saturday, August 25, and Don visualized the city as unreal, made out of cardboard, with so many mindless dolls running around. He lamented his loss of Sabrina. It was not that he had ever had her, or done more than hugged and kissed the girl, it was the sense of a missed opportunity. His future, which had seemed only days ago all bright colors and spinning pinwheels, was a blank page that he was to write on for people to wrap fish in the next day. Nothing seemed duller than what he did, nothing seemed so isolating as this effort to translate events into words for the general and faceless public. What did it matter?

He dressed in his suit, as he was going to see his boss and his boss was going to see him, and it would not do for him not to be well-dressed when re-introduced to the Mayor (to whom he had been introduced a dozen times, after which the Mayor forgot him like an ant he had stepped on). He wondered if anybody present in the frolicking, roiling crowd could possibly feel more empty or meaningless than he.

"You win the prize, boy," he said to himself.

He drove from Davis Square down past the elegant Depauw Café, the railroad depot and the statue of Joan of Arc before the Legion building, down the entirety of the renovated Boulevard, which he thought of as the Boulevard of Broken Dreams now, the stalwart and determined Man at the Wheel, looking seaward, up to a parking area reserved for dignitaries, of which he was allegedly one, where he made a snug berth for his red roadster on the grassy edge of the temporary lot.

He then joined a mass in motion on their way up to the top of the hill, and past the pavilion, where he could see the large bronze tablet devoted to the glories of 1623, when this flat rock was a key step in the fish processing operation of the international Dorchester Company, where codfish were split, salted, and set out to dry.

Gloucester, the city in which over the centuries so many lovers' stories had unfurled like a mainsail, began in 1623 as a big rock stage for drying codfish. From the smack of the first split cod on that rock, it had been three hundred years. Don pondered the passage of three hundred years, more centuries than any three men could live. He was but fifth generation, his people only went back in Gloucester to 1775, supposedly to "the last boat over from London before the Revolution." Tonight, events would be re-enacted in which his ancestors had actually taken part or at least witnessed during their own lives. Part of the pageant—the opening —would be narrated in scripted flowery words he had written, although the volunteer actor's voice might not carry far, especially if and as this huge crowd got restive. His words would fall flat, he became certain. It had been for nothing.

Don spotted, among those in the front row at the railings around the pavilion, the artist from

New York, Ed. Don hesitated between moving through the crowd to get up to talk with a kindred spirit and staying in the crowd until, in any case, he was duty-bound to move up to the speakers' platform and say a few words to his boss and the Mayor. Don considered Ed. Ed was somewhat cynical but nonetheless held himself to preserve a chronicle of a sort in his artworks. How did Ed do it?

Don made his move, and was soon speaking with Ed, both of them pressed together on the railing. Everybody wanted the front-row view of the pageant, and to hear the choruses when they began.

"You got a good spot, Ed," Don said.

"Came early. I had nothing else to do, everything else is shut down."

"Everybody's here, the island might flip over."

Don found it a relief to tell a joke.

"Seventeen," Ed said.

"Seventeen what?" Don asked.

"You asked me to tell you how many watercolors I painted this summer. I got to seventeen before I quit."

"All houses?"

"All but two. I painted two trawlers, or at least I painted as much of them as they would let me. Difficult subjects."

"You said two. What was the other one?"

"It was," Ed said, feeling an unexpected reluctance to say, "one of my friends. At Good Harbor."

Don, so familiar and surrounded himself by loss, interpreted that it was the portrait of a "former" friend, but said nothing of his surmise.

"When does anything happen?" Ed asked.

Don said that in about ten or fifteen minutes the dignitaries ought to begin to arrive and to fill up the flag-decked platform. Honored guests, well-heeled or bohemian civilians, and Civil War vets in bemedaled uniforms, driven over from the G.A.R. residence a stone's throw from the Legion Hall, members of Company G, and survivors from Over There were already up on stage. Don pointed out several familiar to him, including Elias Hayworth, James Centennial Nutt, and Roscoe Knowlton.

"Imagine what their eyes have seen, what their bodies have felt," Ed said.

"They could never tell all of it. I try and get some of the details, and I was just ill and delirious in France, but it is like another world closed to the public."

"Of course, it is, the past, too."

"But Gloucester's past will be on exhibit today."

"Don't be so sure. I am an artist. I know about artist's license and the difficulty of getting a moment right. You can only come so close and no closer. The past keeps its secrets well."

Don shared the pageant's opening, "In 1623, as bullheaded breakers crashed stubbornly upon rocks and splintered themselves back into drops—you understand the poetry? I scripted the first scene of the pageant."

Ed nodded.

"Fishing crews employed by the Dorchester Company, yare, yare hoisted sails, crossed the seas, fished the banks and then oared it to shore in boats from their ships, to split, to salt and to dry codfish, making a stage in the center of a large flat rock in the center of what would become the Fort in the center of what would become the town, then the city, of Gloucester, Massachusetts. Shall I go on?"

Ed nodded.

"No less than their brethren in the South, they,

too, were here in the New World to make money for their owners before they dared to strive, to seek, to find and not to yield."

"Does this go all the way up to 1923?"

"In skips and jumps, yes. Not every year, not every decade, was eventful."

"Ed. Ed," someone was saying repeatedly until Ed finally spotted her and nodded and waved. Jo. Surprise. This was an eventful evening after all.

Chapter Fifty-Two

Jo took Ed's wave as an invitation to join him up on the pavilion porch. Previously, when Jo had been in love with someone, she had thought that she knew how it would end—happily—and previously she had always been wrong. Now, she had no idea where her feelings for Ed would lead, what would take place, and she did not care.

"I'm glad we met again once more," she said. They did not embrace, nor shake hands, but it was suddenly as if the crowd was gone, and everybody around them had disappeared.

"You helped me, you know," Ed said.

"I was glad to."

"You helped me to see."

He found his hand coming up toward her face, although he only inclined her broad-brimmed summer hat a bit to see her eyes easier. The one she had worn at Good Harbor, the one in his watercolor of her. He did not touch her. Their eyes met, however, seeing what there was to see.

"You have been seeing for years, Mr. Hopper."

"Maybe houses. But not people."

At this moment, the first graders in the tradi-

tional shrill, off key raggedy way of children's choruses, began to sing.

*O beautiful for spacious skies, For amber waves of
grain...*

She told him that she loved him. There.

"You love me?" Ed asked, which was neither
the response she had expected nor the response she
had wanted. Apparently, it was a question to which
the learned fool actually expected an answer.

*America! America! God mend thine every flaw
Confirm thy soul in self-control, Thy liberty in law!*

She said, "Yes, dear."

"Will it pass?" he asked. Damn him, he was
being funny, or trying to, his kind of humor.

She glared, then narrowed her eyes and said,
after a quick inhalation of breath, "Like a summer
storm."

"Well, that's too bad because I was starting to
have some feelings for you."

"Starting?" she asked, still angry and unmolli-
fied. Would Ed *never* be normal and speak normally? It was 1923, in Henry Cockeram's old
book a *jubilie,* when normal people spoke
normally.

Don, who had been watching and listening, was
now summoned to shake hands with the Mayor. He
was not going to see how things turned out.

"You know that I am slow," Ed said.

"You painted me fast enough at Good Harbor."
She thought about but did not conjure their com-
plete carnival ride through the entire summer to or
through West Gloucester, Stage Fort Park, the
Boulevard, the Fort, Gloucester Harbor, Rocky
Neck, East Gloucester, Riverdale, Dogtown, An-
nisquam, Bay View, Lanesville, Pigeon Cove and
Rockport.

Ed was going to tell her how the novelty of watercolors had excited him, then realized it would be better to speak more directly to the point.

"Bear with me, Jo. I think you know better than I do that we two are a pair."

O beautiful for patriot dream That sees beyond the years
Thine alabaster cities gleam Undimmed by human tears!

That remark finally did mollify her. Given that much warrant, she seized his neck and drew his face toward her for a kiss. After they kissed and embraced, Ed looked about and asked Jo, "Can we do this in public?"

"In Gloucester, all is possible. Ed, do you not know that?"

"No."

"You know what all of your paintings say? You don't, do you, you lummox? They tell me, 'You are not alone.'"

"How so, Jo?"

"How so? Your houses are empty, they look deserted, no sign of occupancy, no clothes on the line, no children playing, nobody in the street."

"I'm confused."

"But what about the viewer? *The viewer counts.* The one standing beside you, alone in your aloneness. You painted alone and bravely, and you passed your visual notes along to that lone viewer, who says, 'Well, I see what he saw. He is not alone. And I have a friend after all.'"

"A distant friend, wouldn't you say?"

"You genius, you are saying to them that this community in their head is illusion anyway, that we are all alone. The Emperor has no clothes."

"I'm deep but you're deeper, Jo," Ed said, in a tone hat wavered, neither an assertion nor a question but both at the same time.

"You are people more than one person, Ed Hopper. Your eyes, their eyes. If you ever draw and paint people, I know they will be alone, at night, naked, thoughtful, sad, dreamy."

"Or standing alone outside of an empty house."

"You've accomplished that implicitly this summer. It's your theme, your world."

America! America! God shed his grace on thee,

And crown thy good with brotherhood From sea to shining sea.

The children were applauded and cheered, as children happily are, beyond their actual accomplishment. Ed and Jo smiled at one another, two cosmopolitans in a city by the sea. From the sophisticated city of fashion and of the new and novel, they could realize past centuries in Gloucester, within its people now flowing out into the streets, into Stage Fort, and all around the harbor.

Gloucester's insistent eccentricity and self-satisfaction would have been lost in New York but here, where no single church, no single language, no single culture united people, Gloucester was where everybody could do as they liked. They faced east to the infinite and west to the whole country. They were themselves on the edge, neither of the sea nor of the land but an island of survivors and persisters. They lived more as they liked than others elsewhere and knew it. They talked their own way, they looked at things differently, and here, on this day, they remembered their crazy-quilt past of three hundred years in parades, songs, pageants, and dances.

Suddenly looking down and in an apologetic tone, Jo said, "I'm sorry, I don't know what else to say."

"Oh, no, you always know what to say. I am the

one who cannot talk. Do you know what Emerson said was the highest of arts?"

"Painting?"

"Emerson said that the highest of arts is to affect the quality of the day."

"Do you mean—"

"I mean you, yes."

"I really affect the quality of your day?"

"And night."

Matilda Markham Miller, who was Clam Miller's granddaughter, sixteen, was announced to recite a poem that she wrote herself entitled "Homeward Bound." She stood to great applause and cheers.

"I still do not know what to say," Jo said.

"Perhaps that is because I have not asked the question."

"And what question is that, Mr. Hopper?"

"If you would like to become Mrs. Hopper."

Under starry skies tonight we're beating homeward...

Jo froze, her mouth open, her eyes caught between flight and forward, the image of "Woman, Confused." Dazed though she was, she managed to utter, "Now I really do not know what to say."

Ed placed both of his hands upon her shoulders, again as if the two were all by themselves on the pavilion stand rather than amidst a crowd of thousands surrounding them.

"You could try, 'Yes.'"

And together 'round the fire we'll sit and talk...

"I'm scared."

"So am I, dear heart. I might be leading you into destruction. You have something going, Jo, everything going. I have nothing. I may never have anything."

"You don't want to hurt me."

"I don't."

"I think I was hurt when you left me alone."

"You had Arthur."

"I'm serious."

"So am I."

But the mates we lost at sea we shall remember…

"Do you really think you and I could make a life together?"

"Look into my eyes. Don't I look alone without you?"

She looked and felt the electricity that she had felt only once before in her life, when they had looked into one another's eyes that night. She decided then.

"Look, Ed, right in front of you. Somebody else standing alone."

"Are you being a comedian?"

"You bet."

As those at home in Gloucester we shall meet.

Applause and cheers for the reciter distracted most people from seeing them hug and kiss in a way uncommon in public anyplace else in America in 1923, except in Gloucester, the wildest city in the East, where love lived free as air.

They then listened to the Mayor, who was too loud to be ignored. His speech, actually written by the *Times* editor, Garret Bean, was nonetheless unsuccessful because he attempted to say what could not be put into words. Gloucester in a day, let alone in centuries, could not be pinned down verbally. What was true then is true today, no matter how many news accounts and feature articles newspapers and periodicals print of people and events. Historical novels that try to whip up the taste of Gloucester always disappoint, too. Any such scribbling is so much picking up water with a sieve. Neither prose nor poetry, Gloucester's representation requires a master chef or a major artist. Its best representation is either a plate of steaming hot fried clams dipped to taste in ketchup, with fresh French fries and onion rings, along with ice cold Twin Lights ginger ale, or it is artwork. Thus, enter the one person out of everybody that summer, the one who came closest to expressing Gloucester at the time. He was an out of towner, a New Yorker, and he beat the Mayor without uttering a single word, relying solely on brush strokes on paper and canvas, raising Gloucester fragile and delicate on a surface, a bubble that did not pop after all, a vision that could be framed and seen again in a hundred years and still be recognized.

Although the bargain would never be quite even, always a bit fairer to Ed than to Jo, she would help him, for she loved him. Jo found that, properly primed, he could sometimes talk. He could also be quietly present. She did not need to teach him better manners than he had. He would do as is. And, likewise, she would do as is.

Even as early as that night, in Ed's arms, she foresaw that she would select the props, find sites of interest, and talk out with Ed the best angle and structure suited for his subject. The paperwork he never knew he needed she would take care of handily. No other artist would have a better documented record than Ed, thanks to Jo. If he so much as picked out a frame without her, she felt that he would get it wrong. No, it went beyond feeling. She *knew* it and, eventually, *he* would know it, too. He would be so successful. But he must not sit for an interview without her, and he would surely rely on her for half of the answers. They would grow into one. It was starting. The oneness of Mr. and Mrs. Hopper started here in Gloucester, before thousands of unwitting witnesses in Stage Fort Park, people who knew that Gloucester was 300 but not that they surrounded a couple for whom 1923 was Year One.

And so the story of love, art and Gloucester in the summer of 1923 comes to its conclusion but—wait for it—Gloucester's Tricentennial remains the beating heart of modern American art. Gloucester that summer may still be seen on the walls of museums and glowing in Ed's much-replicated Gloucester paintings. As long as no course in modern American art is complete without Ed's Gloucester paintings, that summer has yet to end. As long as authors grapple with the challenge of describing the beginning of Ed's career, that summer has yet to end. And as long as readers—thank you!—visualize the vibrant summer of '23 and Ed and Jo in love, that summer has yet to end.

Epilogue

Although Edward Hopper would eventually become famous for his oils, it was nonetheless with watercolor, the medium that Jo suggested that he try, that he first made his name and began to make his fortune. The winter of 1923 happened to be the scheduled Brooklyn Museum's biennial juried show for watercolor artists. Jo had been invited before she left New York. Ed had not been considered but as soon as she got back to New York, Jo wangled an invitation for him, which led to six of Ed's Gloucester watercolors being displayed.

His watercolors were a surprise sensation. One critic asked the public to go and see "what can be done with the homeliest subjects." Another mentioned Hopper in the same sentence with Winslow Homer. The jury was no less than awed. Hopper's "The Mansard Roof" won "Overall Best" in the show and, thus, this now iconic representation of a wind-swept Rocky Neck house was purchased and became part of the Museum's permanent collection. Jo's watercolors, including one of "Arthur of Ninth Street," her cat, did not find their footing.

"The Mansard Roof," Ed's first sale since 1913, barely preceded the sales of his five other watercolors of Gloucester, which sold as well, and the critics who began to chirp as his paintings flew off the walls. One of the country's outstanding agents, Frank K. M. Rehn, took Ed on as a client. With Jo's encouragement, Ed felt wind enough in his sails to drop commercial illustration completely. First, he devoted himself full time to fine art; next, he married Jo. On July 9, 1924, two weeks before Ed turned 42, he and Jo wed in a church ceremony at which Guy Pène Du Bois served as best man.

(Guy left the country with his family to live and work as an expatriate American artist in France for the next six years. He wrote an autobiography, published in 1940, entitled *Silly Things Artists Say*.)

Ed and Jo never went to Europe. On a working honeymoon, Ed and Jo returned to Gloucester in 1924. After another summer of more watercolors, Rehn Galleries in Manhattan mounted an exhibition of "Recent Watercolors by Edward Hopper," featuring eleven high-priced Gloucester watercolors from 1923 and 1924, which promptly sold out again. Fellow artist George Bellows shrewdly bought Ed's miraculous "Haskell's House." Ed's Gloucester series won an acclaim and praise that began then but never ceased thereafter. To this day, people all over the world marvel at the Gloucester works that stand at the beginning of his fame.

The Hoppers returned to Gloucester one final time in 1928, the actual summer that Ed painted "Adam's House," which I backdated to 1923. After the stock market crashed in 1929, Jo managed to route regular contributions to her former home, the Church of the Ascension, for the poor as Ed enjoyed a prosperity that improved by the day all but magically. As a result her old home church was kept open day and night, its doors never locked on the homeless, who were permitted to sleep indoors on its pews. Tim Tolman, *incognito*, passed through the church and its soup kitchen after his gallery failed.

As the Depression got worse, the art works of the earlier impoverished and ignored artist only became ever more valuable. The market proved unlimited for Ed's gaunt, stiff figures with blank or puzzled faces, his unpeopled cityscapes and empty or nearly empty transit cars and streets, by day or by night. With Jo at his side, Ed did what Henri, who died in 1929, had advised and they together reaped what Henri promised to those who follow their own visions. Ed painted what interested him, disregarded "fine art" subjects, poured his feelings into his lines, colors and strokes, imbued each canvas with himself, that is, with such reserved emotions he cared to share, however lonely, sad, weary, stale, and—he made a stir.

Ten years to the day after his completion of "Adam's House," thinking of it as an anniversary, Ed took Jo out to a restaurant in New York for a quiet meal at a candlelit table covered with white linen. He said nothing about the anniversary, although he guided the conversation to Gloucester, to Arthur, and to their first summer together, the summer that they fell in love.

At first, Jo was puzzled and seemed too tired or full of business to respond in kind, but once he resurrected Arthur, she smiled, her eyes lit up and she said, "Wasn't he the most wonderful cat?"

Ed lied and said, "I'd have been lost without him."

Jo laughed and said, "He'd have been lost without you."

Poor Arthur had been lost (again, with finality) at that point for nine years. But Ed and Jo found themselves beside one another every morning. Their partnership continued into each day. Whenever Ed included women in his paintings, Jo modeled for him. In addition, she managed their finances, kept a record of sales, and regularly cooked by opening cans and warming things up. She also fed Arthur fish as long as her favorite pet lived with them, as he had acquired a taste for fresh flounder and turned up his nose at anything else.

NOTE: Actually, Arthur did not turn up his nose. What he did was paw around a non-fish meal, imitating burying it as one might bury something vile. In fact, as Jo reported in her diary, Ed and Arthur never got along and often "exchanged glances," seeing one another as bitter rivals for her affection. One morning in the spring of 1925 Jo came into her studio and found Arthur gone. The mystery was never solved. Jo's LOST CAT posters did not work this time. Her tomcat never returned to complete the love triangle. Perhaps Arthur finally found his Mehitabel. Adding insult to injury for Ed, he and Jo had to stay put in New York and delay their planned trip to the Southwest for six weeks while Jo in vain hoped against hope to see Arthur again. See Gail Levin, *Edward Hopper, An Intimate Biography*, (New York: Alfred A. Knopf, Inc., 1995), 176-77, 190. ("The tension between Edward and Arthur was real" and it found expression in Ed's caricature—included in Levin's book—of Arthur seated at table with Jo as "The Great God Arthur," both of them feasting and ostentatiously ignoring starving Ed.)

Both of them argued like Don Quixote and Sancho Panza, frequently and loudly, often over nothing, but the lord idealist and his practical squire remained together for forty-three bumptious years, soulmates until the end. Two years before Ed died, he designed and painted his last oil on canvas, a painting that he called "Two Comedians."

In it, an imagined audience from a low vantage point looks up at two small mimes in clown costumes which are completely white, although the man is crowned in a "royal purple" hat. The pair seem to be stepping forward to take a final bow. Their feet and the stage beneath them are unseen, behind a huge side of the stage. They seem like passengers boarding a ship, transforming viewers into a group seeing friends off on a departing ocean liner. The diagonal line of the solid wood stage splits the canvas in half and simultaneously separates the couple from the world they are leaving, and from everybody else.

But the man and the woman are joined, they are together. Unlike sets of characters who populate works like "The Nighthawks," each of them impenetrably occupying a world of one even if seen together, the "comedians" are depicted almost woven together: the man's right hand firmly and encouragingly holding the woman's left hand, as if to bring her forth over her resistance or modesty, his left hand ostentatiously gesturing toward his partner. He wishes to invite the crowd's admiration and appreciation to her while she, emphatically in retreat, a step behind her man, with her right hand, palm up, makes an unspoken plea. Hers, as the last "word," is a clear wish that attention be paid to her partner. Their faces are bravely earnest, their eyes fondly on the audience. Nothing stands behind them now but the dark, the great, the empty abyss. But they have had their show, and they were leaving together.

If it is a metaphor for life, staged at life's end, even if human existence is in the end revealed (by their costumes and his title) as laughable, the painting says that life is nonetheless redeemed by its moments of absolutely arresting grace. We know from Ed's final effort that the stage will continue to transport us all, artists and audiences. It is by his twilight view, as the fourth wall breaks and actors resume their ordinary, bowing *personae*, that we see them behind their outfits, mentally unencumbered by costumes and—dare we prophesy—we also foresee that the memory of these comedians shall last beyond their performance, even long after the two vanish from the stage forever.

Jo, although she never stopped painting, made no efforts after 1923 to market her own colorful paintings. She accumulated a collection of hundreds of watercolors at the time she executed the terms of Ed's will. He had wanted his remaining works on hand to go to the Whitney Museum. Seeing an opening, Jo arranged for the Museum to receive not only Ed's collection but also hers. This gambit she played shortly before she herself died, (only a year after Ed). However, after Jo died, although the Museum staged exhibitions of Ed's works (while, offstage, its administrators toyed with the idea of selling Ed's paintings piecemeal), of Jo's paintings, only one was retained, not displayed, and the Museum otherwise gave away, loaned out permanently and discarded the rest. (Ed's works remain; the museum sold but a few of his etchings.)

Yet one more story might be told of the comedians in conclusion. Once soon after they married, Jo asked Ed how much German he knew. He said that he had memorized a poem by Goethe and when she had asked him to recite it, he did, along with a translation into English by Longfellow, which he also knew by heart.

"Über allen Gipfeln ist Ruh," Ed said, translating, "O'er all the hilltops is quiet."

Then, "In allen Wipfeln spürest du Kaum einen Hauch; Die Vögelein schweigen in Walde."

He turned to Jo, saying, "Is quiet now in all the treetops, hearest thou hardly a breath, the birds are asleep in the trees."

"Warte nur balde, Ruhest du auch," he said to her in conclusion. "Wait, soon like these thou too shall rest."

When Jo touched his face, caressing his chin, and told him that it was beautiful, he said, "Their word 'schweigen' is interesting. We say that someone stops talking or silences himself. They use an active verb, 'schweigen.' 'Ich schweige' means 'I silence,' as if I broadcast it. Their silence is not just the absence of speech, or ceasing to yammer. A person positively emanates silence."

"I think," Jo said on that occasion, smiling broadly, "that you schweige a lot."

Wordless, Ed smiled.

We must imagine them both content.

Postscript

Ed and Jo, though based on a mountain of facts, is nonetheless more than half fictional. Dialogue so essential to any novel has had to be made up for lack of documentation. Nefarious Tim Tolman was invented, and many other culprits, including the crabby trolley conductor who wanted Ed to pay for the cat's portage. As to recognizable names, nobody should look for "real" people to match characters herein. Actual people's names (such as Edward Hopper, Josephine Nivison, Guy Péne Du Bois, Leonard Craske, Howard Blackburn, Roger Babson, etc.) are applied to characters who are only spottily factual. The *good* stuff is usually true, such as Dr. Pett's charitable way of practicing medicine, but the *bad* stuff—a murder at sea, gangsters, and a local doctor in league with them, corruption high and low—is fabricated. Carol's and Ed's misbehavior is not to be imputed to any woman or man in reality. Readers interested in real stories about real people are invited to biographies and histories to find the facts—with the author's assurance that Gloucester's true stories are fascinating and addictive. Nobody can ever get too much *real* Gloucester.

Novels like this one fulfill other wishes than non-
fiction and aim to entertain.

In this book, a novel, the author mainly and
modestly tried to communicate the sparking, quirky
and murky love story of two eccentrics who had
met before infrequently but not fallen in love earlier, along with the story of a wonderful city, my
hometown, that remains a mecca for artists. (Also, a
mecca for centennial buffs—Gloucester is running
up to 400 years, now straight ahead without having
missed a single dawn.) Because the Hoppers' romance is poorly documented, logic and probabili-
ties suggested to me that they bonded in Gloucester
over walks, during days sketching, at the movies
(Gail Levin suggests a puppet show performed in
Rocky Neck, "Frog Goes A-Courtin'") and, not
least, at the activities of the Tricentennial.

On this point, Gloucester itself must be singled
out to take a bow. It is the author's core belief that
this older couple's love in particular thrived because
they were both elated by a subsurface love of beautiful Gloucester. Adam and Eve went back to the
Garden for a summer. Although Arthur the cat will
protest loudly at being outranked by a city, I think
that in the scheme of things it was less important
that Arthur went out tomcatting one full moon in
June to be found and returned by Ed the next
morning and much more important that Ed and Jo
happened to choose for their summer sanctuary in
1923 the same city and that that city was Gloucester, Massachusetts.

I invented details about Ed's affair with Jeanne.
He did love and lose Jeanne, but there was no letter
from New Orleans that he never opened. Her
pledge to be his shepherdess was likewise my invention. Per Gail Levin Jeanne left Ed not a wool scarf
but a book of poems by Paul Verlaine in the orig-

inal French. Although Ed—who rarely did portraits
—kept his sketches of Jeanne for the rest of his life,
Jo was his one and only love beginning in 1923, as
he was hers, (at least once Arthur left her in 1925).

Jo was beyond question a better known and financially successful artist than Ed up to 1923, but
Ed's monetary situation was not as dire as I outlined in Chapter One. Chiefly, although he had
money in the bank, Ed really did *hate* what he was
doing. Again per the indefatigable and careful researcher Gail Levin, Ed once defined himself dis-
couragingly as a "salesman" for a city directory,
although he labeled himself "commercial artist"
more often. Neither view of his occupation satisfied
him professionally.

I discovered no eyewitness accounts or confes-
sions about the kisses and hugs which I imagine
graced the scene in Gloucester, but it is documented and certain that during this pivotal summer
Jo did insist that Ed try her watercolors.

On another point, I have neither doubt nor
documentary proof that Jo read Anita Loos's short
stories about Lorelei Lee in *Harper's Bazaar* (stories
later gathered and published as 1925's best-selling
book, *Gentlemen Prefer Blondes*)—they were so wildly
popular that the magazine's sales tripled in any
edition in 1923 and 1924 that featured a Lorelei
Lee story. Single women like Jo faced deciding
whether to advance toward "flapper" independent
success outside of marriage or, even within marriage, to claim their rights. In the Penn station
scene, I also backdated *Liberty*. Although *Liberty* was
the second most popular magazine after the *Saturday Evening Post* in the 1920s, it did not come out
until 1924.

Admittedly, Ed Hopper and Jo Nivison may
have been different, even very different from the Ed

and Jo of this novel. So much is unknown, and the
couple were reclusive. Their devotion to one another and their simultaneous fractious bickering,
paradoxically contradictory characteristics of the
couple later, I surmise to have sprung up between
them in 1923. I am not intentionally inaccurate
about the way they lived—with constant ups and
downs—through their otherwise magical and life-
changing summer of 1923 in Gloucester. Although
Arthur was incorrigible, I think that each of them,
Ed and Jo, evolved. Just reaching forty, they took
giant steps that summer to turn into the sophisticated and perceptive people that each one was for
the rest of their lives. If they reached perfect har-
mony while in Gloucester, their success proved
brief. Instead, as seems to me true, life began at
forty for them, life with all of its contradictions,
mess, drama, conflict, and comedy.

From the high to the humble. Floyd the Clammer, the nickname of an actual later local character, I confabulated into fiction in this novel. Floyd
was an honest and earnest man whom one could
see and hear shuffling about Gloucester in oversized boots during the 1940s through the 1970s. Although I backdated his existence, I realistically
reflected his simple and hardy lifestyle. People said
of Floyd in winter, "I don't know how he survives."
Floyd was a favorite of artists in all media—I remember seeing portraits at Gloucester's once-an-
nual, now lamentably lapsed Festival of the Arts—
and of countless tourists with cameras, but he was
not a Federal agent. (Speaking of Prohibition,
someone really did concoct a scheme to use delivery trucks of the United States Post Office for an
unsuccessful rum run that was ambushed in 1924
by Feds on Western Avenue.)

Dr. Adam Blythe never existed, and his body

was never found. Manga Campagna, "Bag o' rocks" Birkelder are likewise characters not based on real people. The *Times* editor and reporter are invented, too, although not the *Gloucester Daily Times* and there were (and are) colorful and irrepressible *Times* editors and reporters, both then and now. These latter facts notwithstanding, no character in real life ought to be confused with Garrett Bean or Donny Nash, not even colorful and witty Paul Kenyon wearing his tan scally cap and jaunty plaid scarf as he sped about Cape Ann in his bright red 1952 MG sports car, who puckishly recalled interviewing "an opera lady" in *dishabille* on her visit to Gloucester in the Twenties.

Regarding fictional Donny, the news is good. In 1933 he was assigned to write up Carol's life after she became known for organizing a soup kitchen and a shelter on Duncan Street for Gloucester's homeless families. A romance developed that led to a life-long marriage and three children as Don's parents reconciled with him and became wonderful grandparents to the Nash children, all of whom thrived and undertook a profession, one a doctor, another an English teacher and the third an artist.

The Boulevard looks out on Ten Pound Island to this day, but the Coast Guard station and the old sea plane's hangar exist on it no more. I went to third grade at the Beeman Memorial School with Eddie Enos, last of the children of Coast Guardsmen stationed on the island, who had sketched sea gulls and rocks while on the island, with Gloucester on the other side of the water. I hope that Eddie held on to his drawings, now irreplaceable historical artifacts.

Leon Kroll (distinct from the fictional party organizer depicted here) was the name of a leader of Gloucester's artistic community and a fine gentleman whose education in art went back to New York, where he and Ed were members of "The Independents," a group founded by Robert Henri. He lived to be almost 90 when he died in Gloucester in 1974. Jerome Myers, a contemporary of Kroll's, said of him that he had "the eye of a hawk and the heart of a dove," connoting his exceptional intelligence and sensitivity. Many writers about Ed depend on the recollections of Leon Kroll, who was interviewed often about their friendship.

I wavered between using a pseudonym or running with Guy Péne Du Bois for Ed's sidekick's name and decided to renew public awareness of a great and witty art critic who also painted exceptionally well, and was a devoted friend and family man. I hope that the name will stimulate readers to learn more about the genuine Guy Péne Du Bois. Guy Pène Du Bois, best man at the Hoppers' wedding, did not in fact join Ed and Jo for any part of the summer of 1923, but I found him a character too useful to leave behind in New York with his family. Kindly disregard the man who gawked at women on Back Beach, and bought a straw hat with a blue ribbon. Look further than fiction. Indeed, look into his paintings, which stand among the great pictures of the Twenties. Du Bois was a genius analogous to F. Scott Fitzgerald with a brush and canvas.

Dr. Morris "Mo" Pett lived on as a great asset to his city and to his Temple, marrying and having two sons. The City presented Dr. Pett with a key to the city, a testimonial dinner and entry into Gloucester High School's Athletic Hall of Fame for his forty years of voluntary support of the football team and other athletic teams. As long as Dr. Pett lived, he was welcome to a seat of honor on the sidelines of any Gloucester games.

Federal intervention by way of monitoring and eventually regulating fishing really did begin in Gloucester in 1923 with a report by the expert whom I call "Dr. Biggs" in Chapter Forty-Two. There was a small article in the *Times*. Nobody knew how big that news really was, or would come to be.

Federal agents enforcing Prohibition disappeared from Gloucester and everywhere else shortly after the election of President Franklin D. Roosevelt, who, incidentally, visited Gloucester on a yacht between his election in 1932 and his inauguration ("we have nothing to fear but fear itself") in 1933.

Roger Babson, noted philanthropist and sage, enjoyed recognition in many business books and periodicals and ran for President as the nominee of the Prohibitionist Party in 1940. He won more votes in Ward 4, where more Babsons lived than anywhere else in Gloucester. His name is memorialized by Babson College, which he founded in Wellesley, Massachusetts. He lived into his nineties, dying in 1967. By the way, Prohibition prevailed a long time in Rockport, a dry town into the 21st century.

Fred Foster's talk about an unassisted triple play in Braves Field was a remarkable prediction. "You hear about it? Guy just came up from Rhode Island to play on the team, his first game, Ernie Padgett. He went out to play shortstop, and bang, right into the record books," described an event that only happened near the season's end, on October 6, 1923.

Another thing I could not leave out was Old Man Foster's paean to baseball. Certainly, lots of people in Gloucester were Braves fans. In the 1950s, I recall the black-and-white tiny television in Roy Wilbur's barbershop in Lanesville tuned in for games and the fun rhyme I learned by heart, "Spahn and Sain and pray for rain." Some readers will note that Fred adverted to future events, and not least quoted without credit another writer's fabulous achievement, the monumental and (in my judgment) unsurpassed classic "Hub Bids Kid Adieu," by John Updike. No other baseball tribute comes closer to the mark than Updike's.

Although the Foster Brothers' Drug Store is long gone, the building remains, in which the current Lanesville Post Office operates. Jacobson's family sauna by the sea at Lane's Cove is closed, as are all of the former saunas open to the public in 1923. If you know a Finn who still stokes up the fire on Saturdays, you might be in luck. Otherwise, the discussion in this book must simply read like a quaint reference to the old days.

James Centennial Nutt really was the Captain of Company G, all volunteers, in the War of 1898. I had the honor of meeting him when he was in his late eighties, as he was a guest of honor with other Gloucester veterans at an assembly held at Gloucester High School on Veteran's Day, 1963. He had worked for the Boston & Maine Railroad most of his life and lived until 1967. I wanted to give him a speaking role, in the voice of the modest man that he was, on his birthday, the Fourth of July. Contrary to this novel, I regret to report that there was actually no Marine Band concert, no speech, and no playing of Strauss's "Anniversary Waltz" during which he and his wife danced down by the Stage Fort.

Henry Gould and his wooden leg were real. I like to think that he and Ed, had they met, would have liked one another. I made the encounter happen that never happened in life. If it had, just as in this novel, Ed would have wanted to tell Jo.

Mrs. Post existed and I heard her heroic story of obtaining a loan directly from the banker who approved it, and gave her much credit for raising a family with her guest house, which was actually not on Middle Street but closer to Grant Circle. As kids, my sister and I used to say aloud, "See Mrs. Post, Guests," the simple message on two or three signs posted around the rotary as one arrived in Gloucester from "over the Bridge." Mrs. Murphy and her guest house were invented for the other characters' convenience, as was the aspiring biographer of Franklin Pierce.

Hollywood studios really did make use of Salt Island at Good Harbor beach as a location for a now-lost silent movie, a pirate swashbuckler at the climax of which the "Moorish *hacienda*" built on it was burned. President Wilson really was almost grounded on the *George Washington* in the fog off of Good Harbor upon his return from the Versailles Peace conference in February, 1919.

Dogtown's history, while a bit oversimplified, is pretty well reflected in the history summarized for Jo. The same is true of the docent's recounting of the life of Howard Blackburn, who died in Gloucester in 1932. The incredible tales about him, told in this book by the fictional docent, are all true. Joseph Garland, a brave veteran of World War II, a gifted Gloucester author and a quite competent sailor himself, wrote Blackburn's definitive biography, *Lone Voyager*.

Twin Lights tonics—which is what real Cape Anners call "soda pop"—are history, literally, as the factory's last owner, Pierce Sears, donated his factory near Five Corners to the Rockport Historical

Society. You still might find a souvenir, though. Bottles imprinted with the last operating twin lights
along the East Coast turn up as valued collectibles
that one may spot occasionally on such online sites
as ebay.

Gloucester in summer has been synonymous so
long with the St. Peter's Fiesta that I put it into
1923 even though it technically began as a community celebration, including its outdoor Mass, carnival, banquets, processions, and the greasy pole
competition, only in 1927. You see, I would rather
not be asked, "Why did you ignore the Fiesta?" and
instead use this preference as my excuse for including it in 1923. I think it is the key omission that
all living residents would detect and otherwise
doubt that I really lived in the same city as they did.

Even more sinfully, I backdated the "Fishermen's Monument." I simply wanted to place
Leonard Craske and the monument itself squarely
in the middle of this novel about the summer of
1923 even though Craske won the competition in
September, 1923, and the statue of the "Man at the
Wheel" was itself not unveiled until 1925. The
magnificent man at the wheel overlooking the
harbor went back to 1923 by my fiat. Craske, in
fact a British immigrant whose life history is mir-
rored by what the character in this book tells fictional Don Nash, designed and sculpted a young,
open-collar brash fellow at the wheel on his first try
but, after he won the competition, Craske had
second thoughts and delivered a monument that
embodied the doughty but cautious fighter against
the sea's fury. We know today the man battered and
clothed for a storm who sails over the apt borrowed
Biblical verse, "They that go down to the sea in
ships, 1623-1923."

Craske actually never said, "The tides go in, the

tides go out, storms and fair weather, net-breaking, back-breaking hauls, empty nets and bad trips, all the rhythm of Gloucester. The man at the wheel is not dated. My man at the wheel stands the same now as men at sea a hundred years ago, nay, three hundred years ago, and I predict, a hundred years from now."

That is, he did not say it; he *sculpted* it.

Gloucester Abides

A closing essay in honor of the Gloucester400
Committee and its many volunteers

Let us now praise famous Gloucester, which
surrounds the story of Ed and Jo. The reader, if
unfamiliar with the city, must someday visit this
unique place and, at journey's end, crack a chicken
lobster over melted butter, or how about a cup of
clam chowder? You'll find lobster and clam
chowder in name only outside of our beloved
Gloucester. And if you want Italian rolls, a slice of
warm Portuguese sweet bread, Finnish nisu or
Anadama toast, well, look no further north, west or
south. Come to where the light is better, and the
shadows of cornices are sharper than anywhere
else. And stay long enough to look up at those stars
that surprise your eyes because city lights elsewhere
make it hard to see what the universe really is.
Artists know the secret and make the trek: if you
miss this stuff, my friend, you miss life itself.

This book was written because in Gloucester in
1923 a commercial illustrator became an artist for
the rest of his life. His technique was singular. He

led the way. "Be still," Ed said, and the world abruptly obeyed and stood motionless before him. The success and durability of his vision is indisputable. Ed called a halt to the carnival.

And the magic worked. Omitting people, halting the sea breezes, ignoring the Tricentennial parades, pageants, and fireworks when at his easel, even turning from the ships, the sea, and the rocks, Ed said, "Let there be houses," and there were houses, his vision of unoccupied houses. It was something new under the sun. As a result, as Ed breached his forties, everything in his previously fragmented life came together for him. From fishing shacks around Lane's Cove, from Lanesville "mansions" and clotheslines, from a canopied crazy-quilt house on Rocky Neck, from Adam's house high up on Portagee Hill, Ed spun straw into gold. His partner from that decisive moment forward was Jo. In despair no longer, Ed, with Jo, went about the country playing "freeze tag" with many other houses, people, storefronts, twilight, and, of course, nighthawks.

Oh, but our artists come and go, playing God, making and remaking Gloucester in their own image, while Gloucester people, whose lives can be hard, living and working where countless dangers abound, find nectars and ambrosias to savor, magic alive in their salt air, and a long boulevard to walk to check out the Norway ducks and reports of a sea serpent in their harbor. The Gloucester400 Committee and its many volunteers are dedicated to demonstrating in innumerable activities, exhibits, parades, pageants, shows, concerts and competitions that it remains true, as it has for hundreds of years, that those who live exactly here on the great globe dwell and roam in a special light when not nestling snugly under their exceptional canopy of bright stars, by the deep blue sea, gliding and schooning between their *jubilies.*

In sum, the tide comes in, and the tide goes out, but Gloucester, Gloucester abides.

Acknowledgments

Many people helped me to realize between covers on paper in black and white my otherwise vague and dreamy ambition to recover the story of Ed and Jo in Gloucester in 1923. Thanks and kudos first to Gail Levin for her classic biography, *Edward Hopper*, the masterful tome which constitutes the factual foundation for many of this novelist's reveries; however, nobody should blame her for my invented dialogue, events, and characters. It was Gail Levin who, after over fifty years of obscurity, traced Hopper's Gloucester paintings back to their original streets and houses. We all owe her for her energy and ingenuity in doing that, and for her detailed and highly readable Hopper biography. She scaled the mountain.

Nobody encouraged me to accomplish this novel more than lucid Laura Ventimiglia, a far better writer than myself, lucid Laura Ventimiglia, who saw this book's initial shape, before it was any good at all. Her wisdom helped me all along to avoid many errors, and find to better ways to say what I said between these covers. *Grazie mille!*

Other Gloucester people all over the place helped me as I went on with this project. Ray Hildonen, one of my oldest and truest friends, being a Renaissance man, assisted with lots of hair-splitting historical and literary *arcana*, while essayist and journalist Laura Plummer was my virtual line editor for several chapters, and a circle of wonderful and generous writers who meet online and at the Sawyer Free Library under the auspices of Susan Oleksiw, an accomplished editor in her own right, offered helpful comments and suggestions. Thanks also to Betty Ann Tettoni Maney, English teacher *extraordinaire*. If factual, grammatical, and spelling errors nonetheless remain, it's none of their faults.

Thanks to John W. Erkkila and Betty Kielinen Erkkila for research on old Lanesville. Likewise, my classmate, Catherine Bayliss, a staunch Democrat, and President of the Jonathan Bayliss Society founded in honor of her late father's novels, kindly permitted me to borrow from the *Gloucesterman* tetrology several fictional geographic names to drop into the narrative here "just for fun." Arley Pett and Barry Pett kindly looked over the chapter in which I presented a depiction of their late father, the physician and *Mensch* Morris Pett. I only wish I was better able to convey than I did this representative of the best of Gloucester people, charitable to a fault, the living foundation of Gloucester High School's athletic teams.

Thanks to Dorinda Hartmann, a brilliant and insightful researcher on staff at the Library of Congress, through whom I was enabled to learn that "St. Elmo" was a popular movie in 1923. Although it did not come out until late September, because of the letter test in its plotline, a letter determinedly *not* read by Bessie Love, a decision on which everything turned, I used "St. Elmo" as the movie that Ed and Jo saw at the North Shore Theater. They were, in fact, both great film enthusiasts, beginning during the silent era. Although there is no documentary evidence that they went to any movies at the old North Shore (which did employ a visiting organist at the time), I cannot imagine them spending the summer, and inevitable rainy days, without doing so. It is historically and nationally true that, in the Twenties, movie theaters sold more tickets than they ever would again, some twenty million a year.

For an eyewitness of the Hoppers in life, the author specially thanks a Boston area man who prefers anonymity, who lived in Cape Cod as a child. Their South Truro neighbors Ed and Jo borrowed the family's catboat on nice days each summer. (His family's boat is the sailing craft in "Groundswell," now in the National Gallery.) He told me that his sister, at age ten or eleven, once came up to "Uncle Eddie" with her artwork to ask him what was most important in painting. "Knowing what to leave out," he told the girl, and neither she nor her overhearing brother ever forgot it. That is why I put that remark, which was just begging *not* to be left out, into this novel. From Ed to this man to you, you're one degree from Ed Hopper.

Thanks to Robert Ranta, Director of the Cape Ann Finns, for information on his family's store, a welcoming place which was one of the highlights of Lanesville socially as much as commercially from the Thirties to the Seventies. Although the "Suomi Cooperative Store" actually occupied the building in 1923, with six rooms over the store later occupied by the Ranta family, then to let by the week to Finn quarrymen, I moved them in early. I installed Ranta's Market so that I could describe the old-style cash register that I personally so vividly remember. Mr. Ranta valued it so much that he placed the store's money in a brown paper bag on the counter overnight, and left the register wide open and empty. Any nefarious burglars were thus encouraged to take the money and leave the valuable and fragile register alone. (Perhaps expecting slim pickings, no burglars ever did appear.)

My old friend, Jay O'Connell, a noted author in his own right, kindly helped shape the manuscript into the correct format through his technological know-how and, because he can, he also designed a great cover for this book. As much of any book's success derives from its cover, Jay's role cannot be overstated.

Last but not least, thanks to all readers and to many people who helped me but vanished via my bathtub memory that fills up and works fine until the plug is pulled and then everything, names, events, and all go down the drain.

What was that again?

Hey, just—thanks, everyone.

———

P.S. Your comments, questions and complaints are invited. My email is:
williamshakespeareaww@gmail.com

Made in the USA
Middletown, DE
26 March 2022